WHEN THE EARTH STARTS TO WAKE

WHEN THE EARTH STARTS TO WAKE

The Hollow-Eyed were only the warning.

by

P. HARTWELL

WHEN THE EARTH STARTS TO WAKE

Cover art and design by P. Hartwell

ISBN: 978-1-969929-24-3 (eBook)

ISBN: 978-1-969929-25-0 (Paperback)

ISBN: 978-1-969929 -26-7 (Hardcover)

Dedication

For the people who kept walking even after the world stopped making sense.

For the ones who learned that fear does not always scream—sometimes it waits quietly in the dark, patient enough to let you come closer on your own.

For every soul who has stood awake at night listening to a house settle, a floor creak, or water move somewhere it shouldn't… and felt, for just a moment, that something was listening back.

And for those still carrying old wounds beneath calm surfaces—

may you never face the darkness alone.

"The Hollow-Eyed stand where the world grows thin.
They do not call your name.
They wait for you to hear the river instead."

— Final entry recovered from the Blackwater Survey Logs

Chapter One

The Ground Remembers

The dirt beneath Jonas's cabin floor moved like something with lungs. He lay still for a long minute, listening to the slow push and settle of soil against the boards. It wasn't the wind. The wind didn't sound like it had a shape. He sat up and reached for his boots, pulling them on without lighting the lamp. The sound followed him to the door, a faint rhythm that matched the pulse in his own neck.

Outside, the pre-dawn air cut sharp across his face. The settlement sat quiet under a sky that still held the last of the stars. Jonas walked toward the woodpile at the side of the cabin, boots crunching frost. The ground there had changed. What had been flat dirt the day before now rose in a soft mound, several inches higher than the surrounding earth. He crouched and pressed his palm to the surface. It gave slightly under his weight, then pushed back with a slow, steady beat.

He stayed there until the cold worked through his gloves. When he stood, his hand came away dusted with fine soil that smelled like copper and old leaves. He wiped it on his coat and turned toward the creek path that ran behind the row of cabins. The settlement looked smaller in the half-light, every roof and fence line drawn thin against the trees.

Widow Grier met him on the path. She carried her shotgun broken open across one arm, shells visible in the chamber. Her face was set in the same hard lines it always wore, but her eyes looked tired in a way that went deeper than one night of lost sleep.

"Three more families left while we were sleeping," she said. "Doors standing wide. Beds still made. One of them left a pot on the stove with beans half cooked."

Jonas nodded once. "Which houses?"

"The Coopers, the Brecks, and the old man who came in last month with the mule cart. All on the east side where the ground started sinking last week."

"Anyone see them go?"

"No one admits to it. I checked the stable. Three horses missing. They didn't even bother with the harnesses. Just led them out bareback."

Jonas looked past her toward the empty cabins. The doors did hang open, dark rectangles in the gray light. He thought about the families who had arrived with wagons full of tools and children and hope. Now the wind could walk straight through their kitchens.

"We need to talk to the ones who stayed," Widow Grier said. "Before the rest decide the same thing."

"Pricket won't like that."

"Pricket can choke on it. He's still telling new arrivals the sinkholes are just old mining shafts. Let him explain why the dirt is moving on its own."

They walked together toward the creek. The path narrowed between stands of pine that leaned at odd angles, roots exposed where the soil had shifted. Jonas kept his eyes on the ground. Every few steps he saw small mounds like the one by his woodpile, none of them there yesterday.

Sera Redwillow stood at the water's edge. She wore a wool coat over her usual layers, hair braided tight against the cold. She did not turn when they approached. Her attention stayed fixed on the creek, which should have been running south toward the settlement's lower fields. Instead thin streams of water moved in the opposite direction, sliding against the current like fingers tracing backward through the flow.

"How long has it been doing that?" Jonas asked.

"Since before first light. I watched it start slow. Now it's steady."

Widow Grier stepped closer to the bank. "Red water?"

"Not yet. But it's warm. Feel it."

Jonas crouched and dipped his fingers. The water carried a faint heat that shouldn't have been there in winter air. It smelled of metal and something sweeter underneath, like spoiled fruit left in a cellar.

Paul Murdock came out of the treeline on the far side of the creek. His face looked bloodless even from a distance. He moved like someone who had forgotten how to trust his own legs. When he reached the water he stopped and stared at the backward flow without speaking.

"Paul," Jonas called. "You all right?"

The young man blinked several times before answering. "I heard them again. All night. Under the boarding house floor."

"What did they say?"

"I don't know. The words don't stay. They sound like water moving over stones. Like someone trying to speak with their mouth full of dirt."

Widow Grier crossed her arms. "You tell anyone else about this?"

"No. I came straight here. I didn't want to wake the others."

Jonas studied the boy's hands. They shook even when he pressed them against his coat. The tremor ran up his arms and into his shoulders. It wasn't just cold. It looked like something trying to crawl out from under his skin.

"Show me where you heard them," Jonas said.

Paul nodded and led them back across the creek on the narrow footbridge. The boards creaked under their weight. On the far side the boarding house sat dark, its windows shuttered. Paul pointed to a patch of ground near the rear wall where the dirt had settled lower than the rest of the yard.

"Right there. It started around midnight. I put my ear to the floor and the sound came up through the boards like they were breathing on me."

Jonas knelt and pressed his palm to the ground. The earth felt soft, almost warm. He thought he could feel the same slow rhythm that had moved beneath his own cabin floor. When he lifted his hand a fine red dust clung to his glove.

"That's new," he said quietly.

Sera crouched beside him. She touched the dust with one fingertip and brought it close to her face. "The color comes from deeper down. It's not just surface iron."

"How deep?"

"Deeper than any of us have dug. The land is pushing old things up."

They left Paul at the boarding house with instructions to stay inside and keep his door barred. Widow Grier walked with them toward the blacksmith's shop at the center of the settlement. The forge fire had already been lit, sending a thin column of smoke into the morning air. Behind the building a fresh sinkhole had opened overnight, a ragged circle maybe four feet across. Jonas approached the edge and looked down.

The hole went straight down into darkness that the morning light couldn't reach. Along the upper rim, what should have been broken rock showed instead the pale curve of something that looked like bone. Not animal bone. These were longer, thicker, with the wrong angles for anything that walked on four legs. Some of them still held fragments of what might have been leather or dried sinew.

"That's not natural rock," Widow Grier said.

"No." Jonas reached down and touched one of the curved shapes. It felt smooth under his glove, colder than the surrounding earth. "These were put here."

Sera stood at the opposite side of the sinkhole. She studied the bone shapes with the same careful distance she used when reading old trail signs. "The land is remembering what was buried. It's bringing it up to show us."

"Show us what?"

"That we aren't the first to stand here. And we won't be the last if this keeps going."

A metallic smell rose from the hole. Jonas recognized it as the same scent that had clung to the red dust on his glove. He stood and stepped back from the edge. The ground felt unstable beneath his boots, as if the soil might give way at any moment.

They returned to the main street. A few early risers had already emerged from their cabins. Most kept their heads down and moved quickly between buildings. Two men stood outside the general store arguing in low voices about whether the new families had taken any supplies with them. No one looked at the ground for long.

Widow Grier stopped near the center of the street. "We need to gather everyone who stayed. Tonight if we can. Before more decide to run."

"Pricket will call it panic," Jonas said.

"Let him. Panic is what happens when people don't know what they're running from. We're past that now."

Sera looked toward the creek again. The backward flow had grown stronger, thin ribbons of water visible even from this distance. "The land is responding to us. Every step we take, every word we speak, it hears. It answers by changing."

"Changing how?" Widow Grier asked.

"By pushing us out. Or pulling us under. I don't think it cares which."

Jonas thought about the mound near his cabin and the bone shapes in the sinkhole. He thought about the water that had moved against its own current. None of these things had happened in the years he'd lived alone in the valley. They had started after the first deaths, after the first thin places opened. The entity wasn't waiting anymore. It was working.

"We meet at the schoolhouse after dark," he said. "Tell the ones who will listen. Leave the rest to Pricket's lies if that's what they want."

Widow Grier nodded and turned toward the remaining cabins. She moved with purpose now, the shotgun still held ready across her arm. Sera stayed beside Jonas for a moment longer.

"You felt it under your floor too," she said.

"Yes."

"It's learning how to reach us. The floorboards are just the beginning."

Jonas looked at his hands. The red dust had worked its way into the seams of his gloves. He could feel it against his skin, warm and slightly gritty. "How long do we have before it gets through?"

"Not long enough to run. Not far enough to hide."

She left him there and walked back toward the creek. Jonas stood in the street until the cold began to bite through his coat. Then he turned and headed toward his cabin. The mound by the woodpile had grown taller while he was gone. It rose now like a small hill, the surface moving in slow, even waves. He placed his palm against it one more time. The beat came steady and patient, like something that had all the time in the world to finish what it had started.

Inside the cabin he built a fire and set water to boil. The sound of the dirt still reached him through the floor, a quiet rhythm that matched the one beneath his ribs. He sat at the table and listened. Outside, the settlement continued its slow waking. Doors opened and closed. Voices called across the street. The ground beneath all of it kept moving, pushing upward, remembering.

Jonas closed his eyes and tried to picture the valley as it had been when he first arrived. Trees in straight lines. Water running the right direction. Ground that stayed flat and still beneath a man's feet. The picture wouldn't hold. Every time he tried to fix it in his mind the new shapes intruded. The sinkhole. The backward water. The mound breathing against his palm.

He opened his eyes. The cabin looked the same as it always had. The fire crackled. The kettle began to steam. But the floor beneath his chair moved with a rhythm that belonged to something else entirely. Something that had been waiting a long time to wake.

He stood and walked to the window. The settlement stretched out before him, cabins and fences and the thin line of the creek. Everything looked ordinary in the growing light. But Jonas knew better now. The ordinary was already gone. What remained was the slow work of something ancient learning how to wear the world like a second skin.

He turned from the window and began to gather what he would need for the meeting that night. Rope. Lanterns. The old map of the valley that showed trails no longer visible on the surface. He worked without hurry, each motion careful and deliberate. The dirt beneath the floor kept its steady beat. Jonas matched his breathing to it without thinking. Outside, the sun rose over a valley that was no longer the same place it had been the day before.

The ground had started to remember. And it would not forget again.

CHAPTER TWO

Red Water Rising

The settlement woke to the smell of metal. Jonas stood in his doorway and watched the morning light turn the frost on the ground a dull red. The color came from deeper than the surface. It rose through cracks in the soil like something had been cut and left to bleed out overnight.

He pulled his coat tighter and stepped into the street. Widow Grier was already there, her shotgun cradled across one arm. She looked at the ground the way a person looks at a wound that might start bleeding again.

Widow Grier gestured with the barrel of her shotgun toward the center of the road. "The well. Come see."

They walked without hurry. Every boot print left a mark that seemed to fill in slower than it should. Jonas kept his eyes on the buildings. Doors stayed shut. Windows stayed dark. The ones who had stayed through the night were waiting to see what the morning brought.

The well stood at the center of the main street. A ring of settlers had gathered around it. They held back from the edge, as if the stone itself might reach up and pull them in. Jonas pushed through and looked down.

The water was the color of rust. It moved in slow circles even though there was no wind. When he leaned closer he could feel the warmth rising from it. The smell was thick and sweet, like pennies left in a closed fist too long.

Harlan Pricket stood on the far side of the well. He wore his good suit and the practiced, hollow smile he saved for land buyers—the kind that didn't reach his eyes and stayed fixed on his face a second too long to be real. Two new families had arrived the night before, their wagons still loaded with supplies. They stood close to him now, listening.

"Seasonal minerals," Pricket was saying. "The ground gets cold and the iron leaches up. Happens every year. Nothing to worry about. The horses will drink once they get used to it."

One of the newcomers, a thin man with a red beard, shifted his weight. "My mare already tried. She took one sip and dropped where she stood. The others won't go near it."

Pricket's smile held. "We'll bring fresh water from the creek. Just a temporary inconvenience."

Jonas looked at the dead horse lying beside the well. Its eyes were open and already filmed over. The tongue hung out black. The smell of metal came from the animal too.

Sera Redwillow arrived with a strip of cloth. She dipped one end into the water and pulled it back. The cloth darkened in seconds. Within a minute the whole strip had gone the color of old blood.

Sera let the ruined cloth drop back into the dirt. "Not minerals."

Pricket's eyelid twitched. He kept talking to the newcomers. "The water will clear by midday. These things always do."

More people gathered. A woman holding a child stepped closer to the well and then pulled back when the smell reached her. The child pointed at the water.

"It's moving wrong," the child said.

No one answered.

Jonas walked the edge of the crowd. He kept his hands in his pockets and his eyes on the ground. The red dust clung to every boot. It left prints that looked like someone had walked through drying blood.

Paul Murdock lay beside the well. His face was turned toward the stone. His mouth was open. Red water ran from the corner of his lips and pooled beneath his cheek. Jonas knelt and rolled him over. The boy's eyes stayed closed. His breathing came shallow and fast.

Jonas slapped the boy's face once, then twice, the wet cold of the red water transferring to his own palm. "Paul. Wake up."

Paul's eyes opened. They were not his eyes. The color had gone out of them. What remained was the same rust shade as the well water. His mouth moved before any sound came out.

"The caverns run beneath every root," Paul said. His voice was deeper than it should have been. The words came out wet, like he spoke through a mouthful of the same water that stained his lips. "They remember the weight of every foot that ever walked here. They are learning the shape of you."

Jonas pulled his hand back. The boy's skin felt warm, too warm for the morning air.

"Paul," he said again. "Come back."

The voice continued. "We drank from the same seam. We will drink again. The stone waits. The stone listens."

Widow Grier pushed through the crowd. She grabbed Paul under both arms and hauled him to his feet. The boy sagged against her but kept talking.

"The water carries the memory of every death. Every fear. Every name. You cannot wash it out. You cannot drink it clean."

She dragged him away from the well. The crowd parted. No one tried to stop her. Pricket watched them go but stayed where he was, still speaking to the newcomers about seasonal minerals and temporary inconvenience.

Jonas stayed by the well. He watched the water move in its slow circles. A horsefly landed on the surface and died instantly. Its body sank without a ripple.

Sera stood beside him. She held the blackened cloth between two fingers.

"It ate through the fibers," she said. "Whatever is in there wants to reach bone."

"Pricket will keep lying until someone stops him."

"He has to. If the new families leave, the settlement dies. He knows that."

Jonas looked at the dead horse again. Its legs had already stiffened. The smell of metal and spoiled fruit rose from its open mouth.

"We need to get the children away from the well," he said.

"Grier is already moving them. She'll keep them inside today."

They walked together toward the boarding house. The red dust followed their boots. It left tracks that pointed back toward the well like arrows drawn in drying blood.

Inside the boarding house Paul sat on a bench with his head in his hands. Widow Grier stood over him with her shotgun resting against the wall. She had a basin of creek water and a cloth. She wiped the red stain from around his mouth.

Widow Grier threw the stained cloth into her basin, where the water swirled into a dark, muddy pink. "He stopped talking when we got him inside. But he won't drink anything clean. Keeps reaching for the red water like he's thirsty for it."

Paul lifted his head. His eyes were still wrong. The rust color had not faded.

"I can hear them moving," he said. His own voice had returned, thin and shaking. "They are under the well now. They are under every house. They are counting the living and the almost living."

Jonas pulled a heavy wooden chair close, the legs scraping hard against the floorboards. "Who is counting?"

"The ones who drank before us. The ones who became part of the stone. They want us to join them. They say the water remembers our names better than we do."

Sera crouched in front of the boy. She studied his face the way she studied the creek when it ran backward.

"How long have you been hearing them?"

"Since the first sinkhole. They got louder after I touched the bone in the ground. Now they don't stop. Even when I sleep I hear them under the floor."

Widow Grier wrung out the cloth. Red water dripped into the basin and turned it the color of old rust.

Widow Grier wrung out the cloth a final time, her knuckles white. "Pricket will come for him. He'll say the boy is spreading panic. He'll want him locked up before the new families hear what he said."

Jonas stood and looked down at the shivering boy. "Then we keep him here. Out of sight until we figure out what to do."

Paul shivered. His hands shook against his knees. "They showed me the caverns. Miles of stone and water. No light. No air. Just the memory of every person who ever died here, pressed into the walls like fossils. They are waiting for the rest of us to join them."

Jonas stood. He walked to the window and looked out at the street. Pricket was still talking. The newcomers listened with the careful attention of people who wanted to believe the lie.

Jonas turned back from the window, his face in shadow. "We tell the truth tonight. At the schoolhouse. Anyone who stays after that knows what they're staying for."

Widow Grier nodded. She picked up her shotgun and checked the shells. The sound was loud in the small room.

"I'll stand guard here," she said. "If Pricket comes, he'll leave with less than he arrived."

Jonas and Sera left the boarding house. The red dust had spread farther during their time inside. It coated the steps and the path. Every footprint they left filled with the same rust color.

They walked to the creek. The water still moved against its own current. Thin ribbons of it climbed the bank and soaked into the soil. Where it touched the ground the red dust rose like steam.

Sera dipped her fingers into the flow. She pulled them back quickly.

Sera wiped her wet fingers on her trousers, her expression hardening. "Warmer than before. It's heating up from below."

Jonas watched the backward movement. It reminded him of something trying to return to its source. The water did not want to leave the valley. It wanted to stay and be absorbed.

"The entity is using the water like blood," Sera said. "Carrying its memory through every vein in the ground."

Jonas kept his eyes on the dark red ribbons bleeding into the bank. "Can we stop it?"

"We can slow it. We can seal some of the thin places. But the water will find another way. It always does."

They returned to the main street. The crowd at the well had thinned. Most people had gone back to their cabins. The two new families were unloading their wagons with slow, careful movements. They kept glancing at the dead horse.

Pricket approached Jonas. His smile had thinned to a line.

Pricket blocked his path, his chest rising and falling too fast. "You saw what the boy said. You heard him."

Jonas stopped, refusing to step around him. "I heard him."

"Then you know we can't let that kind of talk spread. It will empty the valley faster than any sinkhole."

Jonas looked at the man's twitching eyelid. "The water is poison. Lying about it won't change that."

"The water will clear. These things pass."

"Not this time."

Pricket stepped closer. His voice dropped. "I have families arriving every week. I have contracts. If word gets out that the water is killing horses and turning boys into prophets, everything I've built here dies. Do you understand that?"

"I understand that the ground is moving and the water is rising. I understand that lying will only make the dying worse."

Pricket's mouth worked. He looked like he wanted to say more but could not find the words. He turned and walked back toward his office. His shoulders were tight under the expensive wool.

Jonas stood in the street until the sun climbed higher. The red dust dried on his boots. It left a crust that cracked when he moved. The smell of metal stayed in his nose.

That night he returned to his cabin. He built a fire and set water to boil from the creek. The water stayed clear. He drank it slowly, tasting the cold and the pine.

He lay down on his cot without undressing. The floor beneath him moved with the same slow rhythm as the night before. He matched his breathing to it without thinking. The sound followed him into sleep.

In the dream he stood waist-deep in black water. The surface reached his ribs and stayed there. The water was warm. It moved against his skin like something alive. Around him the cavern stretched in every direction. Stone walls rose into darkness. The ceiling dripped with slow, steady drops that echoed like footsteps.

Eyeless figures stood in the shadows. They watched him without eyes. Their faces were the color of old bone. Their mouths moved but no sound came out. They stood perfectly still except for the slight rise and fall of their chests. They were breathing the same water he stood in.

One of them stepped forward. Its feet made no sound on the stone floor. It reached toward Jonas with a hand that had too many joints. The fingers brushed his face. The touch was cold and dry.

"You are almost ready," the figure said. The voice came from everywhere and nowhere. "The water has already begun to know you."

Jonas woke with his heart hammering. The cabin was dark. The fire had burned down to coals. He sat up and looked at his boots. They stood by the door where he had left them.

Red mud caked the soles and the sides. It was the same rust color as the well water. It had not been there when he went to sleep. The mud was warm to the touch. It smelled of metal and spoiled fruit.

He stood and walked to the window. The settlement lay quiet under the stars. No lights burned in any cabin. The well stood at the center of the street like a wound that had not yet closed.

Jonas looked at the mud on his boots again. The entity had reached him through the dream. It had left a mark. The water was no longer content to stay beneath the ground. It wanted to climb.

He sat at the table and stared at the cooling coals. The floor beneath his chair moved with its patient rhythm. He placed his palm against the boards and felt the slow push and settle of soil against wood.

The entity was learning how to reach them through the water. It had used the well as a mouth. It would use every seam and crack and thin place until the entire valley drank from the same poisoned source.

Jonas closed his eyes and tried to picture the valley as it had been. The image would not hold. Every time he tried to fix it the new shapes intruded. The rust water. The dead horse. The boy speaking with a voice that was not his own. The red mud on his boots.

He opened his eyes. The cabin looked the same. The fire crackled low. But the floor beneath his chair moved with a rhythm that belonged to something else entirely. Something that had been waiting a long time to wake. Something that was beginning to understand how to wear the world like a second skin.

Outside, the settlement continued its slow breathing. Doors stayed shut. Windows stayed dark. The ground beneath all of it kept moving, pushing upward, remembering. The water had risen. The water had tasted them. The water would not forget.

CHAPTER THREE

The Hollow-Eyed Gather

The morning came hard and gray over the settlement. Jonas stepped out of his cabin and saw the frost had turned the color of old rust again. The red dust had spread during the night. It coated the steps and the path and the edges of every boot print left in the dirt. He pulled his coat tight and walked toward the center of town. Widow Grier stood at the far end of the main street with her shotgun resting across one arm. She watched the tree line the way a person watches a wound that might start bleeding again.

People came out of their cabins slow, keeping their voices low, and a woman carrying a bucket stopped halfway to the well before turning back. A man with a beard stood in his doorway, watching, and did not step outside. Jonas kept his hands in his pockets and his eyes on the ground. The red dust clung to every surface it touched. It left marks that looked like someone had walked through drying blood.

Word had already moved through the settlement before the sun came up. The Hollow-Eyed had been seen again. More of them than before. They stood at the edge of the trees in the places where the frost still held. Their pale shapes stayed motionless against the dark trunks. Their empty sockets faced the buildings. People who had looked out their windows at first light had turned away quick. They pulled their curtains shut and stayed inside.

Jonas found Sera near the boarding house. She held a strip of cloth in one hand. The cloth had gone the color of old blood. She looked at the tree line without blinking. The figures stood exactly where they had been described. They stayed so still they looked like pale, salt-bitten trunks left behind by an old fire, their gray faces catching the weak winter light.

Sera kept her gaze fixed on the gray shapes, her fingers tightening around the blood-colored cloth. "They came closer during the night."

Jonas nodded. He kept his eyes on the figures. The empty sockets seemed to pull at the light. The figures stood where previous victims had fallen. Paul Murdock had marked the locations in his journal. Three of the Hollow-Eyed occupied the exact spots where the stone bodies had been found after the first sinkhole. Their positions matched the pattern of death that had already happened here.

They walked together toward the old graves. The ground there had been disturbed from beneath. Shallow depressions marked the soil in the shape of bodies pressing upward. The earth had split and frayed, looking as though heavy shapes had clawed through the clay and forced the mud aside until the surface gave way. Roots had been pulled loose.

Stones had shifted in their places. The smell of metal rose from the disturbed earth.

Paul Murdock sat on a fallen log with his journal open across his knees. His pencil moved across the page in quick strokes. He sketched the figures that stood at the tree line. His hand worked without pause. The lines came out dark and uneven. He drew the empty sockets with careful attention to the way they caught no light. He drew the positions of their hands and the slight rise of their chests as they breathed the cold air.

Paul didn't look up from his sketching, his pencil tip snapping against the rough paper. "They're standing where the others died. The one near the birch tree. That's where the first man turned to stone. The one by the split rock. That's where the woman fell. They remember the places. They're claiming them again."

Jonas looked at the depressions in the soil. The shapes pressed up from below like bodies trying to surface. The earth had the texture of skin that had been stretched too tight. He knelt and touched one of the depressions. The dirt felt warm beneath his fingers. It pulsed once with a slow rhythm that did not belong to the ground.

Sera stood beside him. She watched the tree line where the figures waited. "They gather when the entity wakes. They mark the thin places. They show us where the memory has collected."

Paul closed his journal. His fingers left red marks on the pages where he had gripped the pencil too hard. He looked at the figures again. His eyes stayed wide. "They know we're watching. They want us to see them. They want us to understand that they're not leaving."

The three of them walked back toward the settlement. The figures at the tree line did not move. They stayed in their positions as the morning light grew stronger. Their pale forms remained visible against the dark trunks. The empty sockets followed the movement of the living.

Eliza Penhaligon arrived that afternoon. She came on foot with a single bag and a veil that covered her face. She walked into the settlement like someone who already knew the way. Her dress was the color of deep mourning. Her hands moved constantly at her sides, touching the string of stone beads she wore around her neck. She stopped in the center of the main street and looked at the well where the red water still moved in slow circles.

Harlan Pricket came out of his office to meet her. He wore his good suit and the practiced smile that did not reach his eyes. He spoke to her in the careful tone he used for new arrivals. She listened without removing her veil. Her hands kept moving along the beads. When Pricket finished his speech about seasonal minerals and temporary inconvenience, she asked him where she might find a man named Jonas Farlow.

Pricket's eyelid twitched. He pointed toward the boarding house. Eliza Penhaligon walked in that direction without thanking him. She moved through the settlement like someone who had already been here before. The people who saw her coming stepped aside. They watched her pass with the same quiet fear they showed the figures at the tree line.

Jonas was inside the boarding house when she arrived. He sat at the table with Widow Grier and Sera. Paul Murdock rested on a bench against the wall. His eyes stayed closed but his hands moved against his knees in small, restless motions.

Widow Grier had her shotgun resting against the wall within reach. She kept her eyes on the door.

Eliza Penhaligon entered without knocking. She stood in the doorway and studied each of them in turn, her veil remaining in place as her fingers traced the cold stone beads. "I am looking for my husband. He came to this valley three years ago. His name was Thomas Penhaligon. I have reason to believe he is still here."

Pricket had followed her inside. He stood behind her with his hands clasped in front of him. "Mrs. Penhaligon, I have already explained that no one by that name has settled here. We keep careful records of all arrivals."

Eliza Penhaligon did not turn to look at him. She stared directly at Jonas, her voice flat and precisely articulated. "You are the one who hears the water. I can see it in the way you stand. The sound has already begun to follow you."

Jonas stayed seated. He kept his hands on the table where she could see them. "I don't know your husband."

Eliza leaned forward slightly, the black veil shifting against her collar. "You will. The water remembers everyone who drinks from it. Your name is already written in the places where the stone listens. When the ground opens, it will speak your name first."

Widow Grier picked up her shotgun. She did not aim it. She simply held it across her lap. The movement was enough to make Pricket step back toward the door. Eliza Penhaligon remained where she stood. Her hands continued their slow movement along the beads.

Eliza's fingers finally stilled on the beads. "The cycle has begun again. I have seen it before. The water turns first. Then the ground remembers how to breathe. Then the witnesses gather at the thin places. Your valley will follow the same pattern as all the others. The only question is how many of you will choose to stay and watch it happen."

She turned and walked back into the street. Pricket followed her with hurried steps. He spoke to her in a low voice that did not carry through the doorway. Jonas watched them go. The smell of metal lingered in the air after they had gone. It mixed with the scent of the red dust that had tracked in on their boots.

Sera pressed her forehead against the cool glass of the window, watching Eliza Penhaligon cross the street toward the boarding house. "She has seen this before. Not in this valley. In another place. The way she speaks of the cycle. She knows the pattern."

Jonas joined her at the window. The figures at the tree line remained in their positions. They had not moved since morning. The light had shifted but their shadows stayed fixed against the trunks. "She asked me what it feels like to hear the water inside my skull."

Sera turned from the glass, her pale eyes dark with a exhaustion she couldn't hide. "The water is learning you. It has tasted you through the dream. It will keep tasting until it knows every part."

Paul Murdock opened his eyes. He sat up on the bench and looked at his hands. The red marks from the pencil had faded. His fingers still trembled. "She smells like the caverns," he said. "Like stone that has never seen light. She has been down there. She has walked in the black water."

Widow Grier checked the shells in her shotgun. The sound was loud in the small room. She closed the weapon and set it back against the wall. "She can stay or she can leave. Either way, we have work to do before night comes."

They spent the afternoon walking the perimeter of the settlement. Jonas and Sera moved along the tree line where the figures stood. The Hollow-Eyed did not react to their approach. They remained motionless. Their empty sockets followed the movement of the living but their bodies stayed fixed in place. The depressions in the old graves had deepened by the time they returned. The shapes pressed higher against the soil.

Paul Murdock stayed inside the boarding house. He drew in his journal with the same restless focus. The pages filled with images of the figures at the tree line. He drew the positions of their hands and the slight rise of their chests. He drew the depressions in the graves and the way the roots had been pulled loose from beneath. His pencil moved without pause. The lines came out dark and uneven.

Evening came early. The light faded behind the trees and the figures at the edge of the forest became harder to see. Their pale forms remained visible against the dark trunks. Three of them had moved closer during the afternoon. They now stood at the boundary where the settlement's cleared land met the wild growth. Their positions matched the places where three victims had been found after the first awakening.

Widow Grier loaded her shotgun and walked to the end of the main street. She stood with her back to the buildings and her eyes on the approaching figures. She did not call out to them. She did not raise her weapon. She simply stood where she could see them clearly. Her presence was enough to keep the fear from driving people inside their cabins.

Jonas and Sera stood at the window of the boarding house. They watched Widow Grier take her position. The figures at the tree line did not advance further. They stayed at the edge of the cleared land. Their empty sockets faced the settlement. The light from the cabins cast long shadows across the ground between them.

"She will stand there all night if she has to," Sera said.

Jonas nodded. He kept his eyes on the figures. The way they stood reminded him of the dream. The black water. The cavern walls. The eyeless shapes watching from the shadows. The memory of the voice that had come from everywhere and nowhere at once. "You are almost ready," it had said. The words stayed with him like a taste he could not wash out.

They left the boarding house together. The red dust had spread farther during the day. It coated the steps and the path and the edges of every boot print. They walked toward the end of the main street where Widow Grier stood guard. The figures at the tree line remained in their positions. They stayed so still they looked like pale, salt-bitten trunks left behind by an old fire, their gray faces catching the weak winter light.

Widow Grier acknowledged them with a nod, keeping her shotgun resting across one arm as her eyes remained locked on the pale shapes in the dark. "They've been moving closer every hour. By morning they'll be at the doors if we let them."

"We won't let them," Jonas said.

The three of them stood together at the edge of the settlement. The figures at the tree line stayed where they were, their pale forms visible against the dark trunks, empty sockets following the movement of the living. The ground beneath their feet pulsed once with a slow rhythm that did not belong to the soil. The sensation traveled up through their boots and settled in their bones like a memory they had not known they carried.

Paul Murdock came out of the boarding house, clutching his journal tightly under one arm. He walked to where they stood, his wide eyes fixed on the figures. "They're breathing with the ground. I can hear it. The same rhythm. They're part of it now."

Jonas placed his hand against the ground. The pulse came again. It moved through the soil like something learning how to reach them. The red dust rose slightly where his fingers touched the earth. It settled back into place when the pulse faded. The smell of metal lingered in the air.

They remained at the edge of the settlement as the last light left the sky. The figures at the tree line stayed in their positions. They did not advance. They did not retreat. They simply watched. Widow Grier kept her shotgun ready. Sera stood with her hands at her sides. Jonas kept his eyes on the empty sockets that followed their every movement. The ground beneath them continued its slow breathing. The water had risen. The witnesses had gathered. The entity beneath the valley was learning how to wear the world like a second skin.

CHAPTER FOUR

Shared Nightmares

The boarding house sat quiet when Jonas pushed through the door. His boots left red prints on the worn floorboards, and the mark of the frost still clung to his coat. Sera followed close behind, her braid heavy with crow feathers that moved when she turned her head. Widow Grier stood at the stove with her iron skillet already in one hand, and Paul Murdock sat on the bench near the window, his journal open across his knees though the pencil rested still between his fingers.

They had come back from the tree line when the light began to fade. No one spoke much on the walk. The figures stayed where they had moved to during the afternoon, three pale shapes that watched without blinking. Widow Grier kept her shotgun low but ready, and when they reached the porch steps she set the weapon against the wall within reach of her chair. The room smelled of wood smoke and the faint iron scent that had followed them from the disturbed graves.

Paul looked up first. His eyes moved from one face to another as though measuring how much each person already knew. "I couldn't sleep last night," he said. His voice came out thin. "I kept seeing the same place. Underground. Water moving under stone that never saw daylight."

Sera pulled out a chair and sat. She kept her hands flat on the table. "Black river," she said. "Cavern ceiling low enough to touch if you reached up."

Paul nodded once. His pencil began to move across the page again, slow at first, then faster. The lines came out dark and certain. He drew the curve of water against rock and the way the current pulled at shapes that might have been bodies or might have been something else entirely. His grip tightened until the pencil creaked in his fingers.

Jonas watched the drawing take shape. He had seen the same water in his own sleep, the same black surface broken by ripples that moved against the pull of any current he understood. The cavern walls had pressed close around him, and something large had moved through the depths below, displacing water that rose and fell in steady rhythm.

Widow Grier set the skillet down. The metal rang against the stove. "My husband was there," she said. Her voice stayed even. "Not the way he was when he left. Stone all the way through his hands and up his arms. Reaching toward the surface like he could still climb out."

The room held the words without answering them. Paul kept drawing. The cavern took clearer form on the page, the ceiling low and the water deep enough to swallow a standing man. A shape moved through the middle distance, larger than anything that should fit in such a space, and the surface of the river rose and fell with its passing.

Jonas felt the memory settle behind his eyes. The sound came next, a low grinding that traveled through the water itself rather than through air. It had no words. It carried only weight and direction and the certainty that something beneath the valley had noticed them.

Sera broke the silence first. "I have seen this place for months," she said. Her fingers pressed harder against the table. "I kept it to myself because I thought if I said it out loud the cycle would already have me. But the details match. Every one of them. The sound. The movement under the water. The way the stone feels warm when you press your hand to it."

Paul's pencil snapped. The broken end rolled across the table and stopped against Widow Grier's forearm. He stared at his hand as though it belonged to someone else, then opened his fingers and let the remaining piece fall. Blood welled at the base of his thumb where the wood had cut him, but he did not seem to notice.

"I need to draw it again," he said. His voice had gone distant. "The same one. I have to get the shape right."

Widow Grier tore a strip from an old cloth and wrapped his thumb without asking. Paul let her do it. His free hand reached for another pencil from the tin on the table, and the drawing began once more on a fresh page. The cavern appeared identical to the first, down to the angle of the water's surface and the position of the dark shape moving through the middle.

Jonas stood and moved to the window. The settlement lay quiet under the weak moonlight, and the figures at the tree line remained visible as pale suggestions against the darker trunks. He watched them for a long moment, then turned back to the room.

"We all saw the same thing," he said. "That shouldn't be possible."

"The entity doesn't care what should be possible," Sera answered. "It wants us to carry the memory together. The more of us who hold it, the stronger the connection becomes."

Paul finished the second drawing and set the pencil down. His fingers left small red prints on the paper. He flexed his hand once, then again, as though testing whether it still answered to him. "The water moved wrong," he said. "Against the slope. Like it had somewhere else to be."

Widow Grier checked the shotgun shells without opening the weapon. Her hands moved in the old pattern, counting without looking. "My husband died in the mine collapse three winters back," she said. "They told me the shaft gave way and the water came in too fast. But I saw his hands in the dream. They were stone all the way to the elbows, and the fingers were still moving."

The words hung in the room. No one reached for comfort or offered any. The truth settled between them like another presence at the table.

Jonas felt the pull behind his thoughts first, a tug toward the creek that had no reason attached to it. He blinked and the sensation passed, but when he looked at the door he could not remember why he had stood. The others watched him without speaking. He sat again and kept his hands on the table where they could see them.

"I lost time just now," he said. "I was thinking about the water and then I was standing."

Sera's expression did not change, but her shoulders tightened. "The missing time comes when the connection strengthens. The entity learns how to reach through the shared memory and pull at the parts of you that are already open."

Paul turned the journal so the others could see the second drawing. The cavern matched the first in every visible detail, and the dark shape in the water had moved slightly closer to the foreground. The surface rippled in the same pattern as before, rising and falling with the passage of something too large to name.

"I didn't choose this one," Paul said. "My hand just kept going until it looked right."

Widow Grier stood and moved to the stove again. She poured water into the kettle and set it to heat, though none of them had asked for tea. The routine motion seemed to steady her. When the kettle began to steam she poured four cups and set them on the table without comment.

They drank in silence. The warmth did nothing to ease the cold that had settled into the room with the drawings. Outside, the wind moved through the trees and carried the faint sound of something shifting beneath the ground, a low grinding that matched the rhythm Paul had drawn in the water.

Jonas finished his cup and stood. The pull toward the creek had returned, stronger this time, and he recognized the sensation now for what it was. He walked to the door without explaining and stepped outside. The cold air cleared his head for a moment, then the missing time took him again.

When he became aware of his surroundings he stood at the creek's edge with water lapping at his boots. The red tint had spread farther upstream during the day, and the surface moved in slow circles that had no source he could see. He stepped back from the bank and turned toward the settlement. His legs ached as though he had walked farther than the distance between the boarding house and the water.

Sera found him there. She carried a lantern that cast a weak circle of light across the disturbed ground. She did not ask how he had come to be standing in the dark with no coat and no weapon. She simply held the lantern higher so he could see the path back.

"How long?" she asked.

"Long enough to get here," Jonas answered. "I don't remember the walk."

They returned to the boarding house together. Paul had started a third drawing while they were gone, and this one showed the cavern from a different angle. The low ceiling curved overhead, and the water filled the lower third of the page. The dark shape had moved closer still, and its outline suggested bulk and weight rather than any recognizable form.

Widow Grier sat with her shotgun across her lap. She had not loaded it, but the shells lay in a neat row on the table beside her cup. "Pricket came by while you were gone," she said. "He heard about the dreams. He says anyone who talks about them openly will answer to him."

Jonas sat again. The warmth from the stove had not reached the far side of the room, and his hands felt stiff from the cold creek air. "He can't stop people from sleeping," he said.

"He can stop them from saying what they saw," Widow Grier answered. "He already threatened to lock up anyone who spreads panic. His words."

Sera set the lantern on the table. The flame wavered and settled. "The entity wants the dreams shared," she said.

"Pricket can threaten all he likes. The connection is already made."

Paul finished the third drawing and pushed the journal away. His fingers bled from the pressure he had put on the pencil, and small red drops marked the page near the edge. He wrapped his hand in the same cloth Widow Grier had used earlier and sat back against the wall.

"I can feel it moving," he said. "Not just in the dream. Under the floorboards. Like it learned the shape of the settlement and now it wants to match it."

The ground answered his words. A single pulse traveled through the soil beneath the boarding house, strong enough to rattle the cups on the table and send the lantern flame leaping. Dishes shifted on the shelf behind the stove, and one plate fell to the floor and broke into three pieces. The sound rang loud in the small room.

No one moved at first. The pulse faded and left a stillness that felt wrong after the movement. Widow Grier picked up the broken plate pieces and set them on the counter without comment. Sera adjusted the lantern wick until the flame steadied. Paul stared at his journal as though the drawings might have changed while the ground moved.

Jonas felt the pulse in his bones long after it had passed through the floor. The rhythm matched the movement he had heard in the dream, the slow displacement of water by something too large for the cavern that contained it. He looked at the others and saw the same recognition in their faces.

"It wants us to dream together," he said. "Not just the same dream. The same moment. The same witness."

Sera nodded. Her hands had gone still on the table. "The cycle feeds on shared memory," she said. "The more people who carry the same image, the more the entity can use that image to reach outward. It is learning how to wear us like clothing."

Widow Grier loaded the shotgun with slow, deliberate motions. The shells clicked into place one after another. She closed the weapon and set it against the wall again, but she did not move her chair back to its usual place by the stove.

"My husband reached up through the stone," she said. "In the dream his fingers broke through the surface and kept reaching. I think he wanted me to pull him out. I think he still wants that."

The words settled into the room like the pulse had settled into the ground. Paul picked up his journal and turned the pages until he found the first drawing of the cavern. He traced the line of the water with one finger, careful not to smudge the pencil marks.

"The sound came from everywhere at once," he said. "Like the stone itself was speaking. I couldn't tell where it started."

Jonas stood and moved to the window again. The figures at the tree line had not moved since he last looked, but their positions seemed closer now, as though the darkness had brought them forward without anyone noticing. He watched them for a long moment, then turned back to the room.

"We need to tell the others," he said. "Not all of them. The ones who will listen without running to Pricket."

Sera gathered the drawings and stacked them in the journal. She closed the cover and tied the leather cord that held the pages together. "They will know soon enough," she said. "The ground will tell them before we do."

The pulse came again while she spoke, weaker than the first but steady enough to move the lantern flame. Widow Grier's shotgun shifted against the wall and settled again. Paul kept his hands flat on the table as though the wood could anchor him against whatever moved beneath.

Jonas felt the missing time threaten again, a tug at the edge of his thoughts that wanted to pull him toward the creek. He stayed where he stood and counted the seconds until the sensation faded. When it passed he sat again and kept his hands visible on the table.

"The entity is no longer content to dream through us," he said. "It wants us to dream together."

The room held the statement without answer. Outside, the wind moved through the trees and carried the faint sound of water moving against stone somewhere far below. The figures at the tree line watched the settlement with empty sockets that caught no light. The ground beneath the boarding house settled into stillness that felt temporary rather than permanent.

Widow Grier poured another round of tea. The kettle had gone cold, but the routine of pouring gave her hands something to do. They drank without speaking, and the broken plate remained on the counter where she had left it. The drawings stayed closed inside the journal, but the memory of the cavern and the black water and the shape moving through the depths remained clear in each of their minds.

Paul's hands had stopped trembling. He flexed his fingers once and winced at the cut on his thumb. Widow Grier rewrapped the cloth without comment. Sera kept one hand on the journal as though the drawings might escape if she looked away. Jonas watched the door and listened for the next pulse that would come from beneath the settlement.

The night stretched long around them. The wind moved and the figures watched and the ground waited. The shared dream had already begun its work, and the entity beneath the valley had made its first demand clear. They would carry the memory together, whether they chose it or not.

CHAPTER FIVE

The Voice Beneath Stone

The collapse hit without warning. One moment the old mine sat quiet in the gray light, its timbered mouth sagging against the hillside. The next, the ground buckled inward with a wet tearing sound that rolled through the dirt like a massive, rotted root snapping far below. Dust lifted in a thick cloud that caught the low sun and turned the air the dull red of drying blood.

Paul Murdock stood ten paces from the edge when it happened. His sketchbook hung open in one hand. The pencil had already begun to move across the page on its own, tracing lines that made no sense until the earth opened and revealed what he had been drawing. Stone walls curved inward beneath the surface. They pulsed once, slow and heavy, like ribs drawing breath.

He dropped to his knees. The book fell beside him and the pages fluttered open to the same cavern he had drawn three times the night before. His lips shaped words without sound at first. Then his voice came through, thin and raw, carrying a tone that did not belong to him.

"Jonas Farlow will be the next to join the collection."

The sentence left his mouth and hung there. Around him, the men just kept leaning on their shovels, wiping sweat from their necks and staring down into the shifting dirt. Nobody turned their head. Nobody looked at Paul as he repeated the words, even as the blood ran from his nose in a steady line that reached his chin and fell in dark drops onto the open sketchbook.

At a dead run, Jonas burst onto the scene. He had been checking the creek when the ground shook, sending ripples across the red surface. Behind him, her braid swinging against her shoulder as they crossed the last stretch of open ground, came Sera.

They found Paul still kneeling. His hands rested on his thighs and his eyes stayed fixed on the hole. The stone inside the chamber had a wet sheen. Thin lines of the same red water that now filled the creek ran through cracks in the rock like veins under skin. The surface rose and fell in a rhythm that matched no wind or heartbeat anyone could claim as their own.

Jonas crouched beside him. He kept his distance from the edge. The drop fell straight for twenty feet before the pulsing stone was swallowed by a thick, heavy darkness that seemed to drink the light itself. "What did you hear?"

Paul's mouth worked. Fresh blood welled at his nostril. "It knows your name. It said you would be next."

The words landed like cold water. Jonas stayed low and studied the stone. The veins pulsed again, stronger this time, and a thin thread of red water broke free and ran down the wall in a slow line. It reached the bottom and disappeared into a seam that had not been there moments before.

Sera moved to the lip of the collapse. She pressed one palm flat against a jutting piece of rock that had not yet fallen. Heat rose through her skin. The stone felt alive under her hand, not warm from sunlight but from something moving inside it. She pulled her hand back and wiped it against her leggings. The red smear stayed on the fabric.

Harlan Pricket arrived with two men carrying hammers and planks. He wore the same stained wool suit he had worn the day before, his fingers restlessly picking at a loose thread on his cuff, pulling and winding it until the skin of his thumb showed raw and white as he took in the scene.

"Board it. Now. No one goes near until I say otherwise."

The men hesitated. One of them looked at the pulsing stone and took a half step back. Pricket's voice rose.

"I said board it. We cannot have every fool in the valley staring into that hole and carrying tales back to new arrivals."

They set to work. The hammers rang against wood, but the sound died instantly in the open air, swallowed between strikes as though the ground itself were drinking the noise. The first plank went across the opening. A second followed. Then something on the far side pushed outward. The wood bowed. Splinters flew from the edges where the nails held. The plank cracked down the center and fell inward, vanishing into the dark.

Pricket swore. He grabbed one of the hammers and swung at the remaining boards himself. Each blow landed with a dull thud that traveled up his arms and left his face pale. The wood held for three strikes, then split. Another plank dropped away. Something moved in the shadows below, slow and heavy, pressing against the last barrier.

Widow Grier stepped forward. She did not raise the shotgun, but her voice cut through the hammering.

"Pricket, those boards will not hold. Whatever is down there has already learned the shape of the settlement. It will find another way out before the day ends."

Pricket lowered the hammer. His hands shook once, then steadied. He looked at the remaining families who had gathered at a distance, children pressed against mothers' skirts and fathers holding axes that would do nothing against what waited below. His voice took on the false brightness he used when trying to sell land to newcomers.

"We seal what we can and keep the rest quiet. Panic solves nothing. The mine has always been unstable. This is just another collapse."

No one answered him. The silence stretched until Sera spoke without looking up from the stone.

"The rock is warm. Veins run through it carrying the red water. This is not a mine anymore. It is something the earth has grown around the old tunnels."

Paul's nosebleed slowed. He wiped his face with the back of his hand and left a red streak across his cheek. His voice returned to its usual softness, though it still carried the echo of what he had heard.

"It spoke inside my head. Not through the air. It said the collection grows. It said Jonas would be the next piece."

Jonas stayed crouched. He watched the last plank bow outward again and then settle as whatever pushed from below withdrew. The motion left a faint tremor in the ground that traveled up through his boots. He stood and moved back from the edge.

"We need to move the children first. Widow Grier, take whoever will listen and get them to the northern ridge. The ground there has not shifted yet."

She nodded once. Her shotgun stayed ready, though she had not chambered a shell. She turned toward the gathered families and began calling names. Some mothers gathered their children without argument. Others stayed rooted, hands tightening on their skirts as though leaving their homes would make the horror real rather than imagined.

Pricket watched the division spread through the small crowd. His eyelid twitched faster. He pointed at Jonas with the hammer still in his hand.

"You spread this. You and the woman with her feathers and her stories. If more families leave because of what you say, the settlement dies. Remember that when you decide what to tell them next."

Jonas met his stare without answering. The hammer trembled in Pricket's grip. After a long moment the man lowered it and turned away, barking orders at the two workers to fetch more lumber from the mill shed. They left without looking back at the hole.

Sera stayed at the edge. She studied the exposed stone again, tracing the pattern of the red veins with her eyes. One of the lines pulsed stronger than the others, and a small bubble of water formed at a crack before bursting and running down the wall. The scent of iron rose from it, thick enough to taste.

Paul gathered his sketchbook. The pages showed the cavern from below now, drawn in lines so dark the pencil had torn the paper. He closed the book and held it against his chest as though the drawings might escape if left open.

"The voice said the collection remembers every witness. It said the stone keeps them all."

Jonas turned toward the settlement square. The ground between the mine and the main cluster of cabins felt uneven under his boots, as though the surface had already begun to settle into new shapes. He walked slowly, counting each step to keep his mind anchored in the present moment. The pull toward the creek had not returned yet, but he expected it with every breath.

Widow Grier had gathered seven children and three mothers by the time he reached the square. She spoke in low tones, directing them toward the northern path with practical gestures rather than promises. One woman refused. She stood with her arms crossed and her youngest child clinging to her leg, shaking her head each time Widow Grier named the dangers.

"My husband built this cabin with his own hands. We buried our first son behind the smokehouse. I will not leave either of them for something that may or may not crawl out of an old mine."

Widow Grier did not argue. She simply moved to the next family and repeated the offer. Two more agreed to go. The rest stayed, and the square grew quieter as the light faded toward evening.

Jonas found Sera already waiting near his cabin. She had brought a basin of water from the well and set it on the stump he used for chopping wood. The water looked clear for now, though the iron smell had begun to reach even this distance from the creek.

Sera poured a thin stream of water over his wrists. "You need to wash the dust from your hands before it settles into the cuts."

He dipped his hands into the basin. The water turned pink as the red clay dissolved. He scrubbed until the skin showed raw beneath the dirt, then dried them on the cloth she offered. The silence between them felt steady rather than empty.

Paul joined them after a while. He carried his sketchbook under one arm and kept glancing back toward the mine as though expecting another collapse. His nose had stopped bleeding, but the dried blood remained on his upper lip like a faint mustache.

"Pricket will try to seal the entrance with more than boards tonight," he said. "He cannot afford for anyone to see what is growing inside."

Jonas nodded. He sat on the chopping stump and rested his elbows on his knees. The ground beneath his boots felt too still, as though it held its breath between pulses. He listened for the next one without wanting to hear it.

Evening came slowly. The families who had refused to leave lit their lanterns early and kept the flames low. The square held a hush that had nothing to do with ordinary nightfall. Even the dogs stayed close to their masters instead of ranging through the trees as they usually did.

Widow Grier returned once the last of the willing families had started north. She carried her shotgun in one hand and a bundle of blankets in the other. She set the blankets on the porch of the boarding house without comment and checked the shells in her weapon again, though she had done so only an hour before.

"Three more cabins are empty now," she said. "The people inside walked out without taking anything. Their doors stand open and the stoves are still warm."

Sera stood near the porch rail. Her fingers moved along the wood grain as though reading something written there. "The entity pulls memory the way a river pulls at loose stone. Some cannot hold against it. They walk toward whatever calls them."

The first stars appeared. The air cooled but did not bring the usual relief after a long day of work. Instead it carried a dampness that settled into clothes and skin and stayed there. Jonas pulled his coat tighter around his shoulders and kept watch on the tree line beyond the square.

The figure stepped out just after full dark. It moved without sound, its pale shape separating from the darker trunks as though the shadows themselves had decided to walk. No eyes caught the lantern light. The sockets remained empty, yet the head turned with purpose toward the small cluster of people still gathered near the boarding house.

It stopped twenty paces from the nearest cabin. The ground between it and the settlement held perfectly still. Then the mouth opened. The sound that emerged carried no human tone. It scraped like stone grinding against stone, low and steady, forming words that should not have fit through any throat.

"Jonas Farlow, we have been waiting for you."

The sentence ended. The figure did not move closer. It simply stood with its arms at its sides and its empty face turned toward the man who had once been only a trapper passing through the valley. The words hung in the cold air long after the mouth closed again.

Jonas felt the cold reach deeper than his coat could block. He did not step forward. He did not speak. The knowledge that the entity beneath the stone knew his name settled into his chest like a second heartbeat, heavier and slower than his own.

The figure retreated without hurry. It melted back into the tree line until the darkness swallowed it completely. No footprints marked the ground where it had stood. The lanterns flickered once and steadied. Widow Grier's shotgun remained lowered, the barrel pointed at nothing.

Paul sat down hard on the porch steps. His sketchbook slipped from his hands and landed open on the boards. The latest drawing showed the same cavern, but now a new shape stood among the others in the water, its arms reaching upward through the red veins. The face had no eyes.

Sera moved to Jonas's side. She did not touch him. She simply stood close enough that her presence anchored him to the moment.

Sera watched the dark gap between the pines where the figure had stood. "It has named you. That means the cycle has already marked you as part of what comes next."

Jonas kept his gaze on the place where the figure had disappeared. The trees stood still. No wind moved through the branches. The ground beneath the square waited, and somewhere far below, the stone continued its slow pulse, drawing breath for whatever waited to rise.

Widow Grier broke the silence first. She chambered a shell with a sharp click that carried across the empty square.

"Whatever it wants from you, it will not take you without a fight. Not while I still have shells and breath to spend."

Paul picked up his sketchbook. He closed it gently, as though the pages might tear if handled too roughly. His hands left faint red prints on the leather cover from the cut on his thumb that had never properly healed.

The lanterns burned lower. Families that remained in their cabins kept their windows shuttered. The mine entrance, half a mile away, stayed dark except for the faint red glow that sometimes leaked between the remaining boards when the stone inside pulsed strongest.

Jonas stayed where he stood until his legs grew stiff from the cold. The name the figure had spoken remained in his ears, repeating with each heartbeat. He turned finally and walked toward his cabin without looking back at the tree line. Sera followed at a distance that gave him room to breathe. Widow Grier stayed on the porch with her shotgun across her lap, and Paul sat beside her with his journal held tight against his chest.

The night settled around them. The ground beneath the settlement held its rhythm, slow and patient, waiting for the next witness to add to the collection it had already begun to gather.

CHAPTER SIX

Missing Hours

Jonas woke to a sky that had not been there when he closed his eyes. Gray light pressed through the cabin window, but the angle felt wrong. He lay still on the cot and counted the breaths that had already passed without his notice. Three hours, at least. Maybe more. The stove had gone cold and the kettle sat untouched on the hook. His boots were still on his feet, caked to the laces with red clay that had not been there the night before.

He sat up slowly. His right hand ached in a way that suggested it had gripped something hard for a long time. When he opened the fingers, the clay filled the creases of his palm and streaked across the knuckles like dried blood. He flexed them. The skin pulled tight. A small cut ran along the base of his thumb, fresh and clean. He could not remember when he had received it.

The knife was gone from its sheath at his belt. The leather loop hung empty, the stitching still tight. He stood and checked the floorboards, then the table, then the shelf above the window. Nothing. The cabin held its usual sparse order, but something had shifted during the missing time. The chair near the door sat at an angle that did not match how he usually left it. A single footprint marked the dust near the threshold, pointing inward.

He crossed to the table. His journal lay open there, the pages weighted down by a river stone he kept for that purpose. The handwriting on the exposed page was his own in shape but not in pressure. The letters slanted differently, the lines crowded closer together than he ever wrote them. He read the first sentence and felt the cold settle deeper into his bones.

The entity feeds on what the valley remembers. Every grief, every death, every fear that has soaked into the soil stays there. It gathers them like a man gathers stones for a wall. The more it holds, the hungrier it becomes. It wants the new memories most of all. The ones still warm.

Jonas read it twice. The words did not feel like his own thoughts. They carried a patience that belonged to something older than any trapper or settler. He closed the journal and pressed both hands flat against the cover. The clay on his skin left faint marks on the leather.

The door opened without a knock. Sera stepped inside and stopped when she saw him standing over the table. She took in the clay on his hands, the missing knife, the open journal. She did not ask what had happened. She simply moved to the basin on the counter and poured water from the pitcher. The water ran clear for now, though the iron smell had begun to reach even this distance from the creek.

She dipped a cloth into the basin and held it out. Jonas took it without speaking. He scrubbed at the clay until the water in the basin turned the color of weak rust. The cut on his thumb stung under the cloth. Sera watched his face the way she watched the stone at the mine, looking for movement that should not be there.

Sera didn't look up from the water. "I've seen it before. Three times."

Jonas rinsed the cloth, the water swirling cloudy and dark. "And?"

"Two of them got the hollow eyes. Within the month." She squeezed the rag dry. "The other walked into the creek. We only found his boots."

The words settled between them like dust. Jonas flexed his hand again. The cut had stopped bleeding, but the ache remained. He could feel the missing hours pressing at the edges of his mind, waiting to be filled with something he had not chosen.

Paul Murdock appeared in the doorway next, breathing hard from the run. His sketchbook hung from one hand, the pages flapping against his leg. He had not washed the dried blood from his upper lip since the day before. It cracked when he spoke.

"The ridge trail," Paul panted, clutching his ribs. "It isn't there. I kept ending up back at the water. The trees... they aren't where they belong, Jonas."

Jonas moved to the door and looked past him. The tree line beyond the cabin looked the same as always from this distance, but something about the spacing of the trunks felt off. A stand of pine that had always marked the eastern boundary now sat too far to the left. He counted the visible trees twice. The count did not match what he remembered.

Sera stepped outside with him. She studied the ground between the cabin and the trees. A faint depression ran through the dirt, barely visible, as though something heavy had been dragged across the surface during the night. The depression pointed toward the creek rather than away from it.

Paul stayed on the threshold. "I tried to reach Widow Grier's place first. The path shifted under me. I walked for an hour and ended up back where I started."

Jonas nodded once. He checked the sky for the sun's position and found it higher than it should have been. The missing hours had taken more than time. They had taken direction as well.

They walked together toward the settlement square. The ground felt uneven beneath their boots, rising in small swells that had not been there the day before. Jonas kept his gaze on the path ahead. He did not want to see how many other changes had taken root overnight.

Widow Grier met them at the edge of the square. Her shotgun rested across one forearm, and her free hand gripped the handle of an iron skillet as though she expected to need it. Her face carried the same grim set it always did, but something new had settled behind her eyes. She jerked her head toward the small graveyard beyond the boarding house.

Widow Grier spit into the dirt. "Someone dug up Thomas. Or tried to."

Jonas followed her through the square. The few remaining families watched from their doorways but did not approach. A child clung to her mother's skirt and stared at the red clay still streaking Jonas's hands. He wiped them on his coat as they walked.

The graveyard sat on a slight rise behind the boarding house. Only twelve graves remained marked, the rest lost to time and weather. Widow Grier's husband's plot lay near the center. The mound of earth had been disturbed, the dirt pushed upward in a low dome. A single crack ran across the wooden coffin lid, wide enough for a hand to fit through if anyone had been willing to reach down and test it.

Sera knelt in the wet clay, her fingers hovering an inch above the split wood. "The wood's splintered upward. From the inside."

A sharp metallic slide echoed as Widow Grier chambered a round. "He's been under for eight years. That's not Thomas pushing."

Paul stood at the edge of the graveyard, his sketchbook open again. His pencil moved across the page without his full attention. The lines he drew showed the same cavern from the mine, but now a shape stood beside the pulsing stone, its arms pressed against the underside of a lid. The face had no eyes. The mouth hung open in a silent push.

Harlan Pricket arrived with two men at his back. He wore the same stained wool suit, though the cuffs had frayed further since the day before. His left eyelid twitched faster than Jonas had ever seen it. He stopped ten paces from the grave and pointed at the cracked lid with a shaking finger.

"You're behind this." Pricket's finger shook as he pointed at the mound. "You and your damn warnings. You want them packing up. You want the whole place to yourselves."

Jonas didn't blink. "I didn't touch it."

"Look at your hands!" Pricket stepped closer, his chest heaving. "People are loading wagons because of your mouth. I won't have it."

The two men behind Pricket shifted their weight but did not speak. One of them glanced at the cracked coffin lid and took a half step back. The other kept his eyes on the ground between his boots.

Pricket fumbled with his coat, his fingers twitching so hard he dropped his iron-headed hammer into the dirt. He didn't pick it up. "Get out. By dark. Take the boy and the girl and hit the road east. If I see you tomorrow, I'll have the boys throw you in the creek."

The words hung in the air. Jonas felt the weight of them settle across his shoulders, heavier than the missing hours. He looked past Pricket to the square beyond. A single figure stood in the shadow of the boarding house porch, watching. Eliza Penhaligon held her stone beads between her fingers, the string clicking softly with each small movement. A small leather book rested open in her other hand. She wrote without looking down at the page.

Widow Grier raised the barrel of her twelve-gauge just enough to clear the dirt. "Try it, Harlan. See who goes in first."

Pricket snatched his hammer from the mud, wiping his hand on his trousers. "There's rules here. We keep them or we're finished."

He turned and walked back toward the square without waiting for an answer. The two men followed. One of them looked back once at the cracked grave, then hurried to catch up.

Eliza Penhaligon remained in the shadow of the porch. She closed her small book and slipped it into a pocket of her dark dress. The beads continued their soft clicking as she watched Jonas across the distance. Her veil stayed down, but her head tilted slightly, as though she were listening to something beneath the surface of the square.

Sera watched them go. "He won't do anything. He's too scared."

Jonas nodded. He looked down at the cracked coffin lid again. A thin line of red water had begun to seep through the split, slow and steady, as though the grave itself had started to bleed. He stepped back from the edge.

They returned to the square together. The families that remained kept their distance, though Widow Grier spoke to each of them in turn. She offered the same practical advice she always gave, directing them toward the northern ridge with gestures rather than promises. Two more agreed to leave. The rest stayed, their faces turned toward their own doorways as though the wood could keep out what had already begun to move beneath their feet.

Paul stared down at his boots, his pencil scratching aimlessly. "The mine... it said you're next. Maybe if you go, it stops."

Jonas shook his head. "The cycle does not break because one man leaves. It waits. It has waited before."

The afternoon stretched long and quiet. The sun moved across the sky without warmth. Jonas checked the position of the trees again and found another stand that had shifted during the missing hours. A path that had once led to the smokehouse now curved toward the creek instead. He marked the change on a scrap of paper and folded it into his pocket.

Evening came without the usual sounds of settlement life. No children played near the well. No dogs ranged through the trees. The remaining lanterns burned low, their flames kept small against the growing dark. Jonas sat on the chopping stump outside his cabin and listened to the ground beneath his boots. It held still for now, but the stillness felt like held breath rather than rest.

Sera brought a basin of water from the well and set it beside him. She poured a thin stream over his wrists again, washing away the last traces of clay. The water ran pink, then clear. She did not speak until the basin had emptied.

"They always ask the same things," Sera whispered, looking at the empty basin. "Where they went. Why their bones ache. Then they stop asking."

Jonas dried his hands on the cloth she offered. "I do not feel different yet."

"For now." She touched the damp cloth to her apron. "Then the dreams start. Then you start hearing it."

Paul came around the corner of the cabin. "Widow Grier's sitting by the grave. She's got her lantern out."

Jonas nodded. He stood and stretched the stiffness from his legs. The cut on his thumb had begun to scab over, but the ache remained. He flexed the hand once more and felt the missing hours press against the edges of his mind again, waiting.

Night settled over the square without the usual comfort of stars. Clouds moved in from the west, low and heavy, carrying the dampness that had followed them since the mine collapse. Jonas stayed near his cabin, watching the tree line. The pines stood in their new positions, still and patient, as though they had always been there.

Eliza Penhaligon appeared at the edge of the square just before full dark. She walked slowly, her dark dress brushing the dirt with each step. The stone beads clicked between her fingers, steady and rhythmic. She stopped twenty paces from Jonas's cabin and watched him across the distance. Her veil stayed down, but her head tilted again, listening.

Jonas did not move toward her. He stayed where he stood and waited. The beads continued their soft clicking. After a long moment, Eliza turned and walked back toward the boarding house. Her small leather book remained in her pocket, but Jonas could feel the weight of what she had written there, the record of every change the valley had shown that day.

He entered his cabin when the last light faded. Sera stayed on the porch with her back against the wall, her gaze on the tree line. Paul sat on the chopping stump, his sketchbook open across his knees. Widow Grier remained at the graveyard, the shotgun across her lap and the iron skillet within reach.

Jonas lay on the cot without removing his boots. He closed his eyes and waited for sleep to come. The missing hours pressed at the edges of his mind, patient and hungry. The ground beneath the cabin held its rhythm, slow and steady, drawing breath for whatever waited to rise.

The dream came without warning. He stood among the Hollow-Eyed in a place that had no sky and no ground, only the red water that filled the space between. His arms hung at his sides. His face turned upward toward a surface he could not see. The sockets where his eyes had been felt empty and cool. Around him, the other figures stood in the same posture, waiting. The water moved against his legs, warm and metallic, carrying the taste of iron with every breath.

A voice rose from the water, low and grinding, like stone against stone. It spoke his name. The sound filled the space and echoed back from every direction at once. Jonas

Farlow. The collection grows. The memories wait. Your eyes will see what comes next.

He tried to move his hands, but they remained at his sides. The water rose higher, reaching his waist, then his chest. The other figures turned their empty faces toward him. Their mouths opened in the same silent push he had seen on the coffin lid. The red water pulsed around them, slow and heavy, matching the rhythm of the stone beneath the mine.

Jonas woke to the sound of his own breathing. The cabin remained dark. The stove sat cold. His hands rested at his sides, and the cut on his thumb had begun to bleed again. He sat up and wiped the blood on his coat. The missing hours had returned during the dream, though he could not say how long they had taken this time.

He stood and moved to the door. The square outside lay quiet under the low clouds. Sera still sat on the porch, her gaze fixed on the tree line. She did not turn when he stepped outside. Paul remained on the chopping stump, his sketchbook closed now, his hands resting on his knees. Widow Grier had returned from the graveyard and stood near the boarding house, the shotgun held ready.

Jonas looked down at his hands. The clay had returned during the missing hours, streaking across his knuckles in the same pattern as before. He flexed the fingers and felt the ache settle deeper into the joints. The ground beneath his boots held still for now, but the stillness carried the same held breath he had felt since waking.

The night stretched on without relief. The clouds stayed low and heavy, pressing down on the square like a second sky. Jonas stayed near his cabin and watched the tree line. The pines stood in their new positions, still and patient.

Somewhere beneath the surface, the stone continued its slow pulse, drawing breath for whatever waited to rise.

He did not return to the cot. He stayed on his feet and counted the hours that remained before dawn. The missing time pressed at the edges of his mind, waiting to be filled. The ground beneath the settlement held its rhythm, slow and steady, patient as the stone that waited below.

CHAPTER SEVEN

The Land Shifts

The valley floor gave way sometime between midnight and dawn. Jonas heard it from inside the cabin, a low, wet sound like ice breaking on a frozen creek. He sat up on the cot and listened. The sound did not repeat. Outside, the square remained dark and still. He pulled on his coat and stepped through the door.

Sera already stood in the open space between the boarding house and the well. She held a lantern low, the flame barely reaching past her boots. Paul came around the corner of the cabin with his sketchbook clutched against his chest. None of them spoke at first. The quiet felt thicker than it should have been.

Widow Grier appeared last. She carried the shotgun in both hands and kept the barrel pointed at the ground. Her face looked older in the lantern light. She jerked her chin toward the southern slope beyond the graveyard. "Something broke open down there. Felt it through the floorboards."

They walked together without hurry. The path sloped gently at first, then steeper as they left the square behind. Jonas kept his boots on the harder ground where the frost still held. Red clay smeared the lower edges of his coat from the previous night, and he could feel the weight of it with each step.

The collapse showed itself before they reached the bottom. A wide section of earth had dropped inward, leaving a ragged pit maybe thirty feet across. Steam rose from the bottom in thin threads. The smell that came up with it reminded Jonas of wet stone and old iron. Roots hung from the broken edge like torn sinew.

Sera held the lantern higher. The light caught on something pale beneath the loose dirt. Flat surfaces. Edges too straight to be natural. Stone blocks lay exposed at the bottom of the pit, their surfaces carved with lines that caught the flame and threw it back in broken patterns.

Paul moved closer to the edge, his boots sliding in the loose gravel. His sketchbook slipped from his fingers and landed in the dirt. He did not pick it up. His eyes stayed fixed on the stone below, his jaw trembling. "I can hear it. Same sound from the mine. Only louder."

Jonas tested the ground near the rim with the toe of his boot, watching the red dirt crumble and slide into the dark. "We go down slow or not at all."

Sera set the lantern on a flat rock and tied a length of rope around a nearby stump. She tested the knot twice before she threw the free end into the pit. The rope uncoiled with a soft hiss. "I can reach the bottom from here. You follow if you want."

She went first, her boots finding purchase on the broken dirt. Jonas waited until she reached the stone floor, then followed. The pit walls pressed close on either side. The air grew warmer the lower he went. When his boots touched stone, he felt something shift beneath the surface, a slow pulse that traveled up through his legs and settled in his chest.

The carvings covered most of the exposed blocks. Circles within circles. Figures without eyes. The same shape repeated across the surface, always facing inward toward a central form that the carver had left unfinished. The stone felt warm under Jonas's palm. Not from the sun. Something else.

Sera traced one of the outer rings with her finger. "These match the marks my grandmother showed me. The ones she said belonged to the first watchers. They marked the places where the boundary thins."

Paul remained at the rim above them. He had retrieved his sketchbook but had not opened it. His hands stayed pressed flat against the dirt as if he needed the contact to stay upright. "The stone is breathing," he said. "I can feel it through my feet."

Jonas crouched near one of the larger blocks. The carving there showed more detail than the others. The central shape had arms that reached upward, though the hands were only suggestions. Around it, the eyeless figures stood in a ring, their mouths open in the same silent push he had seen on the coffin lid the day before. Red water had collected in the depressions between the lines. It smelled metallic and warm.

A sound rose from deeper in the pit. Not wind. Something lower, like stone grinding against stone. It came in slow intervals. Jonas counted the spaces between each pulse. They matched the rhythm he had felt through his boots.

Sera straightened. "We should not stay long. The carvings are old, but the water is new. It means the boundary is moving."

They climbed back up using the same rope. The dirt gave way under their hands in small showers. When Jonas reached the surface, he turned and looked back down. The stone at the bottom reflected the lantern light in a way that made the carvings seem to shift when he blinked. He shook his head and stepped away from the edge.

Paul had not moved from his place at the rim. His eyes looked unfocused. A thin line of red clay marked his left cheek where he had leaned against the dirt. Jonas touched his shoulder. Paul flinched, then blinked several times before his gaze cleared.

"I was at the well," Paul said. His voice sounded distant. "Then I was here. I do not remember walking."

Widow Grier checked the shotgun again, though she had not fired it. "Three hours at most since I left the house. You could not have covered that distance in the dark without falling in."

They walked back toward the square in silence. The sun had begun to rise, but the light stayed thin and gray. No smoke rose from the chimneys of the remaining houses. The families that had not left kept their doors closed. Jonas counted the visible windows. Three showed movement behind the glass. The rest stayed dark.

Harlan Pricket met them at the edge of the square. Two men stood behind him with rifles held across their chests. Pricket's suit looked more rumpled than usual, and his left eyelid twitched without pause. He pointed at the southern slope. "You will cover that hole. Tarps. Boards. Whatever you have. No one goes near it."

Jonas stopped ten paces from him. "The stone underneath predates the settlement. It predates everything we know."

Pricket's mouth tightened. "Stories. We deal in facts here. The fact is that families are leaving because of what you say. I will not have more damage done."

One of the men behind Pricket shifted his weight. He glanced toward the slope, then back at the ground. "We heard voices down there last night," he said. "Calling names. Mine was one of them."

Pricket turned on him. "You keep quiet or you walk. We do not need more panic."

The man looked at Jonas instead. "It knew my brother's name too. He died in the mine two years ago."

Pricket waved a hand as if brushing away smoke. "Cover the pit. That is an order. If I see anyone near it without a tarp in their hands, they answer to me."

He turned and walked back toward his office. The two men followed, though the one who had spoken looked back once. His face had gone pale beneath the dirt.

Widow Grier watched them leave. "He will try to bury this like he buried the last trouble. It will not work."

They gathered what tarps they could find from the storage shed behind the boarding house. The fabric smelled of mildew and old grease. Jonas and Sera carried the first one down to the pit while Widow Grier stayed above with the shotgun. Paul followed at a distance, his sketchbook open again but his pencil still.

They spread the tarp across the opening as best they could. The wind caught the edges and tried to pull it free. Jonas weighted the corners with stones from the slope. The fabric sagged in the middle, but it covered the view of the carvings below. Red water had begun to seep through the lowest point, staining the canvas in slow circles.

A voice rose from beneath the tarp. It sounded like a man calling from a great distance. The words were unclear, but the tone carried the shape of a name. Jonas recognized the rhythm of his own name in the sound. He stepped back from the edge.

Sera tied the last corner down. "Pricket's men will not stay long once they hear that. The stone knows who listens."

They returned to the square. The sun had climbed higher, but the cold had not lifted. Widow Grier's house stood where it always had, though something about the angle of the front door looked different. Jonas stopped and studied the building. The door faced slightly more toward the creek than it had the day before. The foundation stones had shifted during the night.

Widow Grier noticed it at the same moment. She walked to the door and pushed it open, her hand lingering on the rough wood. The hinges moved without resistance, but the threshold now sat at an angle that did not match the path leading to it. "The whole house moved. I felt the floor tilt this morning but thought it was my head."

Inside, the furniture had slid against the far wall. A chair lay on its side near the stove. The iron skillet that usually hung by the door now rested on the floor. Widow Grier righted the chair and set the skillet back on its hook. She did not comment on the change.

Jonas checked the ground around the foundation. A faint line ran through the dirt where the house had dragged itself sideways. The movement had been slow and steady, not sudden. The earth beneath the boards still pulsed with the same rhythm he had felt in the pit.

Eliza Penhaligon appeared at the corner of the boarding house. Her veil remained down, but her hands moved constantly, the stone beads clicking between her fingers. She watched the shifted house without surprise. When she turned toward the southern slope, her head tilted as if she could hear something the others could not.

She walked past them without speaking and continued toward the pit. Jonas followed at a distance. Sera stayed close behind him. Paul remained near Widow Grier's door, his sketchbook pressed against his chest.

Eliza reached the edge of the covered pit and stopped. She lifted one corner of the tarp and looked down. The red water had pooled deeper since they left. She studied the surface for a long moment, then let the fabric fall back into place. When she turned away, her veil had been lifted. Her eyes reflected the red water in the same way the stone had reflected the lantern light. The color did not belong to her.

She walked back toward the square without looking at Jonas or Sera. The beads continued their steady rhythm. Her expression remained empty of any feeling Jonas could name.

They returned to the square as the sun reached its highest point. The remaining families stayed indoors. No one approached the pit. Pricket's men had not returned with more tarps. The one who had heard the voices stood near the well, his rifle held loosely in both hands. He did not meet Jonas's eyes.

Sera studied the carvings she had copied onto a scrap of paper. Her finger traced the outer circle. "The symbols tell of a time before the first settlers. The earth held memory then as it holds it now. What was done upon the surface stayed beneath."

Jonas sat on the chopping stump outside his cabin. The pulse from the pit traveled through the ground and reached him even here. It came slower now, but each beat felt heavier than the last. He pressed his palm flat against the dirt. The warmth beneath the surface matched the warmth of the stone blocks.

Paul approached from the direction of the boarding house, his fingers twitching against the seams of his trousers. His face looked pale beneath the coal dust. "I was at the well again. Then I was at the pit. My hands were on the stone. I do not remember leaving."

Widow Grier came out of her shifted house with the shotgun under one arm. She had wrapped the iron skillet in a cloth and tied it to her belt. "Three more families packed their wagons this morning. They left before sunrise. The rest are staying because they have nowhere else."

Jonas nodded. He watched the tree line beyond the square. The pines stood in their new positions, still and patient. A faint depression ran through the dirt between the square and the slope, the same line he had seen the day before. It pointed toward the pit now rather than the creek.

Sera folded the paper with the carvings and slipped it into her coat. "The entity does not need to climb out. It only needs us to look down. Each witness adds to what it holds."

The afternoon passed without further movement from the pit. Pricket remained in his office with the door closed. His men took turns watching the covered hole from a distance. None of them stayed long before they moved farther back. The one who had heard the voices sat near the well and stared at his hands.

Jonas returned to the cabin when the light began to fade. Sera stayed on the porch with her back against the wall.

Paul sat on the chopping stump again, his sketchbook open but his pencil unused. Widow Grier checked the foundation of her house once more before she went inside. The door still faced the wrong direction, but the floor had settled.

Jonas lay on the cot without removing his boots. The pulse from the pit reached him through the floorboards. It matched the rhythm of his own heartbeat now. He closed his eyes and listened to the sound. The missing hours pressed at the edges of his mind, waiting to be filled with something he had not chosen. The ground beneath the settlement continued its slow breath, drawing closer to whatever waited beneath the stone.

The night settled without stars. Clouds moved in from the west again, low and heavy. Jonas stayed on the cot and counted the pulses that traveled through the wood. Each one felt slightly stronger than the last. He did not sleep. The entity beneath the valley had begun to move in earnest, and the witnesses it had gathered would not be enough to satisfy what it sought next.

CHAPTER EIGHT

The Witness Remembers

Sera waited until the square emptied. The last of Pricket's men had taken their posts farther back, rifles slung low, eyes avoiding the southern slope. She touched Jonas's sleeve once, a quick pressure that meant follow without asking. He fell in step behind her as she moved between the silent cabins. The pine scent on his coat mixed with the damp earth smell that clung to everything now.

She led him past the shifted house where Widow Grier's door faced the wrong direction. The line in the dirt still showed where the whole structure had dragged itself sideways during the night. Neither of them spoke. The air felt thicker the farther they walked from the square, as if the trees themselves pressed inward.

They crossed the low ground near the creek bed. Red water had pooled in the shallows, warm to the touch, metallic in the nose. Jonas kept his boots on the harder ground where the frost still held. Sera moved with the same steady pace she always used, though her shoulders stayed tight beneath her coat.

The thin place appeared without warning. One moment they walked between ordinary pines. The next, the ground opened into a shallow depression ringed by stones that looked too regular to be natural. Moss grew thick along the inner curve. The air above the depression shimmered faintly, like heat rising from summer rock even though the morning stayed cold.

Sera stopped at the outer ring of stones. "This one has been quiet since I was small. My grandmother showed it to me. Told me never to stand inside the circle after dark."

Jonas studied the depression. The stones formed a broken ring maybe twelve feet across. Inside the ring, the ground looked darker than the surrounding soil, almost black. No grass grew there. The depression itself sat lower than the rest of the slope, a scooped-out bowl that shouldn't have formed on its own.

Jonas spat into the weeds, his eyes never leaving the dark bowl. "How many of these exist?"

"Too many. Some we sealed. Some we watched. This one we left alone because it never grew larger. Until now."

She stepped over the outer stones. The shimmer in the air thickened as she moved. Jonas followed, boots sinking slightly into the soft earth inside the ring. The temperature dropped the moment he crossed the boundary. Not by much, just enough to notice against his face.

They stood at the center. Sera knelt and pressed her palm to the ground. Jonas did the same. The soil felt warm beneath his fingers, the same warmth he had felt from the carved stones in the pit. A low sound rose from below, too faint to shape into words yet steady enough to recognize as something that breathed.

His own voice came up through the ground.

The words formed slowly, each syllable stretched like something pulled through water. They described the square at dawn, the way Widow Grier would stand with the shotgun across her forearms, the way Paul would clutch his sketchbook too tightly. They described three settlers found in their beds with their eyes removed and their bodies turned rigid as stone. The voice spoke of things that had not happened yet, but the tone carried the weight of memory already recorded.

Jonas pulled his hand back. The voice stopped. He looked at Sera, who kept her palm flat against the soil. Her face stayed calm, though the muscles along her jaw stood out.

Sera didn't look up, her fingers digging slightly into the dark soil. "It knows us. It learns from every witness it touches."

Footsteps approached from the tree line. Paul Murdock emerged between the pines, his coat unbuttoned, his sketchbook clutched against his chest. He stopped at the outer ring of stones and stared into the depression. His eyes looked unfocused, the same distant expression he had worn at the pit the day before.

Paul didn't look at them. He kept staring down into the dark depression, clutching his book like a shield. "I heard it from the boarding house. Same voice that called from the mine. Only clearer."

He stepped over the stones without waiting for permission. The shimmer thickened around him. When he reached the center, he dropped to his knees and pressed both hands to the ground. His mouth opened. Words came out in a language Jonas had never heard, a rolling cadence that sounded like water moving over stones far underground. Paul did not seem to notice he was speaking. His eyes stayed fixed on the dark soil beneath his palms.

Sera listened without interrupting. The words continued for nearly a minute before Paul drew a shaking breath and spoke in English again.

"It wants what we carry. Every grief. Every death. Every memory that sinks into the soil. It collects us. We become part of the remembering."

Paul's hands trembled against the ground. A thin line of red water seeped up between his fingers, warm and metallic. He did not pull away. His voice shifted back into the unknown language, the syllables tumbling faster now, as if something beneath the surface pushed the words through him.

Jonas watched the younger man's face. Sweat gathered along Paul's hairline despite the cold. His lips moved without pause, translating things Jonas could not understand. The air inside the ring grew warmer. The shimmer above the depression pulsed once, matching the rhythm Jonas had felt through the ground since the collapse.

More footsteps. Widow Grier appeared at the outer stones, the shotgun held loosely in both hands. She studied the depression, then the three figures already inside the circle. Her face showed no surprise, only the same grim set she wore when facing Pricket's men.

Widow Grier didn't look at the stones. She kept her eyes on the tree line behind them, her thumb resting on the shotgun's safety. "Three more. Found this morning. Two in the boarding house, one in the cabin behind the well. Eyes gone. Bodies stiff as boards. Pricket has his men moving the remains to the storage shed. Says he'll deal with them after he handles the pit."

She stepped over the stones. The shimmer parted around her without resistance. She stopped a few feet from the center and looked down at the dark soil.

"He barricaded himself in the office. Won't come out. Won't let anyone in. His men are scared enough to listen to him for now."

Paul's voice rose again, still in the strange language. Widow Grier listened for a moment, then shook her head once.

"Whatever he's saying, it isn't for us to understand."

Eliza Penhaligon appeared last. She wore the same heavy mourning dress, the veil still lifted from the night before. Her stone beads clicked between her fingers as she approached the outer ring. She studied the depression without speaking, her eyes reflecting the dark soil in the same way they had reflected the red water the day before.

She stepped across the boundary. The shimmer thickened immediately, pushing back against her. A low sound filled the air, like fabric tearing. Eliza continued forward, her hands moving faster on the beads. When she reached the inner edge of the circle, something invisible struck her palms. She jerked backward, a sharp breath escaping her. Burn marks appeared across both hands, red and blistered, as if she had touched hot metal.

She stopped. The beads fell silent. She looked at her palms, then at the center of the depression where Jonas, Sera, and Paul remained. Her expression stayed empty, though the skin around her eyes tightened.

Sera watched the retreating figure, her hand dropping back to her side. "The boundary remembers who belongs inside it."

Eliza did not answer. She turned and walked back toward the outer stones, her hands cradled against her chest. The burn marks stood out against her pale skin. She crossed the ring and disappeared between the pines without looking back.

Paul's voice broke off. He sat back on his heels, breathing hard. Red water streaked his palms. He wiped them on his coat, leaving dark smears across the fabric.

Paul stared at his stained hands, rubbing his palms against his trousers to scrape off the wet grit. "I don't know those words. I don't know how they came out of me."

Sera kept her palm against the ground. "The thin places open the mind. They let the entity reach through. You translated because it needed someone to speak for it."

Jonas stood. The voice from beneath the soil had gone quiet, but the pulse still traveled through the soles of his boots. It matched his heartbeat now, a slow rhythm that felt almost familiar.

"What happens if we stay here too long?" he asked.

"We add to its collection," Sera answered. "Every witness it touches becomes part of the memory it holds. The more we listen, the more it learns us."

Widow Grier checked the shotgun, though she had not fired it. She kept the barrel pointed at the ground inside the ring.

"Pricket will try to bury this too. Same as the pit. Same as the missing families. He thinks if he covers it long enough, the settlement keeps running."

She looked toward the trees where Eliza had disappeared.

"That one knows more than she says. The burns won't stop her. They'll only make her more careful."

Paul remained on his knees. His hands had stopped shaking, but his face stayed pale beneath the coal dust. He stared at the dark soil between his boots.

"It showed me things. People standing in circles. Water rising through stone. A shape in the center that never stops moving. I saw it like I was already there."

Sera finally lifted her hand from the ground. The warmth faded from her palm, leaving it cold again. She stood and brushed the dirt from her coat.

"My people tried to seal these places generations ago. They poured salt. They burned cedar. They left watchers to guard the boundaries. None of it worked for long. The entity always finds another way through."

Jonas studied the depression. The shimmer above it had thinned slightly, though the pulse still moved through the soil. He could feel it in his chest now, a slow beat that matched the one he had heard from the pit.

Jonas turned his collar up against the rising wind, looking back toward the dark pines. "Then we delay it. Same as they did. We keep it from growing until we find a way to stop it."

Sera nodded once. She stepped toward the outer ring, and the others followed. The shimmer parted around them as they crossed the stones. The temperature rose again once they left the circle, the morning cold settling back against their faces.

They walked in silence toward the square. The pines stood in their new positions, still and patient. The line in the dirt that pointed toward the pit had grown deeper overnight, a narrow trench that cut through the frost. Jonas kept his boots on the harder ground, avoiding the soft places where the red water had begun to seep upward.

Paul walked slightly behind them, his sketchbook open now, his pencil moving across the page. He drew the ring of stones, the dark depression, the shimmer that still hung in the air above it. His hand moved without hesitation, as if the image had already formed behind his eyes.

Widow Grier stayed at the rear, the shotgun held ready. She glanced back once toward the thin place, then forward again toward the square where Pricket's men still kept their distance from the southern slope.

Jonas felt the pulse through the ground with every step. It followed him away from the depression, a steady rhythm that settled deeper into his bones. He realized the entity beneath the valley did not need to climb out. It only needed witnesses. Each one added to the collection. Each one became part of the memory that waited below the stone.

The square appeared between the trees. No smoke rose from the chimneys. The remaining families kept their doors closed. Jonas counted the visible windows and found only two that showed movement. The rest stayed dark, the glass reflecting the gray morning light like blind eyes.

They stopped near the well. Widow Grier checked the shotgun again, her fingers moving over the shells with practiced care. Paul closed his sketchbook and pressed it against his chest. Sera looked toward the southern slope where the tarp still covered the pit, red water staining the canvas in slow circles.

Jonas pressed his palm flat against the dirt near the well. The pulse came through clearly, matching the rhythm he had felt inside the thin place. He pulled his hand back and stood. The entity already knew him. It had spoken his name from beneath the ground. Whether he fought or surrendered, he had already become part of what it collected.

The morning light stayed thin. Clouds moved in from the west, low and heavy. The settlement held its breath around them, waiting for whatever came next from below the stone. Jonas turned toward his cabin, and the others followed without speaking. The ground continued its slow breath beneath their feet, drawing them closer to whatever waited in the dark.

Sera paused at the cabin door. She looked back toward the southern slope, then at Jonas. Her eyes carried the same weight they always held when she spoke of the old stories, the ones her grandmother had passed down through the watchers who came before her.

Sera pulled her coat tighter, her gaze fixed on the red-stained tarp in the distance. "We seal what we can. We watch the rest. The cycle has broken before. It can break again."

Jonas nodded. He pushed the door open and stepped inside. The cabin felt colder than the morning air. He sat on the cot without removing his coat. The pulse from the ground traveled through the floorboards and reached him even here. He closed his eyes and listened to the sound. It matched his own heartbeat now, steady and patient, waiting for the next witness to add to its collection.

Outside, the square remained quiet. Widow Grier returned to her shifted house, the shotgun still in her hands. Paul sat on the ground near the well, his sketchbook open again, his pencil moving across the page. Sera stayed on the porch with her back against the wall, watching the trees where the thin place waited beneath the pines.

The entity beneath the valley had begun to move in earnest. Jonas could feel it through the boards beneath his boots, through the soil that pressed against the cabin walls. Every witness it touched became part of the memory it held. He had already added to that collection. The voice that spoke his name from below the ground had made that clear. Whether he stayed or fled, the entity would remember him. It would use what it learned to reach the others who remained.

He opened his eyes and stood. The cabin felt smaller than it had the night before. He walked to the door and looked out at the square. Sera still stood on the porch, her coat buttoned against the cold. Paul remained near the well, his pencil moving. Widow Grier's door faced the wrong direction, the foundation stones shifted during the night.

Jonas stepped outside. The pulse followed him, a steady rhythm that settled into his chest. He looked toward the southern slope where the pit waited beneath the tarp. The red water had spread farther overnight, staining the canvas in wider circles. Pricket's men had moved their posts even farther back, their rifles held loosely, their faces turned away from the covered hole.

The settlement held its silence around them. No wagons left the square. No smoke rose from the chimneys. The families that remained kept their doors closed and their windows dark. Jonas counted the visible movement and found none. The square felt like a place already abandoned, the people inside it waiting for whatever came next from below the stone.

Sera touched his arm once more, the same quick pressure that meant follow without asking. She led him toward the well where Paul sat with his sketchbook. Widow

Grier joined them from her shifted house, the shotgun held ready. They stood together in the gray morning light, four witnesses to something that collected memories and turned them into something new beneath the ground.

The entity beneath the valley waited. It had spoken through the thin place, through Paul's mouth, through the pulse that traveled through the soil. Jonas realized that every witness it had ever touched became part of its collection. He had already joined that collection. The voice that spoke his name from below the ground had made that clear. Whether he fought or surrendered, the entity would remember him. It would use what it learned to reach the others who remained.

The morning light stayed thin. Clouds moved in from the west, low and heavy. The settlement held its breath around them, waiting for whatever came next from below the stone. Jonas turned toward the southern slope and began to walk. The others followed without speaking. The ground continued its slow breath beneath their feet, drawing them closer to whatever waited in the dark.

CHAPTER NINE

The Heart Beneath Stone

The creek had changed again overnight. Where the red water once pooled in shallow pockets, it now flowed in slow circles that defied the slope of the land. Jonas stood at the tree line with Sera and watched the surface turn against itself. The water looked thicker than it had the day before. It carried bits of something pale that caught the weak light and vanished again.

Paul Murdock had not slept. His sketchbook lay open on a flat stone, the latest page filled with lines that curved like ribs around a hollow space. He pointed at the drawing without looking up. The pencil marks showed a chamber beneath the creek bed, walls lined with shapes that might have been people once.

Paul didn't look up from the page. "It opened while I was drawing. The ground just dropped. I heard it from the well."

Jonas moved closer to the bank. The red water reached within a few feet of his boots now. He could smell the metal in it, sharp and wrong. Something moved beneath the surface, not fish, not current, but a steady rise and fall like the breathing he had felt through the thin place.

Sera stepped to the water's edge. She studied the circles without touching them. The stone beads she sometimes carried hung quiet at her belt. She kept one hand near them, fingers ready to count or count out something else.

Sera's hand dropped to her belt. "This is where it chooses. The last thin place that still opens wide enough."

Widow Grier arrived with the shotgun slung across her back. She had wrapped the barrel in cloth to keep the red mist from settling on the metal. Her face showed the same hard set it always held when trouble moved from rumor to fact. She planted her boots in the frost-stiff grass and looked at the turning water.

Widow Grier spat into the weeds. "Pricket's men are clearing the last wagons. They won't go near the creek. Can't blame them."

Jonas nodded once. The settlement square had emptied faster than anyone expected. Three families had left at dawn, their children wrapped in blankets, their eyes fixed forward. No one looked back at the southern slope. The ones who remained kept their doors barred and their lamps low.

The ground beneath the creek trembled. A low sound rose, too deep for words, too steady to be wind. The red water lifted in a single wave that rolled outward and fell back into itself. Then the surface dropped. The creek bed caved inward, a sudden collapse that pulled the water down with it. Mud and stone tumbled into the new opening. The sound of falling earth echoed up from below like distant thunder trapped in rock.

Jonas moved without thinking. He grabbed the coil of rope from Widow Grier's shoulder and tied one end around the nearest pine. The trunk had shifted during the night, its roots pulled halfway from the soil, but the wood still held. He tested the knot and threw the free end into the hole.

Sera caught the rope on its second swing. She looped it around her waist and checked the knot with quick, sure fingers. Paul followed her to the edge. His hands shook, but he gripped the line anyway. Widow Grier stayed above, the shotgun now in both hands, her eyes on the trees that ringed the new sinkhole.

"If it moves again, pull twice," Jonas told her. "We'll come up if we can."

Widow Grier nodded. She did not waste breath on promises. The shotgun barrel tracked the rim of the hole, ready for anything that might climb out.

The descent took longer than Jonas expected. The walls of the sinkhole were not clean earth. They showed layers of stone that looked worked, edges too straight to be natural. Roots grew through the cracks, thick and pale, pulsing with the same rhythm he had felt in the thin place. The air grew warmer as they dropped. It carried the smell of wet stone and something older, like dust that had never known wind.

They reached the floor of the chamber. Jonas's boots landed on something that gave slightly under his weight. He looked down and saw a surface of fused stone and bone. The shapes were human in outline, arms and legs pressed flat, faces turned upward with empty sockets where eyes should have been. The remains had hardened into the floor itself.

They formed a single unbroken surface that stretched into the dark.

Sera touched one of the forms with the toe of her boot. The stone did not shift. She knelt and pressed her palm to what might once have been a chest. Her face stayed calm, but her shoulders tightened.

Sera pulled her hand back, rubbing her fingers against her skirt. "These are the ones who witnessed before. They stayed too long. The land took them the way it takes everything it remembers."

Paul moved to the nearest wall. His sketchbook stayed closed now. He traced the outline of a figure embedded in the stone. The shape showed a woman with long hair, her hands clasped around something small and round. The details stood out even in the low light, every fold of clothing preserved in the calcified surface.

Paul pressed his forehead against the damp stone. "They knew each other. I can feel it. Their memories are still here, stacked like cordwood."

The chamber opened wider than the sinkhole above. It stretched into a broad oval, the ceiling low enough that Jonas had to keep his head down in places. At the far end, a formation rose from the floor like a heart carved from living rock. It pulsed with the same slow rhythm that traveled through the ground. The surface showed veins of darker stone that moved beneath the outer layer. Around it stood the Hollow-Eyed, dozens of them, their empty faces turned toward the beating stone. They did not move. They only watched.

Jonas stepped closer. The nearest figure stood no more than three feet away. Its skin had the texture of dried clay. The sockets where eyes should have been held only darkness, but something in the way the head tilted suggested attention. Jonas felt the weight of that attention settle on him, patient and cold.

The voice came without warning. It rose from the air itself, not from any mouth, not from the stone, but from the space between the figures. The words formed slowly, each one carrying the weight of long use.

"You carry what we need," the voice said. "Every grief. Every death. Every name you have forgotten. We collect them all. The valley is one memory now. It waits for the right witnesses to finish the remembering."

Jonas felt the words settle in his chest. They matched the pulse beneath his boots. The Hollow-Eyed remained still, but the formation in their center beat faster for a moment, then slowed again.

Sera moved to stand beside him. She kept her distance from the figures, but her eyes tracked the walls where more remains lay embedded. She spoke quietly, almost to herself.

"The warnings are carved deeper here. My grandmother's people left markers, but these are older. They say the cycle cannot be broken, only turned. Each time it turns, more witnesses are added. The memory grows thicker."

Paul had dropped to his knees near the edge of the formation. His hands pressed flat against the stone floor. Sweat ran down his face despite the cold. His mouth opened, but no sound came at first. Then words spilled out, the same unknown language he had spoken at the thin place. The syllables rolled and broke against the walls, echoing back in fragments that sounded almost like names.

The Hollow-Eyed turned their heads toward him. The movement was slight, but it carried weight. Paul convulsed once, his back arching, his hands clawing at the stone. The voice that came from his mouth now belonged to something older than language. It spoke in layers, words overlapping words, until the chamber filled with the sound of water moving underground and stone grinding against stone.

Jonas reached for him. His fingers closed around Paul's wrist. The younger man's pulse raced beneath the skin, too fast, too hot. Jonas pulled hard. Paul came upright, eyes wide and empty. The foreign words stopped. He sagged against Jonas, breathing in ragged pulls.

Paul shivered, his teeth clicking together. "It knows your name. It knows all of us. We are already inside the memory. We just don't feel it yet."

The formation pulsed again. A low crack ran through the stone floor, thin and sharp. Red water began to seep upward through the new fissure. It spread across the fused remains, warm and metallic, carrying the same smell that had risen from the creek above.

Above them, Widow Grier's voice called down. The words echoed through the sinkhole, tight with urgency.

"Pricket's men are moving the wagons closer. They have barrels. Red water from the upper creek. He's going to try to flood you out."

Jonas looked up. The circle of daylight at the top of the hole looked smaller now. He could hear the sound of wood scraping against wood, men shouting orders that carried the edge of panic. The rope jerked once, then twice. Widow Grier was signaling them to climb.

They did not have time. The red water rose faster, pooling around their boots. Jonas felt the heat of it through the leather. Sera pulled Paul upright and guided him toward the rope. The Hollow-Eyed remained still, their attention fixed on the beating stone. Only their heads had moved. The rest of their bodies stayed rooted to the chamber floor.

Eliza Penhaligon appeared at the rim of the sinkhole. She wore the same mourning dress, the veil lifted, her stone beads glowing faintly in the gray light. She looked down at the chamber without surprise. Her hands moved over the beads in a steady rhythm. Then she stepped forward. The rope that Widow Grier had braced snapped tight as Eliza grabbed it. She descended without hesitation, her dark skirts trailing through the falling dirt.

Jonas moved to intercept her at the bottom. The red water reached his ankles now. Eliza stepped off the rope and into the chamber. She walked past the Hollow-Eyed without looking at them. Her eyes stayed on the central formation. The beads in her hands pulsed with the same light that came from the stone veins.

Eliza didn't blink. "It remembers me. It has remembered me through every cycle. I only need to stand close enough for it to finish the work."

Sera blocked her path. The two women stood face to face, the red water rising between them. Sera's hand rested on the hilt of the small knife she carried. Eliza smiled, the expression thin and empty.

Eliza's smile didn't reach her eyes. "You cannot stop what has already begun. The witnesses are gathered. The memory is ready. You only delay the moment when the valley opens its eyes."

The formation beat faster. The crack in the floor widened. Red water poured upward in a sudden fountain that splashed across the nearest Hollow-Eyed. The figures did not react. They only watched as the water ran down their calcified faces and pooled at their feet.

Paul staggered. The foreign words returned, louder now, filling the chamber. His body convulsed again, knees buckling, mouth working around syllables that belonged to no living tongue. Jonas caught him before he fell. The younger man's eyes rolled back. His skin burned hot beneath Jonas's hands.

"It is not trying to climb out," Paul said through the other voice. "It needs no body. It needs only to be seen. To be known. To be carried in every mind that has touched the valley. The Hollow-Eyed are its eyes. They witness so that the memory can grow. You are already part of it. Every name you have spoken. Every death you have seen. It holds them all."

The words stopped. Paul went limp in Jonas's arms. His breathing slowed, but his pulse still raced beneath the skin. Jonas lowered him to a patch of stone that remained above the rising water. The red tide reached their knees now.

Eliza continued forward. She reached the edge of the formation and opened her arms. The stone beads glowed brighter. The Hollow-Eyed turned their heads toward her in perfect unison. The movement made no sound, but the weight of it pressed against Jonas's chest like a hand.

Above, the sound of rushing water grew louder. Harlan Pricket's men had begun to pour the red creek water into the sinkhole. It cascaded down the walls in thick streams, adding to the flood already rising from below. The chamber filled faster. Jonas felt the current pull at his legs.

Widow Grier's voice cut through the noise. She had moved to the edge of the hole, the shotgun now aimed downward.

"Get out," she called. "The whole bank is shifting. I can't hold the rope much longer."

Jonas looked at Sera. She had her knife drawn now, the blade pointed at Eliza's back. The water reached their waists. The formation continued its slow pulse, unaffected by the flood. The Hollow-Eyed stood motionless, their attention fixed on the woman who approached them with open arms.

Jonas made the choice without speaking. He grabbed the rope and looped it around Paul first. He tied the knot with hands that shook from the cold water. Sera helped lift the younger man. They pulled once on the line. Widow Grier answered with two sharp tugs. The rope went taut. Paul rose toward the surface, his body limp, his sketchbook still clutched in one hand.

Eliza reached the formation. She placed both palms against the beating stone. The light from her beads flared once, then steadied. The Hollow-Eyed moved closer, their empty faces inches from hers now. She smiled again, the expression almost peaceful.

Eliza's fingers sank into the pulsing stone. "I have waited through so many cycles. This time I will stay. The memory will hold me. It will hold all of us who understand."

The water reached Jonas's chest. He could feel the pull of the current growing stronger. Sera still stood between him and Eliza, the knife steady in her hand. The chamber had become a single pool of red. The remains embedded in the floor disappeared beneath the surface. Only the tops of the Hollow-Eyed heads remained visible, and the beating stone that rose above the flood.

Jonas pulled on the rope. Widow Grier answered. The line went tight again. He looked at Sera. She met his eyes for a moment, then nodded. They climbed together, hands gripping the wet rope, boots finding purchase on the shifting wall. The red water rose behind them. It swallowed the chamber floor. It reached the waists of the Hollow-Eyed and kept climbing.

They reached the surface. Widow Grier hauled them over the rim with both hands. Paul lay on the grass nearby, his eyes open, his breathing shallow. The sketchbook had fallen open beside him. The latest drawing showed the chamber from above, the Hollow-Eyed gathered around the stone heart, Eliza's figure small and distant at the center.

The sinkhole continued to fill. Red water poured from the upper creek in steady streams. Harlan Pricket stood at the far bank with his men, his face pale, his hands clenched at his sides. He did not look at Jonas. He watched the rising water as if it could solve what the land had already set in motion.

Jonas stood on the bank. His clothes dripped red. The pulse still traveled through the ground beneath his boots, but it felt slower now, almost tired. He looked at the trees that ringed the sinkhole. The pines had shifted again during the flood. Their roots stood exposed, pale and wet, reaching toward the water like fingers.

Sera knelt beside Paul. She checked his pulse, then closed the sketchbook and tucked it beneath his arm. Her face showed nothing of what she had seen below. Only her hands, steady and sure, gave any sign that the chamber had touched her at all.

Widow Grier reloaded the shotgun. The shells clicked into place with the same care she always used. She kept the barrel pointed at the ground, but her eyes tracked the tree line where shadows moved between the pines.

Widow Grier wiped the rain and grit from her face. "Pricket will say the flood worked. He'll tell the next wagons that the danger has passed. They'll believe him until the ground opens again."

Jonas did not answer. He watched the red water settle in the sinkhole. The surface had gone still. The circles had stopped turning. The chamber below remained hidden now, filled and quiet, but the pulse still traveled through the soil. It matched the beat of his own heart, slow and patient, waiting for the next witness to add to its collection.

The Hollow-Eyed had not climbed out. They had stayed with the stone heart, their empty faces turned upward even as the water closed over them. Eliza had stood among them with open arms. Jonas could still see the way her beads had glowed against the dark stone. The memory would hold her now, the same way it held all the others who had come before.

He turned toward the settlement square. The remaining cabins stood with their doors closed. No smoke rose from the chimneys. The last wagons had already left, their wheels cutting fresh tracks through the frost. Only the four of them remained near the creek, four witnesses to something that collected names and turned them into stone.

Sera touched his sleeve once. The same quick pressure she had used before. Jonas followed her toward the trees. Widow Grier walked beside them, the shotgun ready. Paul stumbled between them, his eyes still distant, his sketchbook clutched tight against his chest.

The ground continued its slow breath beneath their feet. The pulse traveled through the soil and into their bones. Jonas felt it settle deeper with every step. He realized the entity did not need to emerge into the world of flesh and bone. It only needed to be known. To be carried in every mind that had touched the valley. The Hollow-Eyed were its eyes. They witnessed so that the memory could grow. Jonas had already become part of that memory. The voice that spoke his name from beneath the ground had made that clear. Whether he fought or surrendered, the entity would remember him. It would use what it learned to reach the others who remained.

The morning light stayed thin. Clouds moved in from the west, low and heavy. The settlement held its silence around them, waiting for whatever came next from below the stone. Jonas walked toward his cabin, and the others followed without speaking. The ground continued its slow breath beneath their feet, drawing them closer to whatever waited in the dark.

CHAPTER TEN

The Valley Remembers

The work at the creek bank had taken most of the night. Jonas wiped mud from his palms and studied the last stake Sera had driven into the soil. The wood stood straight where the thin place had shown itself, wrapped in strips of cloth marked with symbols her grandmother had passed down. She moved along the line of markers, checking each knot with careful fingers. The red water had retreated during the hours they worked, pulling back toward the main channel like something reluctant to leave.

Paul Murdock sat on a flat rock nearby, his sketchbook closed beside him. He had come to with the first light, his eyes still clouded from whatever had taken him in the chamber below. He hadn't spoken much since then, only nodded when Sera asked if he could stand. His hands stayed steady now, though the tremor returned whenever he looked toward the water.

Widow Grier had left them hours earlier to organize the last wagons. She returned as the sun climbed higher, her shotgun resting across one shoulder. She carried news in the set of her jaw, the way her boots struck the ground harder than usual. Two more families had slipped away in the dark, their doors left swinging and their animals loose in the pens. The livestock wandered the edges of the settlement, bleating at empty cabins.

Widow Grier spat into the dirt. "Pricket's got guards around the square. Rifles. Says he's protecting the property."

Jonas tested the nearest stake with his boot. It held firm, though the ground around it felt softer than it should. The red clay clung to the leather and refused to flake away when he scraped at it. He had no memory of stepping into the water during the night, but the stains reached past his ankles and disappeared beneath his cuffs.

Sera finished her circuit and returned to the center of their work. She carried a length of braided cord marked with the same symbols as the cloth. Her hands moved through the patterns without hesitation, though her shoulders stayed tight with the effort of remembering each step. The ritual was old, older than the settlement, older than the families who had settled here before them. It had never been meant to hold forever.

The first crack appeared while she worked. It started small, a hairline seam running from the base of one stake toward the water's edge. Jonas watched it lengthen, the soil parting like something pulled from beneath. Red moisture seeped through the opening and spread in a thin line across the clay. He stepped forward and pressed his heel against the seam, but the water found its way around his boot and continued outward.

Paul stood up from the rock. He moved toward the crack with his sketchbook open again, though he didn't draw. His eyes tracked the spreading moisture, and his free hand rose to his temple as if something pressed against the inside of his skull. The pencil marks on the open page showed the same stone formation repeated in overlapping lines, the edges blurred where his hand had shaken.

Paul didn't look at them. His fingers clawed at the edge of the paper. "It won't hold."

Sera didn't pause in her work. She finished tying the cord around the final stake and stepped back to survey the line. Her face showed nothing of what the words meant, but her fingers lingered on the last knot longer than necessary. The cloth strips fluttered in the morning breeze, their symbols already fading where the red moisture touched them.

Jonas walked the perimeter of their work one more time. The stakes stood evenly spaced, each one driven deep enough that only a foot of wood remained above the surface. The symbols on the cloth had been copied from rocks her people had left near other thin places, places where the ground had tried to open before. None of those markers remained intact now. Time and weather had worn them smooth, but the memory of what they meant survived in the stories passed from grandmother to granddaughter.

The settlement square lay quiet when they turned toward it. No smoke rose from the chimneys, and the windows stayed dark behind their shutters. The guards Pricket had posted stood at the corners with rifles across their chests, their eyes following the small group as it approached. One of them stepped forward when Jonas reached the first cabin, but the man stopped short of speaking. His face held the same exhausted look that everyone wore now, the look of someone who had stopped expecting the morning to bring answers.

Harlan Pricket's office door remained closed. The curtains had been drawn across the single window, and the lamp inside burned low enough that only a thin line of light escaped beneath the door. He had barricaded himself with the ledgers and contracts that proved his ownership of the valley. The documents would not stop what moved beneath the soil, but they gave him something to hold while the world changed around him.

Eliza Penhaligon stood at the creek's edge where the red water had risen during the night. Her mourning dress trailed into the moisture, the hem dark with it. She held her arms slightly away from her sides, her stone beads clicking together as her fingers worked through them in a steady rhythm. She did not turn when Jonas and Sera passed behind her, but her posture shifted as if she sensed their presence without needing to see them. The water reached her ankles now, and she made no move to step back from it.

Paul followed a few paces behind, his sketchbook clutched against his chest. He stopped when they reached the edge of the square and turned back toward the creek. His hands shook as he opened the book again, and the pencil moved across the page in quick, unsteady lines. The drawing showed the same formation, the same pulsing stone, the same gathering of empty faces around it. He tore the page free and started again on the next one, the lines overlapping the previous attempt until the paper became a single dark mass of marks.

Widow Grier stayed with the last of the wagons. She had gathered the children into the remaining beds, wrapping them in blankets that still carried the smell of smoke from the cabins they had left. Her shotgun rested within reach, and her eyes moved constantly between the guards at the square and the tree line beyond the creek. She had lost count of how many times she had checked the loads, but the ritual of it kept her hands busy while her mind worked through what came next.

Jonas returned to the creek bank as the light shifted toward afternoon. The cracks around the stakes had multiplied. Thin lines radiated outward from each marker, the soil between them crumbling into fine red dust. The water seeped through in more places now, finding paths around the stakes and the cords that connected them. The symbols on the cloth had darkened where the moisture touched them, the ink bleeding into the fabric until the patterns became unreadable.

Sera knelt at the center of the work and pressed her palm to the ground. The soil felt warm beneath her fingers, warmer than the morning air should have allowed. She traced one of the symbols in the dust with her free hand, following the curves and lines that her grandmother had taught her to draw without looking. The mark held for a moment, then began to fade as the red moisture rose through the soil and washed it away.

Paul's warning came as she worked. He had moved closer to the water's edge, his sketchbook abandoned on the grass behind him. His voice carried the same strained quality it had held in the chamber, though the words now belonged to him rather than the thing that had spoken through him. The seal would hold only as long as the ground allowed it. The entity beneath the soil had already begun reaching outward, following the memories of those who fled into the night. Their dreams would carry pieces of it across the valley and beyond, spreading the knowledge of what waited here.

Jonas felt the pressure against his thoughts as the words settled. It came like the pulse they had felt in the chamber, a steady rhythm that matched the beat of his own heart. The offer formed itself without sound, without language, a simple knowing that pressed against the inside of his skull. He could stay with the others who had witnessed. He would never be alone again. The loneliness that had driven him west would end here, replaced by something older and more complete than any human connection could offer.

He drove the final stake deeper into the soil with the heel of his boot. The wood sank another inch, and the ground convulsed around it. Red water surged upward through the new opening, soaking his trousers to the knee. The pressure in his head sharpened for a moment, then withdrew as if the entity had recognized the refusal and chosen to wait. The pulse continued beneath his boots, slower now, almost thoughtful in its patience.

The surviving townspeople had already begun their flight. The last wagons rolled out of the square while the guards watched without interfering. Some of the families walked beside the wagons, their children carried in arms or walking between the wheels. They did not look back at the creek or the markers that stood along its bank. The road north would take them past the old mining claims and into territory where the ground had not yet learned their names.

A handful remained. They stood at the edges of their cabins, doors cracked just enough to watch the wagons leave. Their faces showed the same exhaustion that Widow Grier carried, the same grim acceptance that came from watching the land turn against them. Some would follow by morning.

Others would stay until the ground opened beneath their floors or the red water reached their doorsteps. The choice belonged to each of them now, and no argument from Jonas or Sera would change what they had already decided.

Jonas and Sera stayed at the creek until the light faded. They reinforced what they could, replacing cloth strips that had bled out and retying cords that had loosened where the soil shifted. The work felt futile even as they performed it, each adjustment lasting only as long as it took the ground to reject the change. Paul remained nearby, his eyes fixed on the water that continued its slow circling. He had stopped drawing, the sketchbook closed and set aside where the moisture could not reach it.

Widow Grier joined them as the first stars appeared. She carried a lantern that threw a weak circle of light across the markers, and her shotgun had been cleaned and reloaded during the afternoon. She reported that Pricket had not left his office, though the guards had changed shifts twice. The men who replaced them carried the same weary expressions, their rifles held with the resignation of soldiers who knew their orders would not matter when the land decided otherwise.

The pulse beneath the stakes had grown stronger as darkness settled. It traveled through the soil in waves now, each one stronger than the last. Jonas could feel it through his boots, a rhythm that matched the beat of his own heart but carried a different weight, a different intention. The red water had risen again, reaching the bases of the markers and lapping at the cloth strips that hung from them. The symbols had disappeared entirely, the ink dissolved into the fabric until only the color remained.

Sera finished the last adjustment and stood back from the line. Her hands hung at her sides, fingers still marked with the red clay that refused to wash away. She had done what her people had taught her to do, and the land had answered with the only response it knew. The cycle could be delayed, but it could not be broken. Each turn added more witnesses, more names to the collection that waited beneath the stone. The memory grew thicker with every person who touched the valley and carried pieces of it away.

Paul moved to stand beside her. His eyes had cleared somewhat, though the tremor in his hands had not entirely left. He watched the water rise around the stakes, and his voice came out steady when he muttered. The entity had already begun reaching into the minds of those who fled. Their dreams would carry it across distances the wagons could not outrun. The seal would hold for now, but the ground would remember what had been done here. It would wait for the next witness, the next moment when the thin place opened wide enough to let it through.

Jonas knelt at the center of the markers and pressed his palm to the soil. The warmth had increased, the pulse traveling through his fingers and up his arm. He felt the offer again, the simple knowing that pressed against the inside of his thoughts. He could join the others who had witnessed. He would never face the loneliness that had driven him west. The refusal came without words, without sound, a simple turning away that the entity accepted with the same patience it had shown before. The pulse continued beneath his hand, slower now, waiting for the moment when the ground would open again.

The water reached the ankles of his boots as he stood. It carried the same metallic smell that had risen from the chamber, the same warmth that had filled the space around the beating stone. He stepped back from the markers and wiped his hands against his trousers, though the red clay remained. Sera moved beside him, her shoulder touching his for a moment before she turned toward the settlement square. Widow Grier followed, the lantern swinging from her hand and casting long shadows across the grass.

Paul remained at the water's edge a moment longer. His eyes tracked the circles that continued to form and dissolve on the surface, and his hands moved through the air as if he could feel the pulse traveling through it. He joined them when they reached the first cabin, his sketchbook tucked under his arm and his steps unsteady on the uneven ground. The guards at the square watched them pass without speaking, their rifles held across their chests and their faces turned toward the darkness beyond the creek.

The cabin door closed behind them with a sound that seemed too final for the work they had left unfinished. Jonas lit the lamp on the table and watched the flame settle into a steady glow. The pulse from the creek traveled through the floorboards and into the soles of his boots, a rhythm that would not let him forget what waited beneath the soil. Sera sat at the table with her hands folded in her lap, her eyes on the window where the light from the settlement square showed through the curtains. Widow Grier stood near the door, the shotgun resting against the frame within easy reach. Paul remained by the window, his eyes on the darkness where the creek continued its slow work against the markers they had placed.

The night settled around them with the weight of things that had been delayed but not stopped. The ground continued its slow movement beneath the cabin, the pulse traveling through the wood and into their bones. Jonas closed his eyes and let the rhythm settle into him, the same patient waiting that had filled the chamber and the thin place and the soil around the stakes. The entity beneath the valley had begun to wake. It would not rest again until the memory it carried had grown thick enough to hold everything the witnesses had brought to it. The seal would hold for now. The ground would remember what had been done. And the cycle would turn again when the time came for the next witness to add their name to the collection that waited beneath the stone.

CHAPTER ELEVEN

The Seal Cracks

The morning came in slow layers of gray light that filtered through the cabin window and landed on the floorboards like something spilled. Jonas stood in the doorway and studied the ground beyond the steps. The stakes from the night before remained visible along the creek bank, but they leaned now where the soil had shifted beneath them. Thin seams ran outward from each one, the red moisture already finding its way through the gaps. He could smell it from here, that metallic tang that clung to everything it touched.

Sera moved past him without speaking. She carried the last length of braided cord from her pack, and her fingers worked at the knots as she walked. The cloth strips they had hung the night before hung limp now, their symbols blurred where the water had reached them. She knelt at the first marker and pressed her palm to the soil. Warmth rose through her skin, stronger than it had been when they finished their work. The ground gave slightly under her weight, then pushed back as if something breathed beneath the surface.

Paul stood at the water's edge with his journal open across his forearm. His pencil moved in short, repeated strokes that layered the graphite into a heavy, metallic sheen, dark as wet slate. The lines overlapped until the paper became a dark mass of marks. His shoulders hunched forward, and his free hand trembled against the leather binding. He did not look up when Jonas approached. The pencil kept moving, the same formation repeated in tighter and tighter circles until the graphite wore through the paper and left only a hole.

"Two families left before the light came," Widow Grier said from the path behind them. Her shotgun rested against one shoulder, and her boots carried fresh mud from the wagon ruts. "Left their doors open and their animals in the pens. The goats wandered into the square looking for feed." She paused and wiped her hand across her mouth. "Pricket's got men posted at the corners. Says we're under quarantine. Won't let anyone in or out."

Jonas tested the nearest stake with his boot. The wood shifted sideways before catching on something deeper. Red clay clung to the leather and refused to flake away when he scraped it against the grass. He had no memory of coming back to the creek after they sealed the markers, but the stains reached past his ankles and disappeared beneath his cuffs. The same warmth he had felt in the chamber pressed against the soles of his feet, patient and steady.

Sera finished checking the first marker and moved to the next. She drew fresh symbols in the dust with her fingertip, following the curves her grandmother had taught her without looking at her hand. The marks held for a few moments, then began to darken where the moisture rose through the soil. The ink bled outward until the patterns became unreadable. She tried again with a longer cord, wrapping it around two stakes and tying the knot tight enough that her knuckles whitened. The ground accepted the cord for a moment, then pushed upward in a small mound that loosened the tension.

Paul tore the ruined page from his journal and started on the next sheet. His breathing came shallow and quick, and the pencil moved faster now, the same stone formation appearing in thicker lines. A thin line of blood ran from the corner of his mouth where he had bitten his lip without realizing it. The red droplet fell onto the page and spread across one of the drawings, turning the black marks into something darker and wetter.

"The guards turned away three wagons this morning," Widow Grier continued. Her voice stayed level, but her fingers tightened on the shotgun stock. "Pricket's telling them there's been a collapse in the old mine. Says the air's bad down there and they're not taking chances with outsiders." She spat into the grass. "One of the men tried to argue, and they put a rifle on him until he backed off."

Jonas walked the line of markers one more time. Each stake stood at the same depth they had driven it the night before, but the soil between them had changed. Small craters formed where the moisture pushed upward, then collapsed inward again as the pressure released. The red water found its way around the barriers they had built, seeping through cracks too small to see until the moisture appeared on the surface. The cloth strips hung heavier now, the symbols completely gone where the liquid had touched them.

Sera tried a different approach. She gathered dry grass and laid it in a pattern between two stakes, then pressed her palm against the center of the design. The grass blackened where it touched the soil, curling inward as if something pulled the life from it. She pulled her hand back and watched the pattern dissolve into the red dust that rose from the ground. Her shoulders remained tight, but she made no sound of frustration. The ritual had never been meant to hold forever. She knew that. They all knew that.

Paul closed his journal and held it against his chest with both hands. His eyes tracked the water as it circled the stakes, and his voice came out hoarse when he finally spoke. The words carried the same strained quality they had held in the chamber below, though now they belonged to him.

Paul's fingers dug into the leather of his journal. "The water... it's not just flowing." He swallowed, his throat clicking in the quiet room. "It knows which way they went. It's following the wagon wheels."

Widow Grier shifted her weight and adjusted the shotgun on her shoulder. "The children are in the last wagon. I told them we're going to visit family up north. They know something's wrong, but they haven't asked yet." She looked toward the settlement square where the guards stood at their posts. "Pricket's still in his office. Hasn't come out since last night. The men say he's burning papers."

Jonas felt the warmth rising through his boots again. It traveled up his legs in slow waves that matched the rhythm beneath the soil. The pressure against his thoughts returned, not as words but as a simple knowing that pressed against the inside of his skull. He could stay with the others who had witnessed. He would never face the loneliness that had driven him west. The offer formed itself without sound, without language, and he turned away from it the same way he had the night before. The refusal came without words, a simple turning that the entity accepted with the same patience it had shown before.

Sera stood and brushed the red dust from her hands. The clay clung to her palms the way it clung to everything it touched. She looked at the line of markers one more time, then turned toward the path that led back to the square. Her steps left prints in the soft soil that filled with red moisture before she had gone ten paces. The cloth strips fluttered behind her, their symbols already unreadable where the water had reached them.

Paul followed a few steps behind, his journal clutched against his chest. He stopped once and looked back at the creek, his free hand rising to his temple as if something pressed against the inside of his skull. The pencil marks on the pages showed the same formation repeated until the paper became a single dark mass. He tore another page free and started again on the next sheet, the lines overlapping the previous attempt until the drawing became unreadable.

Widow Grier remained at the edge of the path and watched the guards at the square. One of them had stepped forward when Jonas and Sera approached, but the man stopped short of speaking. His face held the same exhausted look that everyone wore now, the look of someone who had stopped expecting answers. She adjusted the shotgun on her shoulder and followed the others toward the cabin.

The settlement square lay quiet when they reached it. The livestock wandered between the empty cabins, bleating at doors that no longer opened. A goat had found its way into one of the abandoned pens and stood chewing on the remnants of a feed sack. The guards watched them pass without interference, their rifles held across their chests and their eyes following the small group as it moved toward Widow Grier's door.

Inside the cabin, Jonas lit the lamp on the table and watched the flame settle into a steady glow. The pulse from the creek traveled through the floorboards and into the soles of his boots, a rhythm that would not let him forget what waited beneath the soil. Sera sat at the table with her hands folded in her lap, her eyes on the window where the light from the settlement square showed through the curtains. Widow Grier stood near the door, the shotgun resting against the frame within easy reach. Paul remained by the window, his eyes on the darkness where the creek continued its slow work against the markers they had placed.

The night settled around them with the weight of things that had been delayed but not stopped. Jonas checked the rifle he had left by the door, running his fingers along the barrel to make sure the action remained clear. The metal felt cold against his skin, colder than the air inside the cabin should have allowed. He loaded fresh shells and set the weapon back against the wall where he could reach it from his chair.

Sera unfolded her hands and traced one of the symbols from the ritual on the table surface. Her fingertip left a faint line in the dust that had settled during the day. The mark held for a moment, then began to fade as the warmth from the floorboards rose through the wood. She tried again with a different pattern, one her grandmother had taught her for protection rather than containment. The second mark lasted longer, but the red moisture still found its way through the grain of the table and washed it away.

Widow Grier cracked the shotgun open and checked the shells again. Her fingers moved through the familiar motions without conscious thought, the way a person might count fence posts while walking a familiar path. She closed the weapon and rested it across her knees, her eyes on the window where the guards continued their watch. The men had changed shifts twice during the afternoon, and each new pair carried the same weary expressions.

Paul sat on the floor near the window with his journal open across his lap. His pencil moved in slow, careful strokes now, filling the page with a different pattern than the stone formation. The lines formed a circle with smaller marks around the edge, the same arrangement Sera had drawn in the dust between the stakes. His hand trembled when he reached the center of the design, but he completed the mark and set the pencil aside. The drawing held for a moment, then began to darken where his fingers had touched the paper.

Jonas stood and moved to the window. The settlement square remained empty except for the guards at their posts. The livestock had found their way into one of the empty cabins, and their bleating carried through the thin walls like a complaint. A single lamp burned in Pricket's office window, the light thin and unsteady behind the drawn curtains. The man had not left his barricade since the wagons departed.

The pulse beneath the floorboards grew stronger as darkness settled. It traveled through the wood in waves now, each one stronger than the last. Jonas could feel it through his boots, a rhythm that matched the beat of his own heart but carried a different weight. The red water had risen again at the creek, reaching the bases of the markers and lapping at the cloth strips that hung from them. The symbols had disappeared entirely, the ink dissolved into the fabric until only the color remained.

Sera stood and moved to the door. She opened it a crack and looked out at the square, her shoulders tight with the effort of watching for movement in the shadows. The guards had turned their backs to the cabin, their rifles pointed toward the road that led north. One of them shifted his weight and adjusted his grip on the weapon, the motion slow and deliberate in the growing darkness.

Widow Grier set the shotgun aside and stood. She moved to the stove and checked the kettle, then poured water into three mugs that had been set out on the counter. The steam rose in thin curls that caught the lamplight and turned it into something warmer than the air inside the cabin. She set the mugs on the table without speaking, her eyes on the window where the guards continued their watch.

Paul closed his journal and held it against his chest with both hands. His eyes had cleared somewhat, though the tremor in his hands had not entirely left. He watched the water rise around the stakes in his mind, the same slow circling that had continued throughout the day. His voice came out steady when he spoke, the words carrying the weight of something he had seen rather than something he had imagined.

The seal would hold for now. The ground would remember what had been done. Jonas nodded without speaking and moved back to his chair. The pulse continued beneath his boots, slower now, waiting for the moment when the thin place would open wide enough to let it through. The surviving townspeople had already begun their flight, and the wagons would carry them past the old mining claims before morning. A handful remained, their doors cracked just enough to watch the road and wait for what came next.

The cabin door closed behind them with a sound that seemed too final for the work they had left unfinished. Jonas lit the lamp on the table and watched the flame settle into a steady glow. The pulse from the creek traveled through the floorboards and into the soles of his boots, a rhythm that would not let him forget what waited beneath the soil. Sera sat at the table with her hands folded in her lap, her eyes on the window where the light from the settlement square showed through the curtains. Widow Grier stood near the door, the shotgun resting against the frame within easy reach. Paul remained by the window, his eyes on the darkness where the creek continued its slow work against the markers they had placed.

The night settled around them with the weight of things that had been delayed but not stopped. The ground continued its slow movement beneath the cabin, the pulse traveling through the wood and into their bones. Jonas closed his eyes and let the rhythm settle into him, the same patient waiting that had filled the chamber and the thin place and the soil around the stakes. The entity beneath the valley had begun to wake. It would not rest again until the memory it carried had grown thick enough to hold everything the witnesses had brought to it. The seal would hold for now. The ground would remember what had been done. And the cycle would turn again when the time came for the next witness to add their name to the collection that waited beneath the stone.

CHAPTER TWELVE

The Memory Flood

Jonas woke with dirt under his fingernails and the taste of metal on his tongue. His cabin door stood open to the predawn dark, and his boots were soaked through with something that wasn't rain. He levered himself up slowly, feeling the pull of muscles that had moved without him. The floor felt warm beneath his bare feet, warmer than it should have in the hour before light.

He found his coat on the chair and pulled it on without checking the pockets. Whatever had taken him outside had left marks on the threshold, a scuffed pattern that led toward the old graves beyond the settlement's last cabin. He stepped into the boots and felt the wet clay inside them press against his socks. The smell followed him as he walked, that same iron scent that had been rising from the creek for days.

The graves sat in two crooked rows behind a split-rail fence that had never been repaired properly. Jonas had passed them a hundred times without stopping, but this morning something had drawn him there while he slept. His footprints showed clearly in the soft ground, leading straight to the middle of the second row. He stood where he had stood in his sleep and looked at the markers. Most of the names had worn away, but a few still showed through the moss.

The Hollow-Eyed stood thirty feet from the settlement's edge now. They had been further out the day before, pressed against the tree line where the pines grew thick. Now they occupied the open ground between the last cabin and the old mining road. Their shapes remained still in the gray light, but their positions had changed. Something had moved them closer during the hours he had lost.

Jonas counted them without moving from the graves. Seven figures stood where there had been five. Two more had joined the group while the settlement slept, and none of them had left tracks. The ground between their feet looked undisturbed, as if they had risen from beneath the soil rather than walked across it. He watched them for a long moment, waiting for any sign of movement. None came.

A sound broke the stillness behind him. Paul Murdock came running from the direction of the boarding house, his boots slapping against the packed dirt of the path. His shirt was buttoned wrong, and his hair stood up in wet spikes. Blood showed at the corners of his mouth, dark against his pale skin. He stopped ten feet from Jonas and bent over, hands on his knees, breathing hard enough that the sound carried across the graves.

Paul bent double, his hands clamped to his knees. "I heard you," he spat out between wet, ragged gasps. "Through the wall. All the way from the boarding house. I heard you walking."

Jonas waited for the young man to catch his breath. Paul's hands shook as he straightened, and the same bloodshot look that had haunted his eyes since the chamber beneath the creek burned through his gaze. He wiped his mouth with the back of his hand and stared at the red smear it left on his skin.

Jonas didn't look back at him. He kept his eyes on the open ground. "They're closer."

Paul turned to look at the figures standing in the open ground. His shoulders tightened, and he took a step backward before stopping himself. "They weren't that close yesterday. I watched them from my window until the light went. They stayed at the trees."

"How long were you watching?"

Paul wiped a cold sweat from his forehead. "I couldn't close my eyes. The words... they just started coming. If I didn't get them down, they..." He trailed off, shaking his head.

Paul pulled a folded page from his pocket and held it out. His fingers left red prints on the paper. Jonas took it and opened the sheet under the weak light. The writing covered every inch of the page, the pencil dug so hard into the cheap, fibrous paper that the lead had torn through in several places, leaving gray-rimmed scars where the fibers had split under the pressure. The lines crossed over lines until the words became a single dense, heavy block of graphite. The handwriting belonged to Paul, but the language did not. Jonas recognized none of the characters, though some of the shapes reminded him of the symbols Sera had drawn in the dust.

Paul stared at his own hand. "I don't know what any of it is. I woke up and the pencil was just... stuck in my fingers. My arm was dead to the elbow."

Jonas folded the paper and gave it back. Paul tucked it into his pocket without looking at it again. His breathing had slowed, but the tremor in his hands remained. He looked past Jonas toward the graves and then toward the cabin where the light had begun to show in the single window.

"Sera needs to see this," Jonas said.

They walked back through the settlement without speaking. The guards at the square watched them pass, rifles held across their chests in the same position they had taken the day before. None of the men spoke. Their eyes followed the pair until they reached the cabin door, and then their attention returned to the road leading north.

Sera opened the door before Jonas could knock. She had been awake, and her coat was already buttoned. She looked at Paul's face and the blood at his mouth, then stepped aside to let them enter. Widow Grier sat at the table with her shotgun across her knees, the same position she had held when Jonas left the night before. The kettle steamed on the stove, and three mugs waited on the counter.

Paul sat on the bench near the window and pulled the folded page from his pocket again. He smoothed it flat on the table surface and stared at the dense writing as if seeing it for the first time. His finger traced one of the lines, following the characters without stopping.

Paul's fingernails dug into the edge of the table. "It wasn't like this before. The cabins... they weren't ours. They were smaller. Rounder. The wood was grey, like it had been sitting in the wet for a hundred years."

Sera leaned over the paper and studied the writing. Her finger moved across the page without touching it, following the flow of the characters. She stopped at a cluster of marks near the bottom and traced the shape in the air above the paper.

Sera's finger hovered over a cluster of heavy, dark lines. "They tried to use salt. And fire. It didn't work. The ground just swallowed the heat and turned the salt to grease. It took them three days."

"They didn't even get to run," Paul whispered. "The ground took what they remembered first. Their kids. Their names. It's all down there. Inside the slate."

Jonas poured water from the kettle into one of the mugs and set it in front of Paul. The young man drank without seeming to taste it, his eyes still on the writing. The tremor in his hands had spread to his shoulders now, a fine shaking that made the mug clink against his teeth when he set it down.

"How many cycles?" Jonas asked.

Sera straightened and rubbed her thumb along the edge of the table. "At least four that we can count from the records. Each one left fewer witnesses than the last. The stone takes what it needs and leaves the rest to sink back into the ground."

Paul pushed the paper away and pressed both hands against his temples. His breathing came shallow again, and a fresh line of blood appeared at the corner of his mouth. He swallowed hard and kept his eyes closed.

"They aren't stopping when I wake up," Paul said, his voice dropping to a dry rasp. "I can still feel them. Like they're trying to crowd me out of my own head."

Widow Grier stood and moved to the window. She looked out at the square where the guards had changed shifts again, the new men taking up the same positions as the old.

Her fingers tightened on the shotgun stock, and she turned back to the table without speaking.

The door opened before anyone could reach for it. Harlan Pricket stood in the threshold with two of his guards behind him. His coat was buttoned to the throat, and his hat sat low over his eyes. He looked at each person in the cabin in turn, his gaze lingering on Paul and the blood at his mouth.

Pricket took off his hat and held it against his chest, though his eyes remained hard. "No more talk about the woods. No more talk about the water. Anyone spreading stories goes into the dry-house until the next wagon leaves. I've already told the men."

Widow Grier's hands shifted on the shotgun. She did not raise it, but the movement was enough to make the guards behind Pricket step back half a pace. Pricket's left eyelid twitched, but he kept his voice steady.

"Two more families packed out before dawn," Pricket spat. "I won't have this place empty because of some bad water and nerves."

Sera didn't look up from the table. "The road is six feet narrower than it was on Monday, Harlan. Pretending won't fix the dirt."

Pricket pointed a thick, gloved finger at Paul. "That one's been a rot since the mine collapsed. Put him in the dry-house."

The guards moved forward. Paul stood up from the bench, and his hands clenched at his sides. His eyes went dark for a moment, the pupils expanding until the color disappeared. When he spoke, the voice that came out was not his own.

"Harlan," Paul said, his voice flat and hollow. "The deep slate knows your father's name. It's waiting for yours."

The guard on the left reached for Paul's arm. Paul moved faster than any of them expected, his fist connecting with the man's jaw hard enough to send him stumbling into the doorframe. The second guard grabbed for his rifle, but Paul was already moving again, his hands finding the man's throat and squeezing with a strength that did not belong to his thin frame. The guard's face went red, then purple, before Widow Grier stepped forward and brought the butt of her shotgun down across Paul's shoulders.

Paul dropped to his knees. The darkness left his eyes, and he looked up at the people around him with confusion replacing the emptiness. Blood ran from his nose now, mixing with the red at his mouth. He touched his face and stared at the stain on his fingers.

"I don't remember," he said. "I don't remember what just happened."

The guard on the floor pushed himself upright, rubbing his jaw. The second guard released his hold on his throat and stepped back, breathing hard. Pricket watched the scene without moving, his hands clasped behind his back.

Widow Grier cracked the shotgun open and checked the shells. She closed it again and rested the barrel against her shoulder, the same position she had held all morning.

"He's coming to my cabin," Widow Grier said, resting the heavy barrel in the crook of her elbow. "The dry-house has a dirt floor and no stove. I'm not carrying a frozen boy out of there just to please you."

Pricket looked at the guards, then at Paul still kneeling on the floor. He nodded once, short and sharp, and turned toward the door. The guards followed him without looking back, their rifles held ready but not raised. The door closed behind them, and the sound of their boots faded across the square.

Jonas helped Paul to his feet. The young man swayed but stayed upright, one hand pressed against his nose to stop the bleeding. Widow Grier opened the door again and checked the square before leading them out. They walked in a line toward her cabin at the far end of the settlement, passing the guards who watched without interfering.

Eliza Penhaligon stood in the shadow of the boarding house, her veil pulled low over her face. Her hands moved constantly at her waist, the stone beads clicking together in a rhythm that matched the pulse rising from the ground. She watched the group pass, her head turning to follow their movement, but she did not step forward or call out. The beads glowed with the same red light that had been rising from the creek, faint but steady in the growing morning.

Widow Grier's cabin was larger than most, built with an extra room at the back that had once held her husband's tools. She opened the door and pointed Paul toward the bench near the stove. He sat without argument, his shoulders hunched forward and his hands clasped between his knees. The bleeding had slowed, but the tremor remained in his fingers.

Sera took Paul's journal from his coat pocket and opened it on the table. The pages were filled with the same dense writing that had covered the folded sheet, but newer entries showed drawings that had not been there the day before. She turned the pages slowly, studying each image. The last drawing showed the subterranean chamber beneath the creek, but with details that Paul could not have seen during their visit. New passages appeared in the stone walls, and a second set of symbols marked the floor in a pattern that had not been present when they sealed the thin place.

"These weren't here yesterday," Sera said. "Paul drew them while he was sleeping."

Jonas leaned over her shoulder and studied the new marks. The symbols matched some of the writing on the folded page, though the arrangement was different. The chamber looked larger in the drawing, the walls extending further into darkness than they had in the actual space. A line of figures stood along one wall, their shapes matching the Hollow-Eyed that now waited thirty feet from the settlement.

Paul watched them from the bench, his eyes following Sera's finger as she traced the new symbols. His breathing had steadied, but the blood at his mouth had dried into a dark crust. He touched his lip and winced at the pressure.

"It's watching," Paul whispered, staring at his palms. "Not from the trees. From underneath. It knows what we're saying before the words even leave our mouths."

Sera closed the journal and set it on the table. She rubbed her hands together as if trying to remove something that clung to her skin. The red clay from the graves had dried on Jonas's boots, but it still showed in the creases of his knuckles where he had touched the markers.

"We need to keep him awake," Sera said. "The longer he sleeps, the more the stone can use him."

Widow Grier moved to the stove and added wood to the fire. The flames caught quickly, casting shadows across the cabin walls. She stood with her back to the room, her hands resting on the iron surface of the stove. The heat rose through her palms, but she did not move away.

"Pricket won't let this sit," Widow Grier muttered, staring out at the grey light. "The men are jumpy. Jumpy men do what they're told if you promise them a dry bed."

Jonas stood at the window and looked toward the square. The guards had resumed their positions, but their postures had changed. They stood closer together now, their rifles held ready rather than resting across their chests. One of them glanced toward Widow Grier's cabin, then looked away when he saw Jonas watching.

Paul leaned forward on the bench and pressed his forehead against his knees. His shoulders shook with something that was not quite crying, a dry heaving that made no sound. Jonas moved to stand beside him, one hand resting on the young man's back between his shoulder blades. The warmth from the ground traveled through the floorboards and into his boots, steady and patient.

"The stone remembers every name," Paul whispered against his knees. "It remembers yours."

The words hung in the air between them. Jonas did not pull his hand away. The pulse beneath the cabin continued its slow rhythm, matching the beat of his own heart but carrying a different weight. Outside, the Hollow-Eyed remained in their new positions, waiting for the light to strengthen and the next witness to step forward.

Eliza Penhaligon appeared at the window, her veil still low over her face. She raised one hand and pressed it against the glass, the stone beads clicking against the pane. Widow Grier turned from the stove and raised the shotgun, the barrel steady as she aimed at the figure outside. Eliza held her position for a long moment, then lowered her hand and stepped back into the shadows. The beads continued their quiet rhythm as she walked away, the red light fading with the distance.

Jonas watched her go. The settlement square remained empty except for the guards and the livestock that had wandered into the abandoned pens. The pulse from the ground grew stronger as the morning light strengthened, traveling through the wood and into the bones of everyone who remained. Paul lifted his head from his knees and wiped his face with his sleeve. The blood had dried completely now, leaving dark streaks across his pale skin.

"I can feel them moving," he said. "Not the figures outside. The ones still beneath the stone. They're waiting for the rest of us to join them."

Sera opened the journal again and turned to a fresh page. She drew a single symbol in the corner, one of the protection marks her grandmother had taught her. The ink held for a moment, then began to darken where the moisture from the table surface rose through the paper. She closed the book and set it aside, her hands resting flat on the cover.

The cabin held the quiet of people who had run out of words. Outside, the ground continued its slow work, and the figures in the open field remained still. The morning settled over the settlement like a weight that would not lift until the next witness added their name to the collection waiting beneath the stone.

CHAPTER THIRTEEN

The Witness Breaks

The boarding house smelled of wet wool and boiled cabbage when Jonas pushed through the door. Paul Murdock's room sat at the end of the narrow hallway on the second floor, where the boards creaked under every step and the single window let in the gray morning light. Widow Grier followed close behind him, her shotgun held low at her side, the barrel brushing against the stair rail with each stride.

Sera had already reached the landing ahead of them. She stood with one hand on the doorframe, looking into the small room where Paul lay on his back across the narrow bed. His arms hung limp over the sides, fingers brushing the floorboards. Red water leaked from the corner of his mouth and pooled in the hollow of his throat before dripping onto the sheets below.

Jonas stopped just inside the threshold. The journal lay open on the floor beside the bed, pages scattered with writing that spilled across the margins and onto the back covers. The pencil had snapped in half, the broken pieces still clutched in Paul's left hand. Fresh blood showed beneath his fingernails where he had driven the lead into the paper with too much force.

"He was calling out through the wall this morning," the boarding house keeper said from the hallway. She stayed back, one hand pressed to her apron. "I thought he was talking to someone. Then the talking stopped and the sound just kept going. Like it was coming up from under the bed."

Sera knelt beside the journal and turned the pages carefully, avoiding the wet spots where Paul's hands had rested. The writing covered every available space, the characters packed tight against each other until they formed solid blocks of graphite. She stopped at a page near the middle and leaned closer to study the lines.

Sera looked up, her fingers still hovering over the graphite blocks. "This isn't his hand. Not all of it."

Paul's chest rose and fell in shallow pulls. His lips moved without sound at first, then the words began to form, barely audible over the settling of the old building. Jonas moved closer to hear them clearly. The voice that came from Paul's mouth carried none of the young man's usual hesitation or tremor. It spoke flat and steady, each syllable placed without emotion.

"The last witnesses tried to bind it with their own blood. They drew the circle and spoke the names of their dead. The stone took their offering and gave nothing back. Three days later the ground opened and swallowed the cabins whole. The children went first. Their names were the easiest to take."

Widow Grier shifted her weight in the doorway. The shotgun barrel tapped against the doorframe once, then settled again. She watched Paul's face without blinking, her jaw set hard enough that the muscle stood out along her neck.

"The valley was abandoned before," Paul continued. His eyes remained closed. "They left the tools in the fields and the fires burning in the hearths. The ones who stayed behind became part of the collection. Their fear fed the hunger for twenty years before the next group arrived. The stone remembers the pattern. It waits for the witnesses to fail again."

Jonas crouched beside the bed and pressed two fingers against Paul's wrist. The pulse beat steady beneath the skin, too regular for someone speaking through a throat full of red water. He looked at Sera across the narrow space between them.

She shook her head once, her fingers tightening against the floorboards. "This isn't him."

The door at the end of the hallway slammed open. Harlan Pricket's voice carried up the stairs before his boots reached the landing. Two guards followed him, their rifles held ready, the metal catches on their belts clicking with each step. Pricket stopped at the threshold and looked into the room, his left eyelid twitching once before he controlled it.

Pricket pointed a finger at Paul's limp form. "Get him out of here. Put him in the dry-house. Let him cool off before he starts a panic."

The first guard stepped forward and reached for Paul's arm. Widow Grier moved to block the doorway, her shotgun rising to rest against her shoulder. The second guard hesitated, his hand halfway to his rifle stock.

Paul's eyes opened. The darkness had swallowed the color again, the pupils expanded until only black showed. He sat up in one smooth motion that carried none of his usual stiffness or pain. His hand found the guard's wrist before the man could pull back. The sound of bone grinding against bone filled the small room.

The guard screamed. Paul stood and drove his shoulder into the man's chest, sending him crashing into the wall hard enough to crack the plaster. The second guard raised his rifle but Paul was already moving again, his fingers closing around the barrel and wrenching it sideways with a strength that bent the metal. The guard stumbled backward, his boots sliding on the worn floorboards.

Widow Grier brought the butt of her shotgun down across Paul's shoulders a second time. The impact dropped him to his knees. He stayed there, breathing hard, the darkness fading from his eyes as quickly as it had come. Blood ran from his nose and mixed with the red water already staining his shirt.

"I don't remember," Paul said. His voice sounded small again, the young man's own words returning to him. "I don't remember any of that."

Pricket remained in the hallway, his hands clasped behind his back. He studied Paul for a long moment, then turned his attention to Widow Grier. "The dry-house has a dirt floor and no stove. I'm not carrying a frozen boy out of there just to please you."

She lowered the shotgun but kept her thumb on the hammer. "He's coming to my cabin. You want him locked up, you come try it yourself."

Pricket looked at the guards, then at Paul still kneeling on the floor. He nodded once and turned toward the stairs.

The guards followed without looking back, the injured man cradling his wrist against his chest. Their boots sounded heavy on the wooden steps, then faded across the square outside.

Jonas helped Paul to his feet. The young man swayed but stayed upright, one hand pressed against his nose to slow the bleeding. Widow Grier opened the door again and checked the square before leading them out into the cold morning air. They walked in a line toward her cabin at the far end of the settlement, passing the guards who watched without interfering.

Eliza Penhaligon stood in the shadow of the boarding house, her veil pulled low over her face. Her hands moved constantly at her waist, the stone beads clicking together in a rhythm that matched the pulse rising from the ground. She watched the group pass, her head turning to follow their movement, but she did not step forward or call out. The beads glowed with the same red light that had been rising from the creek, faint but steady in the growing morning.

Widow Grier's cabin was larger than most, built with an extra room at the back that had once held her husband's tools. She opened the door and pointed Paul toward the bench near the stove. He sat without argument, his shoulders hunched forward and his hands clasped between his knees. The bleeding had slowed, but the tremor remained in his fingers.

Sera took Paul's journal from his coat pocket and opened it on the table. The pages were filled with the same dense writing that had covered the folded sheet, but newer entries showed drawings that had not been there the day before. She turned the pages slowly, studying each image. The last drawing showed the subterranean chamber beneath the creek, but with details that Paul could not have seen during their visit. New passages appeared in the stone walls, and a second set of symbols marked the floor in a pattern that had not been present when they sealed the thin place.

Sera tapped the edge of the paper, her voice dropping. "These weren't here yesterday. He did this while he was out."

Jonas leaned over her shoulder and studied the new marks. The symbols matched some of the writing on the folded page, though the arrangement was different. The chamber looked larger in the drawing, the walls extending further into darkness than they had in the actual space. A line of figures stood along one wall, their shapes matching the Hollow-Eyed that now waited thirty feet from the settlement.

Paul watched them from the bench, his eyes following Sera's finger as she traced the new symbols. His breathing had steadied, but the blood at his mouth had dried into a dark crust. He touched his lip and winced at the pressure.

Paul stared down at his raw, graphite-stained fingers. "It's right under us. It hears... everything."

Sera closed the journal and set it on the table. She rubbed her hands together as if trying to remove something that clung to her skin. The red clay from the graves had dried on Jonas's boots, but it still showed in the creases of his knuckles where he had touched the markers.

Sera closed the journal with a sharp snap. "We have to keep him awake. Don't let him drift."

Widow Grier moved to the stove and added wood to the fire. The flames caught quickly, casting shadows across the cabin walls. She stood with her back to the room, her hands resting on the iron surface of the stove. The heat rose through her palms, but she did not move away.

"Pricket won't let this sit," Widow Grier muttered, staring out at the gray light. "The men are jumpy. Jumpy men do what they're told if you promise them a dry bed."

Jonas stood at the window and looked toward the square. The guards had resumed their positions, but their postures had changed. They stood closer together now, their rifles held ready rather than resting across their chests. One of them glanced toward Widow Grier's cabin, then looked away when he saw Jonas watching.

Paul leaned forward on the bench and pressed his forehead against his knees. His shoulders shook with something that was not quite crying, a dry heaving that made no sound. Jonas moved to stand beside him, one hand resting on the young man's back between his shoulder blades. The warmth from the ground traveled through the floorboards and into his boots, steady and patient.

"The stone remembers every name," Paul whispered against his knees. "It remembers yours."

The words hung in the air between them. Jonas did not pull his hand away. The pulse beneath the cabin continued its slow rhythm, matching the beat of his own heart but carrying a different weight. Outside, the Hollow-Eyed remained in their new positions, waiting for the light to strengthen and the next witness to step forward.

Eliza Penhaligon appeared at the window, her veil still low over her face. She raised one hand and pressed it against the glass, the stone beads clicking against the pane. Widow Grier turned from the stove and raised the shotgun, the barrel steady as she aimed at the figure outside. Eliza held her position for a long moment, then lowered her hand and stepped back into the shadows. The beads continued their quiet rhythm as she walked away, the red light fading with the distance.

Jonas watched her go. The settlement square remained empty except for the guards and the livestock that had wandered into the abandoned pens. The pulse from the ground grew stronger as the morning light strengthened, traveling through the wood and into the bones of everyone who remained.

Paul wiped his sleeve across his face, leaving a dark smear of dry blood. "They're moving. Down there. They're just... waiting."

Sera opened the journal again and turned to a fresh page. She drew a single symbol in the corner, one of the protection marks her grandmother had taught her. The ink held for a moment, then began to darken where the moisture from the table surface rose through the paper. She closed the book and set it aside, her hands resting flat on the cover.

The cabin held the quiet of people who had run out of words. Outside, the ground continued its slow work, and the figures in the open field remained still. The morning light settled over the settlement like a wet, gray shroud, thick and suffocating, pressing down on the roofs as if to bury them before the day could even begin.

CHAPTER FOURTEEN

The Ground Breathes

The valley floor moved beneath Jonas's boots like something trying to stand. He had been walking toward the creek when the ground lifted beneath him, a single hard surge that threw him sideways into the frozen weeds. Dirt sprayed upward. A low grinding sound rose from below the surface, stone against stone, deep enough that it reached his ribs before it faded. He stayed down for a moment, hands pressed to the cold soil, feeling the tremor travel up through his palms.

Sera was already on her feet again when he looked. She stood twenty yards ahead near the waterline, one arm out for balance. The creek had stopped flowing. Its surface sat still as glass, reflecting the gray sky without a single ripple. Then the water drew back, slow at first, then faster, until the channel stood empty except for dark mud and scattered stones. A moment later the flow returned from the opposite direction, thick and sluggish, carrying red streaks that spread across the surface like rust.

Jonas pushed himself upright. His ears rang. Every building along the settlement's edge had shifted on its foundation. One cabin listed sideways, its front door hanging open at an angle. Windows cracked in their frames. With a wet slap, a shutter fell from the boarding house and landed in the mud. He could hear people shouting from inside the square, but the sound came muffled, like it passed through layers of cloth.

He wiped his hands on his coat. The right palm came away smeared with dirt and something darker. When he looked down he saw blood beneath his fingernails, already drying in the cold air. He did not remember walking to the thin place. The last clear image in his head was standing at Widow Grier's window, watching the guards take their new positions around the square. After that came only fragments: cold air, the smell of turned earth, the sound of wood splitting somewhere behind him.

The ritual markers lay scattered across the ground. Each stake had been pulled free and thrown aside. The ancestral symbols Sera had carved into the wood were gone, burned down to black char that flaked away when he touched them. He knelt and picked up one of the stakes. The point had been driven deeper than he remembered, the wood split along its length from the force. Fresh splinters clung to the dirt around the hole.

Sera reached him without a word. She looked at the burned markers, then at the creek that now flowed backward in slow, heavy pulses. Her shoulders sagged, her head dropping just enough to let her wet hair fall forward and hide her eyes. She crouched beside him and gathered what remained of the charred wood, stacking the pieces in a small pile at the edge of the clearing.

Sera didn't look up from the pile. "Paul."

Jonas nodded. He stood and followed her back toward Widow Grier's cabin, his boots leaving deep prints in the softened ground. Each step sent small tremors up through his legs. The pulse had not stopped. It moved beneath the surface in slow, steady waves, like something breathing deep in sleep.

Widow Grier met them at the door. She held the shotgun loose in her right hand, the barrel pointed at the floorboards. Her face looked older than it had that morning, lines carved deeper around her mouth and eyes. She stepped aside without asking questions and let them enter.

Paul lay on the narrow bed in the back room. His chest rose and fell in perfect time with the ground's movement, each breath matching the slow lift and fall that traveled through the cabin floor. His eyes remained closed. Sweat covered his forehead despite the cold air coming through the single window. Widow Grier had placed a damp cloth across his brow, but it had already dried at the edges.

"Three more," Widow Grier said. She stood at the foot of the bed, watching Paul's breathing. "Found them this morning inside their own homes. Same as the others. Eyes gone. Bodies arranged like the figures outside. One of them still had a spoon in his hand from breakfast."

Jonas moved closer to the bed. Paul's skin had taken on a gray cast, the same color as the stone formations beneath the creek. His fingers twitched against the blanket in small, rhythmic movements that matched the pulse. When Jonas touched his wrist, the skin felt warm and damp, too warm for the temperature of the room.

"He's not fevered," Widow Grier said. "It's just the breathing. It started an hour ago. Matches the ground exactly."

Sera stood in the doorway, arms crossed tightly over her chest. She watched the slow rise and fall of the boy's chest. "It's using him."

Jonas stared at his own dirty fingernails. "The ground too."

They left the spare room and returned to the main cabin. Widow Grier set the shotgun on the table and poured coffee from a pot that had been sitting on the stove too long. The liquid came out thick and bitter, but none of them complained. They drank in silence while the pulse traveled through the floor and up into their bones.

A knock came at the door. Widow Grier answered it with the shotgun already in her hands. One of Pricket's guards stood on the step, his rifle held across his chest. He looked past her shoulder into the cabin, his eyes settling on Jonas for a moment before moving away.

"Pricket's gone," the guard said. "Office is empty. Left papers behind. Something about selling the valley to people back east."

Widow Grier lowered the shotgun but kept her thumb near the hammer. "When did he leave?"

"Sometime last night. Guards at the office say he packed a bag and walked out. Didn't say where he was going."

The guard turned and left without waiting for an answer. His boots made soft sounds in the mud as he crossed back toward the square. Widow Grier closed the door and leaned against it, the shotgun resting across her forearm.

"Selling the valley," she said. "To people who don't know what's under it."

Jonas set his cup down. The coffee had gone cold against his fingers. "He thinks he can outrun it. Or buy his way out."

"He won't get far," Sera said. She stood at the window, looking toward the creek. The water had slowed again, moving in thick, heavy sheets that carried more red than before. "The land won't let him leave. It never lets witnesses leave once they've seen too much."

They returned to the thin place after finishing the coffee. The walk took longer than it should have. Distances felt wrong, stretched in some places and compressed in others. Jonas counted his steps and came up short of where the markers should have been. When he looked back, the settlement appeared closer than it had a moment before, as if the ground had folded beneath them while they walked.

The creek had changed again. The red water had thickened until it moved like syrup, clinging to the banks and leaving dark stains on the stones. Small bubbles rose from the mud at the bottom, each one carrying a faint metallic smell that stung the back of Jonas's throat. He kept his distance from the waterline, staying on the higher ground where the grass still held its normal color.

Sera examined what remained of the ritual site. The burned stakes lay where they had left them, already sinking into the softening earth. She picked up one of the pieces and turned it over in her hands, studying the char marks that had eaten through the carved symbols. The wood smelled of old smoke and something sweeter, like burned hair.

"They knew we would try to bind it here," she said. "The entity sent the Hollow-Eyed to erase the markers before we could finish the work."

Jonas crouched beside one of the holes. The stake had been driven nearly three feet into the ground, deeper than either of them could have managed by hand. The dirt around the opening showed fresh claw marks, long grooves that ran parallel to each other like something had dragged itself free. He touched one of the grooves and felt the edges crumble beneath his fingers.

A sound rose from the direction of the settlement. Not shouting this time. Something lower, like wood splitting under pressure. Jonas stood and turned toward the sound. One of the cabins near the square had collapsed inward, its roof folding down into the walls as the foundation gave way. Dust rose in a gray cloud that hung over the wreckage before settling back to the ground.

Widow Grier appeared at the edge of the clearing a moment later. She carried her shotgun in both hands now, the barrel pointed toward the ground. Her face had gone pale beneath the weathered skin, and her breathing came hard from the walk. She stopped several yards away and waited for them to acknowledge her.

"Paul's awake," she said. "He's asking for you."

They followed her back to the cabin. The ground continued its slow breathing beneath their feet, each pulse arriving at irregular intervals now, sometimes close together and sometimes spaced out like a failing heart. Jonas kept his eyes on the path ahead, avoiding the places where the dirt had begun to crack open in thin lines.

Paul sat upright on the bed when they entered the spare room. His eyes had returned to their normal color, though the pupils remained too large for the dim light. He held a cup of water in both hands, the surface trembling with each breath that matched the ground's rhythm. When he looked up at Jonas, his expression held a mixture of fear and recognition that made Jonas's stomach turn.

"It's moving," Paul whispered. He didn't look at them, his eyes fixed on the trembling water in his cup. "Under the floor. Inside. It... it knows my name, Jonas."

Sera moved to the side of the bed and took the cup from his hands. She set it on the small table beside the window, then sat on the edge of the mattress. "What do you remember?"

"The deep place. Under the water," Paul muttered, his teeth clicking against the cup. "There are... faces in the stone. New ones. Yours. Sera's. Mine."

Paul's hands shook as he spoke. He pressed them together in his lap, trying to still the movement. The tremor traveled up his arms and into his shoulders, making the whole bed creak beneath him. Widow Grier stood in the doorway, watching him with the same careful attention she gave to wounded animals.

"The Hollow-Eyed are gathering again," Paul continued. "More than before. They're standing in a circle around the stone. Waiting for something to happen."

Jonas leaned against the wall near the window. The pulse from the ground traveled through the wood and into his spine, steady and patient. He could feel it changing him in small ways, shifting his sense of time and distance until the room felt both larger and smaller than it should have been. "How many?"

"I don't know the number. More than we can count. They're bringing something with them. Something that was buried deeper than the rest."

They stayed with Paul until his breathing steadied and the tremor left his hands. Widow Grier brought more water and a bowl of thin soup that Paul drank without complaint. Outside the window, the light had begun to fade toward evening, casting long shadows across the cabin floor. The pulse continued beneath them, slower now but still present, like something settling in for a long wait.

Jonas left the cabin first. He walked toward the square, passing the collapsed cabin on his way. The wreckage had already begun to sink into the ground, the broken boards disappearing beneath layers of mud that rose from below. A single chair remained upright in the middle of the debris, its legs buried halfway in the softening earth.

Pricket's office stood empty when Jonas reached it. The door hung open on broken hinges, and papers lay scattered across the floor inside. Jonas stepped over the threshold and picked up one of the documents. The handwriting was Pricket's, the same tight script that covered the settlement records. The paper described a sale agreement, the valley divided into parcels and offered to investors back east. The dates on the documents ran into the future, months ahead of the current season.

Jonas set the paper down. He moved through the rest of the office, checking the desk drawers and the shelves along the back wall. Most of the records had been removed, leaving only the sale documents and a few scattered notes about timber rights and mining claims. A single ledger remained open on the desk, its pages marked with red clay that had dried into dark stains.

He returned to Widow Grier's cabin as the light failed completely. Sera and Widow Grier sat at the table, a single lamp burning between them. Paul had fallen asleep again in the spare room, his breathing still matched to the ground's slow rhythm. They ate in silence, passing a plate of bread and dried meat between them without speaking.

After the meal, Jonas stood at the window and watched the settlement. The guards had retreated to the edges of the square, their rifles held ready as they scanned the tree line. The Hollow-Eyed stood among the trees at the far side of the clearing, their pale forms visible even in the failing light. One figure stood slightly ahead of the others, arms raised as if reaching for something just beyond its grasp.

Eliza Penhaligon stood among them. Her dark dress blended with the shadows, but her face remained visible, turned toward the settlement with the same cold interest she had shown since her arrival. The stone beads she carried had disappeared from her hands. In their place, dark marks showed on her palms, circular impressions that looked like the beads had pressed into the skin and stayed there.

Jonas turned away from the window. He sat at the table with the others and poured the last of the coffee into his cup. The liquid had gone cold, but he drank it anyway, letting the bitterness settle in his throat.

"We need to decide what happens next," Widow Grier said. She kept her hands flat on the table, fingers spread against the wood. "Pricket's gone. The guards won't hold without someone giving orders. The people left in the settlement are going to start asking questions we can't answer."

Sera's finger traced a rough circle on the wood, over and over until the skin went white. "It's moving faster. It isn't waiting anymore."

Jonas looked toward the back room. "We can't keep him here."

Widow Grier stood and moved to the stove. She added wood to the fire and closed the iron door with a soft click. The flames caught quickly, casting new shadows across the cabin walls. She remained standing with her back to the room, watching the fire through the small glass window in the stove door.

"We keep him here," she said. "And we keep him awake. If the entity wants to use him as a doorway, we make sure the door stays locked."

They sat in silence for a long time after that. The pulse from the ground continued its slow work beneath the cabin, traveling through the floorboards and into their bones. Outside, the settlement settled into an uneasy quiet, the only sounds coming from the creek as it moved backward in thick, heavy sheets. Jonas closed his eyes and listened to the water, trying to remember what it had sounded like before the red stains appeared, before the flow reversed, before the ground began to breathe.

The memory would not come. The creek had always been this way, he realized. The red water. The wrong direction. The slow pulse beneath the surface. Everything else was just something he had told himself to make the valley seem normal, something he had invented to keep the fear at a distance. Now the distance had collapsed, and the fear sat in the room with them, patient and waiting, like the figures at the tree line who had already learned to wear the faces of the dead.

CHAPTER FIFTEEN

The Voice Returns

The morning brought a different kind of quiet. Jonas stood outside Widow Grier's cabin and listened for the usual sounds of the settlement stirring to life. Instead he heard only the slow drag of water moving against its banks and the occasional crack of wood settling into new positions. Three more cabins had shifted during the night. One had lost its entire back wall. The boards lay scattered across the mud like broken ribs.

He walked the perimeter first. The ground felt uneven beneath his boots, rising in places where it had been flat the day before. He marked each change with a stick driven into the soil. By the time he reached the old mine entrance, he had placed twelve markers. None of them matched the positions he remembered from the previous day.

Sera met him at the mine shaft. She carried a coil of rope over one shoulder and a lantern in her left hand. Her braid had come loose during the night, and dark strands clung to her neck. She looked at the sticks he had placed and nodded once. Neither of them spoke. The sinkhole had opened sometime after midnight, its edges still raw and crumbling. Red clay lined the rim like a wound that refused to close.

Jonas tied the rope to a pine stump that had survived the last shift. He tested the knot twice before lowering himself into the darkness. The walls of the sinkhole showed fresh carvings, the same symbols that had appeared on the stakes at the thin place. He touched one of the marks and felt it give slightly beneath his fingers, as if the stone were still soft. Sera followed him down, the lantern casting long shadows that moved independently of their bodies.

The chamber below had changed. Where bare rock had stood before, now a central formation rose from the floor like a spine pushed through skin. Water dripped from the ceiling in steady intervals, each drop landing with a sound that echoed too long. The Hollow-Eyed stood in a circle around the formation, their pale forms pressed close together. Jonas counted thirty-two before he stopped. Their number had indeed doubled.

One of the figures stepped forward. Its mouth opened, and the sound that emerged was not speech in any language Jonas knew. It was a wet scraping, like stone dragged across stone. The words formed slowly, each one carrying the weight of something learned rather than spoken.

"Sera Redwillow," the figure said.

Sera stopped moving. The lantern trembled in her hand, casting shifting light across the chamber walls. Jonas reached for her arm but found only empty air. She had already taken three steps toward the figure before he could stop her.

"Why do you fight what your ancestors could not stop?" the Hollow-Eyed asked. The voice scraped from deep behind its teeth. "They saw. They chose silence. You will too."

Jonas moved to stand beside her. The other figures remained motionless, their eyeless faces turned toward the central stone. He could feel their attention even without eyes to mark its passing. The air in the chamber had grown thick, pressing against his skin like water.

Sera's hands curled into fists at her sides. "They tried to bind it. They failed because they didn't know what it was."

The figure tilted its head. The movement was wrong, too fluid for something that had once been human. "They understood perfectly. They chose survival over truth. The same choice stands before you now."

Jonas studied the chamber walls. Fresh carvings covered the stone, deeper than the marks he had seen during their first visit. His own face stared back at him from the rock, rendered in crude lines that somehow captured the set of his jaw and the line of his beard. Beside it, Sera's profile appeared, her braid marked with the same crow feathers she still wore. Paul's face completed the row, his eyes wide and empty in the stone.

"These were not here before," Jonas said.

Sera turned to look. The lantern light caught the carvings and threw them into sharp relief. She traced one line with her finger, following the curve of Jonas's cheek down to where the stone had been gouged away to mark his mouth. "They know us now. We have become part of the record."

The Hollow-Eyed that had spoken stepped back into the circle. The others shifted to make room, their pale shoulders pressing together like stones in a wall. The chamber grew colder. Water dripped faster from the ceiling, each drop landing with a sound that reminded Jonas of blood hitting stone.

They climbed back toward the surface. The rope had grown slick with moisture, and Jonas had to pause twice to wipe his hands dry. When they reached the top, the sun had moved behind a bank of clouds that had not been there when they descended. The settlement looked smaller from this height, its buildings clustered together as if seeking protection from something larger than walls could hold.

Paul was awake when they returned to Widow Grier's cabin. He sat at the table with a bowl of water in front of him, his hands moving through the liquid in slow circles. The water had taken on a reddish tint that matched the creek. He did not look up when they entered.

Paul didn't look up from the bowl. His fingers kept circling. "The place where memory becomes stone. The Hollow-Eyed... they're just its eyes. Seeing what's buried."

Widow Grier stood by the stove, her shotgun resting against the wall within easy reach. She had not slept. Dark circles marked the skin beneath her eyes, and her hands trembled slightly when she poured coffee into three cups. She set one in front of Paul without asking if he wanted it.

"He woke an hour ago," she said. "Started talking about the chamber before his eyes were fully open. Described every carving. Every face. Even the ones he couldn't have seen."

Jonas sat across from Paul. The boy's skin had taken on a gray cast that reminded him of the stone in the chamber. Paul's fingers continued their slow movement through the water, tracing patterns that left temporary marks on the surface.

"How do you know what's down there?" Jonas asked.

Paul looked up. His eyes had changed. The pupils had expanded until only thin rings of color remained around them. "It showed me. The same way it shows the Hollow-Eyed. We are all part of the same memory now."

Sera moved to the window. She watched the settlement with the same careful attention she had given the chamber walls. Her shoulders had drawn tight, and Jonas could see the tension running through her back like wire pulled too taut.

"Pricket's been found," Widow Grier said. She kept her hands flat on the table, fingers spread wide. "Guards brought him in from the forest an hour ago. His suit is torn. Covered in red clay. He won't say where he's been, but the marks on his hands match the carvings in the chamber."

Jonas stood. "Where is he now?"

"Locked in his own office. Guards are keeping watch. He keeps asking for you. Says he has something to tell you about a deal."

The walk to Pricket's office took longer than it should have. The ground had shifted again during their absence, creating small ridges that caught at their boots. Jonas counted his steps and came up with a different number than the distance suggested. Sera walked beside him without speaking, her hands tucked into the folds of her coat.

Pricket sat behind his desk when they entered. His expensive suit hung from his frame like cloth draped over a skeleton. Red clay stained the fabric from collar to hem, and his hands showed fresh cuts that had not been cleaned. He looked up when Jonas closed the door, and the relief in his face was almost painful to witness.

Pricket gripped the edge of his desk, his voice hoarse. "They offered a deal. To keep the settlement going. Keep the money coming in. All I had to do... I just had to stop interfering."

Jonas remained standing. The office had been cleared of most documents, leaving only the sale agreements scattered across the desk. He picked up one of the papers and studied the handwriting. Pricket's signature appeared at the bottom in a shaky hand that barely resembled his usual script.

"What did you agree to?" Jonas asked.

Pricket's left eyelid twitched. The movement had grown more pronounced since the last time Jonas had seen him. "I told them I needed time to think. They didn't like that answer. The Hollow-Eyed came for me in the forest. I ran. Lost my way. When I stopped running, I was standing at the mine entrance with no memory of how I got there."

Sera moved to the desk and picked up another document. She read the terms without comment, her finger tracing the lines that divided the valley into parcels. "You were selling something that was never yours to sell."

"I was trying to save it," Pricket whispered, leaning his weight onto his hands. "If we fail, everything I built dies. It offered a way. I just had to look away. Just let it take what it wanted."

Jonas studied the cuts on Pricket's hands. They formed a pattern that matched the carvings on the chamber walls. The wounds had not been cleaned, and dried blood flaked away when Pricket moved his fingers. "What did it take from you?"

Pricket stared down at his cut fingers. "Memories. The ones I kept buried. My wife's face. My boy's voice. It pulled them out. Like splinters. Said I wouldn't need them."

The silence that followed pressed against the walls of the office. Jonas could hear the guards shifting their weight outside the door, their boots scraping against the wooden steps. Pricket's breathing had grown shallow, each exhale carrying the smell of red clay and something sweeter, like spoiled fruit.

Pricket's shoulders shook. "They're waiting. One more witness. Someone who has seen enough. Then the chamber opens. It gets its eyes up here."

Sera set the document down. "Who is the witness?"

Pricket's mouth worked for a moment before sound emerged. "Eliza Penhaligon. She joined them at dawn. Her hands were bleeding. The stone beads had worked their way into her palms like seeds planted in flesh. She stood among the Hollow-Eyed and smiled when they touched her."

Jonas turned toward the door. The guards stepped aside as he passed, their rifles held ready but their eyes fixed on the ground. He walked through the settlement without stopping, his boots leaving prints that filled with water behind him. Sera followed at a distance, giving him room to think.

Eliza stood at the edge of the clearing where the forest began. Her dark dress had been torn along one side, revealing pale skin marked with the same circular wounds that covered her palms. The stone beads remained embedded in her flesh, each one surrounded by dried blood that had cracked and flaked away. She turned when Jonas approached, and the expression on her face was almost peaceful.

"You see it now," Eliza said. She spoke with her usual quiet precision, but the rhythm was off. "It doesn't destroy. It preserves. We become part of it."

Jonas stopped ten paces from her. The ground between them had begun to rise in small swells, like breathing that refused to settle. "You knew this would happen. From the moment you arrived."

Eliza lifted her bloody palms. "I've seen this cycle three times. Everyone tries to fight. Everyone fails. And it learns. It gets stronger every time."

Sera appeared at Jonas's side. She studied Eliza with the same cold attention she had given the chamber carvings. "Why join them if you know what happens?"

"Survival isn't enough," Eliza said. Fresh blood welled around the stone beads in her hands. "The valley gives you nothing. The entity offers permanence. To be remembered. Always."

Jonas felt the ground shift beneath his boots. A low tremor traveled up through his legs and into his spine. The sensation reminded him of the pulse they had felt in Widow Grier's cabin, but this one carried a different rhythm. It felt like anticipation.

"The chamber showed us our faces," Jonas said. "Carved into the stone. Part of the record already."

Eliza nodded. "You're marked. It knows your names. It's going to call. You can answer, or... well, it takes what it wants anyway."

Sera took a step forward. Her boots sank into the softening earth, leaving prints that filled with red water. "There must be a way to delay it. Your ancestors found one. You must know what they did."

Eliza's smile went cold. "They offered themselves. One witness for every generation. It bought time. But the hunger always comes back. And it remembers what it lost."

Jonas studied the tree line behind Eliza. The Hollow-Eyed had gathered there, their pale forms visible between the trunks. They stood motionless, their attention fixed on the clearing. He could feel their presence like pressure against his skin, a weight that had nothing to do with air or light.

"We will not offer ourselves," Jonas said. "And we will not let you offer others."

Eliza tilted her head. The gesture reminded him of the Hollow-Eyed in the chamber, the same wrong fluidity that suggested something learned rather than natural. "You cannot stop what has already begun. You can only choose how it ends."

The ground beneath them gave a single hard pulse. Jonas felt it travel through his boots and into his chest, a rhythm that matched nothing he had felt before. Sera reached for his arm, her fingers closing around his sleeve. They stood together in the clearing while Eliza watched them with eyes that had seen this moment before.

"The witness will be chosen," Eliza said. "One way or another. The entity does not bargain. It only takes."

She turned and walked back toward the tree line. The Hollow-Eyed parted to let her pass, their pale shoulders pressing together like stones in a wall. When she reached them, she stopped and looked back one last time. Her hands had begun to bleed again, the blood running down her wrists in thin streams that matched the color of the creek.

Jonas watched her until the trees swallowed her form. The ground had settled again, but the memory of the pulse remained in his bones. He turned to Sera and found her already looking at him, her dark eyes holding the same question that had taken root in his own mind.

"We go back to the chamber," she said.

Jonas nodded. The decision had already formed between them, a shared understanding that needed no words. They walked together toward the mine entrance, their boots leaving prints that the ground slowly filled behind them. The settlement lay quiet in the afternoon light, its buildings shifted into new positions that would never match the maps Pricket had drawn.

Paul met them at the mine shaft. He had followed them from Widow Grier's cabin, his hands still wet from the bowl of water. His eyes had returned to their normal size, but the gray cast to his skin remained. He carried a length of rope over one shoulder and a lantern that matched the one Sera held.

"It's calling," Paul said, his hands trembling against the wet rope. "It wants us down there. It wants us to see."

Jonas took the rope from him and tested the knot at the stump. The pine had grown slick with moisture, its bark peeling away in long strips. He tied a second line and lowered it into the darkness, checking each knot as he worked.

"Stay close," he said. "And if the ground shifts, we leave together. No one stays behind."

They descended into the chamber once more. The water had risen since their last visit, covering the floor in a thin layer that reflected the lantern light like oil. The Hollow-Eyed remained in their circle around the central stone, their numbers unchanged. The carvings on the walls had deepened, the lines cut deeper into the rock as if something had worked at them during the hours they had been gone.

Jonas approached the stone formation. It rose from the water like a bone pushed through skin, its surface marked with the same symbols that covered the walls. He placed his hand against it and felt warmth beneath the stone, a heat that had nothing to do with the temperature of the chamber.

"It is learning us," Sera said. She stood beside him, her lantern held high. The light caught the carvings and threw their faces into sharp relief. "Every witness adds to its knowledge. Every memory becomes part of what it remembers."

Paul moved to the edge of the circle. The Hollow-Eyed did not react to his presence. They remained motionless, their pale forms pressed together like stones in a wall. He studied their faces, his own expression shifting from fear to something closer to recognition.

"They aren't dead," Paul whispered, staring into the dark. "Not really. They're just... eyes. Seeing what the ground remembers."

Jonas stepped back from the stone. The warmth had begun to spread through his palm, traveling up his arm in slow waves that matched the pulse they had felt in the clearing. He wiped his hand on his coat, but the sensation remained, a memory of heat that refused to fade.

"We have seen enough," he said.

They climbed back to the surface. The sun had moved lower in the sky, casting long shadows across the mine entrance. Jonas untied the ropes and coiled them, his hands working through the familiar motions without thought. Sera stood at the edge of the sinkhole, looking down into the darkness that had already begun to fill with shadows.

"The witness will be chosen," she said. Her voice came out quiet, almost lost beneath the sound of water moving through the chamber below. "But we choose who it will be."

Jonas shouldered the rope. The weight felt familiar, a reminder of tasks that could still be completed even when the ground refused to stay still. They walked back toward the settlement, their boots leaving prints that the earth slowly claimed behind them.

Widow Grier waited for them at the cabin. She had prepared food, though none of them felt like eating. Paul sat at the table and traced patterns in the wood with his finger, the same symbols that had appeared in the chamber. His hands moved without conscious direction, leaving marks that would not fade when he stopped.

"The settlers voted," Widow Grier said. She stood by the stove, her shotgun within reach. "They want to leave. Pricket's guards have blocked the road. They say no one goes out until the entity is satisfied."

Jonas set the rope down. The chamber had shown them their faces carved into stone. The Hollow-Eyed had spoken Sera's name. Eliza had joined the circle with blood on her hands. The witness would be chosen, and the entity would take what it needed.

But the choice of who would be taken remained theirs. And that was a different kind of power, one that the earth had not yet learned to claim.

CHAPTER SIXTEEN

The Ancestral Warning

Sera reached her shelter just after the sun cleared the ridge. The low structure sat back among the pines where the ground had not yet begun to buckle. She had built it years ago from stone and timber, a place to keep the old writings away from the settlement's eyes. The door stood slightly open. That alone told her something had changed.

Inside, the single room smelled of wet earth and the bitter herbs she burned to keep the air clean. The wooden chest that held her ancestral texts lay open on the floor. Someone had removed the heavy lid and set it aside. The pages inside were not as she had left them. They had been rearranged into new patterns, the symbols aligned in sequences she had never examined before.

She knelt and lifted the first sheet. The ink had faded to the color of dried blood, but the shapes remained clear. The text described the Hollow-Eyed as something other than victims. They were not people who had been taken. They were pieces of the entity itself, each one carrying a fragment of its awareness into the world above ground. The next page spoke of how these extensions learned from every witness they encountered. They collected memories the way roots collected water.

Jonas arrived while she was still reading. He paused in the doorway, letting his eyes adjust to the dim light. The scent of pine and damp earth came with him. He did not ask what had happened. He simply stepped inside and closed the door behind him.

Sera held up the rearranged pages, her fingers smudging the dry ink. "Someone moved these. The order is different."

Jonas crouched beside her. His broad hands rested on his knees as he studied the text. The symbols meant little to him, but the structure of the pages told its own story. Someone had taken care to place certain passages side by side.

Jonas touched the corner of the dry paper. "What's it say?"

Sera's finger traced the lines. "The Hollow-Eyed don't hunger. They just watch. Each one is a piece of the memory that feeds what's down there. When it has enough... the ground opens."

She turned the page. The next passage described earlier cycles in the valley. Entire settlements had vanished when the entity learned their collective memories. The people had not died in the usual sense. Their thoughts had been pulled downward, absorbed into the larger awareness that waited below the stone.

Jonas listened without interrupting. The words settled into the space between them like cold water. He had seen enough in the chamber to know the warnings were not exaggeration. The carvings on the walls had shown their own faces already marked in the record.

Jonas didn't look up from the floor. "How long ago was the last one?"

Sera searched through the remaining sheets. She found a passage written in a different hand, older than the others. It described a settlement that had stood where Buffalo Creek now stood. The people there had tried to bind the entity with ritual and sacrifice, burying their firstborn children up to their necks in the red mud and leaving them to sing to the earth until the water filled their throats. They had lasted three generations before the ground took them all at once. The final witness had been a woman who carried the same bloodline as Sera herself.

They read in silence for a time. Outside, the wind moved through the pines with a sound like distant water. Jonas shifted his weight and felt the ground give slightly beneath him. The sensation had become familiar, but it still made his skin tighten.

Jonas spat onto the dirt floor. "Every person we lose. It just makes it smarter."

Sera nodded. Her dark eyes remained fixed on the text. "The Hollow-Eyed are not the threat. They are the record. When the record is complete, the thing beneath will have everything it needs to rise into the minds of whoever remains."

A sound from outside made them both look up. Footsteps approached through the pine needles. Widow Grier appeared in the doorway, her shotgun cradled in one arm. She leaned heavily against the jamb for a second, her gaze slipping past them as if she'd forgotten why she came in, before her eyes focused again. She stepped inside and closed the door against the wind.

Widow Grier leaned heavily against the jamb, her shotgun resting in the crook of her arm. "The settlers voted. They're packing. But Pricket's got men on the north road with rifles. Nobody's leaving."

Jonas stood up, his head nearly brushing the low rafters. "How many?"

"Thirty-two. Seventeen kids. The rest are gone or... otherwise." Grier stared out the open door into the gray woods. "Pricket claims he's keeping them safe. Says the thing wants witnesses, not corpses."

Sera gathered the texts and returned them to the chest. She closed the lid but did not lock it. The pages had already shown their secrets. Locking them away would change nothing.

Widow Grier rubbed her temple, her hand trembling slightly. "Paul is carving again. He started on the walls of my cabin while I was gone. His hands move without him watching."

Jonas rubbed his thumb across his palm, feeling the dry skin. "We need to see it."

They left the shelter together. The walk back to the settlement took them along the creek bank where the water had turned the color of rust. Jonas kept his distance from the edge. The red water had begun to give off a metallic smell that reminded him of blood left too long in the sun.

Widow Grier's cabin stood near the center of what remained of the settlement. The structure had shifted during the night, its foundation tilted at an angle that made the door hang uneven. Paul sat on the ground outside, his hands moving across a flat stone he had pulled from the creek. His fingers traced patterns in the mud that coated the surface. The symbols emerged slowly, each one identical to the carvings they had seen below ground.

Jonas knelt beside him. Paul's eyes were open, but they did not track movement. His breathing came steady and shallow. The gray cast to his skin had deepened since the previous day.

Jonas nudged the boy's shoulder. "Paul."

The younger man did not respond. His fingers continued their work, pressing the symbols into the mud with careful precision. When he finished one pattern, he began another. The sequence matched the pages Sera had read in her shelter.

Sera crouched on Paul's other side. She studied the symbols without touching them. "These are instructions. The entity is using him to record what it has learned."

Sera crouched on Paul's other side, watching the dirt gather under his fingernails. "These are instructions."

Widow Grier stood with her back to the cabin wall, the shotgun held ready but not raised. Her eyes scanned the remaining buildings. Several families had gathered near the well, their voices low and urgent. They kept glancing toward the road where Pricket's guards stood watch.

Widow Grier spat into the dry grass. "We can't stay here. The water's red, the ground's moving, and the kids aren't sleeping."

Jonas wiped his muddy hands on his trousers. "We'll find another way."

The square had once been the center of trade and gathering. Now it held only scattered debris and the remains of wagons that had been abandoned during the first sinkhole. Jonas crossed the open ground with Sera and Widow Grier following. The air felt thicker here, as if the space itself had grown heavier.

Eliza Penhaligon appeared from the direction of the creek. Her dark dress dragged through the mud, leaving a trail that filled with red water behind her. Her hands hung at her sides, and fresh blood seeped from the wounds where the stone beads had embedded themselves deeper into her palms. She walked with the same calm precision she had shown in every previous encounter.

She stopped twenty paces from Jonas. The distance felt deliberate, a measured space between witness and extension. Her eyes held no fear, only the same detached interest she had carried since her arrival.

Eliza stopped twenty paces from Jonas. The distance felt deliberate. Her hands hung at her sides, fresh blood seeping from the wounds where the stone beads had embedded themselves. "There's a place it hasn't touched. A thin place from the last cycle. The ground still holds."

Jonas didn't move. "How do you know that?"

"Because I have seen it before. Three times. Each cycle leaves new thin places behind when it retreats. They are the scars from when it tried to rise and failed."

Sera stepped between them, her dark eyes hard. "Why tell us?"

Eliza lifted her bleeding hands. The stone beads caught the light like dark seeds. "Because the cycle is accelerating. If you remain here, the witness will be chosen within days. If you follow me, you may buy time. Not escape. Only time."

Widow Grier shifted the weight of her shotgun. "What's your share in this?"

"I want to see it finish," Eliza said. "I've seen three. I'll see this one, too."

Jonas felt the ground shift beneath his boots. A low tremor moved through the square, subtle but unmistakable. The remaining families near the well fell silent. They had learned to recognize the warning signs.

Jonas looked back toward the quiet cabins, then at the road. "Show us."

Eliza turned without another word. She walked toward the creek bank, her steps leaving prints that filled with red water. Jonas followed at a distance, keeping Sera and Widow Grier between himself and the woman who had joined the Hollow-Eyed. Paul remained behind, still tracing symbols into the mud.

The creek had changed since morning. The water moved slower now, its surface reflecting the sky in shades of rust and copper. Eliza stopped at a bend where the bank had collapsed inward. The exposed soil showed layers of different colors, each one marking a previous shift in the land.

She pointed to a section of the bank where the ground had pulled away from the roots of a fallen pine. A narrow opening showed beneath the roots, barely wide enough for a person to crawl through. The air that emerged from the opening carried no scent, only a pressure that pressed against the skin.

"This is the thin place," Eliza said. "It was not here during the last cycle. The entity does not know it exists yet."

Sera approached the opening but did not enter. She placed her hand against the soil and felt the same warmth Jonas had felt in the chamber. The sensation traveled up her arm and settled in her chest like a second heartbeat.

"How long do we have?" Sera asked.

"Until there's a witness," Eliza said. "Then it will look everywhere."

Jonas studied the opening. The roots that framed it had grown in twisted patterns that suggested they had been shaped by something other than natural growth. He could not see how far the passage extended into the earth.

"We cannot bring the children through that," Widow Grier said. Her voice remained steady, but her free hand had begun to tremble against the shotgun stock.

Eliza turned to face them. Blood continued to seep from her palms, running in thin lines down her wrists. "The children will be the first to change. Their minds are still forming. The entity will take them before the adults."

Jonas felt the weight of the choice settle across his shoulders. The texts in Sera's shelter had described what happened when entire populations were consumed. The memories did not simply vanish. They became part of something larger and older than any single life.

Jonas turned away from the hole. "Let's look at the road."

They left the creek and walked toward the northern edge of the settlement. The road had once been wide enough for two wagons to pass. Now it narrowed where Pricket's guards had placed their wagons across the path. Four men stood with rifles ready, their faces showing the same exhaustion as everyone else in the valley.

Pricket himself was not among them. Jonas searched the line of buildings but found no sign of the man who had once controlled every decision in the settlement. The absence felt like another warning.

The guard at the center of the road didn't raise his rifle, but he didn't move away from the wagon either. "Pricket says nobody leaves. Says running only makes it follow."

"And if we stay here?" Jonas asked.

The guard looked down at his boots. "He says we're part of it. Safe. Just... kept."

Sera moved closer to the wagons. She studied the arrangement with the same cold attention she had given the chamber carvings. The barricade was not meant to keep the Hollow-Eyed out. It was meant to keep the living in.

"This will not hold," she said. "When the ground shifts again, these wagons will fall into whatever opens beneath them."

The guard nodded. "We know. But Pricket pays, and we have nowhere else to go."

Jonas turned back toward the settlement. The families near the well had begun to move, their voices rising in argument. Widow Grier followed his gaze, her shotgun held ready at her side.

"We have to talk to the families," Grier said. "Before they start believing him."

They walked back through the square. The air had grown colder, though the sun still hung above the ridge. Jonas counted the remaining buildings and came up with a different number than he remembered from the morning. The ground had shifted again while they were at the creek.

Paul had finished his work with the symbols. He stood beside the cabin, his hands coated in mud. His eyes had returned to their normal size, but the gray cast to his skin remained. He looked at Jonas with an expression that held both recognition and distance.

Paul didn't look up from the mud. "It won't save us. It just delays things. It always figures a way in."

Sera knelt in front of him. "Paul. How do you know that?"

"I remember," the boy whispered. His fingers dragged through the wet clay. "Not my memories. But they're there. It always ends with the ground opening."

Jonas felt the words settle into his chest like cold stone. The texts had described the same pattern. The entity did not rush. It waited. It collected. It remembered.

Eliza had remained at the creek bank. She watched them from a distance, her bleeding hands held at her sides. The Hollow-Eyed had begun to gather among the trees beyond her, their pale forms visible between the trunks. They stood motionless, their attention fixed on the settlement.

Jonas looked toward the dark treeline. "We read the rest of those pages. Now."

She nodded. The decision had formed between them without need for further words. They walked back toward her shelter, leaving Widow Grier and Paul behind. The ground shifted once more beneath their boots, a subtle tremor that traveled up through their legs and settled in their bones.

The shelter door still stood open. Inside, the chest remained where they had left it. Sera lifted the lid and removed the remaining pages. She spread them across the floor in the order the intruder had arranged them. The patterns became clearer with each new sheet.

One passage described how the Hollow-Eyed had once been witnesses themselves. They had carried the same fears and doubts as Jonas and Sera. The entity had taken their memories and left their bodies as empty vessels. The process had taken years in some cycles, days in others.

Another passage spoke of the thin places. They were not random. They formed where the entity's awareness had been strongest during previous cycles. The scars from its attempts to rise remained in the land, waiting to be discovered by those who knew how to look.

Jonas read each line twice. The words did not bring comfort, but they brought clarity. The entity was not a mindless force. It was something that learned. It adapted. It used every witness to become more than it had been before.

Sera gathered the pages and returned them to the chest. She closed the lid and pressed her hand against the wood. The action felt like a farewell to something she had carried for too long.

Sera gathered the pages and returned them to the chest. She closed the lid and pressed her hand against the wood. "We can't stop it. But we don't have to just wait for it, either."

Jonas stood. The shelter felt smaller than it had earlier. The air pressed against his skin with the same weight he had felt in the chamber. He opened the door and stepped outside, letting the wind clear the scent of wet earth from his lungs.

They walked back toward the settlement together. The families had gathered in the square again, their voices rising and falling in argument. Widow Grier stood among them, her shotgun held ready but not raised. Paul remained near the cabin, his hands still moving through patterns only he could see.

Eliza had not moved from her position near the creek. She watched the settlement with the same detached calm she had shown since her arrival. The blood on her wrists had dried to dark lines that matched the color of the water.

Jonas stopped at the edge of the square. The ground felt uneven beneath his boots, rising in places where it had been flat the day before. He marked each change in his mind, counting the shifts that had occurred since morning.

The choice stood before them as clearly as the barricade on the road. They could follow Eliza to the thin place and buy time. They could remain and face whatever the entity chose to send next. Or they could attempt to break through Pricket's guards and lead the remaining families into the wilderness.

None of the options offered safety. None of them offered escape. They offered only different ways to delay what the texts had described as inevitable.

Sera stood beside him. Her dark eyes held the same knowledge that had settled into his own mind. The entity remembered every witness it had ever touched. It learned from each encounter. It changed its approach with every cycle.

The ground shifted once more beneath their feet. A low tremor moved through the square, subtle but unmistakable. The families fell silent. They had learned to recognize the warning signs.

Jonas looked toward the dark treeline. "The thin place. We look at it first."

She nodded. The decision had formed between them, a shared understanding that needed no further words. They walked toward the creek bank where Eliza waited, her bleeding hands held at her sides. The Hollow-Eyed watched from the trees, their pale forms motionless between the trunks.

The wind moved through the pines with a sound like distant water. The settlement lay quiet behind them, its buildings shifted into new positions that would never match the maps Pricket had drawn. The ground continued its slow work, reshaping the valley one tremor at a time.

They reached the creek bank as the sun began to lower behind the ridge. Eliza turned to face them, her expression showing neither surprise nor concern at their decision. The stone beads in her palms caught the fading light like dark seeds waiting to be planted.

Eliza gestured to the dark gap. "One at a time. Watch the ceiling."

Jonas studied the opening beneath the roots. The pressure that emerged from the darkness pressed against his skin like water. He could not see how far the passage extended or what waited at the other end.

"Sera first," Jonas said. "Then me. Grier, keep watch out here."

Eliza nodded. She stepped aside, leaving the opening clear. Sera approached the thin place and lowered herself to the ground. She crawled forward, her shoulders disappearing into the darkness beneath the roots.

Jonas waited until she had vanished completely. Then he followed, the weight of the decision settling across his shoulders like stone. The ground shifted once more beneath him as he entered the passage, a subtle tremor that traveled up through his legs and settled in his chest.

The darkness closed around him. The pressure increased. The sound of water moving wrong echoed from somewhere ahead, a rhythm that matched nothing he had heard before. He crawled forward, following the sound of Sera's breathing in the darkness.

The thin place held its secrets. The entity had not yet discovered this gap in its awareness. The passage offered a chance to delay what had already begun. Whether it offered anything more remained to be seen.

Jonas continued forward. The ground above him shifted again, a low tremor that sent small particles of soil drifting down onto his back. He kept moving, one hand after the other, following the narrow passage toward whatever waited on the other side.

The air grew colder. The pressure increased. The sound of water moving wrong grew louder, a wet scraping that reminded him of the Hollow-Eyed voice in the chamber. He pressed forward, the weight of the earth above him pressing down with each breath.

"Jonas," Sera's voice echoed back, muffled by wet dirt. "There's light up here."

Jonas moved faster. The thin place had accepted them. The entity had not yet learned of its existence. They had bought time, though he could not say how much. The ground continued its slow work above them, reshaping the valley one tremor at a time.

He reached the end of the passage and pulled himself into the chamber beyond. The space was small, barely large enough for two people to stand. A narrow shaft of light came from above, illuminating the stone walls that had been carved with symbols he did not recognize.

Sera stood near the far wall, her hand pressed against the stone. The warmth from the surface traveled up her arm and settled in her chest like a second heartbeat. She turned to Jonas as he entered, her dark eyes holding the same knowledge that had settled into his own mind.

Sera touched the cold, carved stone. "They left these. The others. The thing hasn't found this spot yet."

Jonas studied the symbols. They matched the patterns Paul had carved into the mud. The same sequence that had appeared in Sera's ancestral texts. The thin place held its own record, separate from the one the Hollow-Eyed carried.

"We can get the kids in here," Jonas said. "Keep them quiet while we figure out the rest."

Sera nodded. The decision had formed between them, a shared understanding that needed no further words. They stood together in the small chamber while the ground shifted above them, a low tremor that sent small particles of soil drifting down from the ceiling.

The thin place had accepted them. The entity had not yet learned of its existence. They had bought time, though Jonas could not say how much. The choice of how to use that time remained theirs.

He turned toward the passage. Widow Grier would be waiting at the entrance. Paul would still be tracing symbols into the mud. Eliza would be watching with the same detached calm she had carried since her arrival. The Hollow-Eyed would be gathering among the trees, their pale forms motionless between the trunks.

The ground shifted once more. A low tremor moved through the chamber, subtle but unmistakable. Jonas felt it travel up through his boots and settle in his chest like a second heartbeat. The thin place had accepted them. The entity had not yet discovered this gap in its awareness.

They had work to do. The remaining families needed to know what they had found. The texts needed to be read again, every passage examined for any detail that might help them delay what had already begun. The thin place offered a chance. Whether it offered survival remained to be seen.

Jonas crawled back through the passage. The pressure increased as he moved, the weight of the earth above him pressing down with each breath. He reached the opening beneath the roots and pulled himself into the fading light.

Widow Grier stood waiting, her shotgun held ready at her side. Her face showed no surprise at their return. She had learned to expect the unexpected in this valley where the ground refused to stay still.

"There's a cave," Jonas told her as he climbed out. "It's clean. We can hide the families there."

Widow Grier nodded. She turned toward the settlement, her shotgun resting against her shoulder. The remaining families had gathered in the square again, their voices rising and falling in argument. Pricket's guards still stood watch at the road, their rifles ready but their faces showing the same exhaustion as everyone else.

Jonas followed her back through the square. The ground felt uneven beneath his boots, rising in places where it had been flat the day before. He marked each change in his mind, counting the shifts that had occurred since morning.

The choice stood before them as clearly as the barricade on the road. They could bring the families to the thin place and buy time. They could remain and face whatever the entity chose to send next. Or they could attempt to break through Pricket's guards and lead the remaining families into the wilderness.

None of the options offered safety. None of them offered escape. They offered only different ways to delay what the texts had described as inevitable. The ground continued its slow work, reshaping the valley one tremor at a time.

They reached the square as the sun dropped below the ridge. The families fell silent when they saw Jonas approach. Their faces showed the same exhaustion that had settled into his own bones. They had learned to recognize the warning signs.

Jonas stopped at the center of the square. The ground felt uneven beneath his boots. He studied the remaining buildings, counting the shifts that had occurred since morning. The thin place offered a chance. Whether it offered survival remained to be seen.

The choice stood before them. They could follow Eliza to the thin place and buy time. They could remain and face whatever the entity chose to send next. Or they could attempt to break through Pricket's guards and lead the remaining families into the wilderness.

Jonas turned to Sera. The decision had formed between them, a shared understanding that needed no further words. They had work to do. The remaining families needed to know what they had found. The texts needed to be read again. The thin place offered a chance.

The ground shifted once more beneath their feet. A low tremor moved through the square, subtle but unmistakable. The families fell silent. They had learned to recognize the warning signs. The thin place had accepted them. The entity had not yet discovered this gap in its awareness.

They had bought time. How they used that time remained to be seen. The choice stood before them, as clear as the barricade on the road and the symbols carved into the stone. The ground continued its slow work, reshaping the valley one tremor at a time.

Jonas felt the weight of the decision settle across his shoulders. The texts had described what happened when entire populations were consumed. The memories did not simply vanish. They became part of something larger and older than any single life. The thin place offered a chance to delay that process. Whether it offered anything more remained to be seen.

He turned toward the creek bank where Eliza waited. The blood on her wrists had dried to dark lines that matched the color of the water. The Hollow-Eyed watched from the trees, their pale forms motionless between the trunks. The ground shifted once more beneath his boots, a low tremor that traveled up through his legs and settled in his chest like a second heartbeat.

The thin place had accepted them. The entity had not yet learned of its existence. They had work to do. The remaining families needed to know what they had found. The texts needed to be read again. The choice stood before them, as clear as the barricade on the road and the symbols carved into the stone.

Jonas walked toward the creek bank. Sera followed at his side. Widow Grier remained in the square, her shotgun held ready at her side. The ground continued its slow work, reshaping the valley one tremor at a time. The thin place offered a chance. Whether it offered survival remained to be seen.

CHAPTER SEVENTEEN

The False Prophet

The settlement square lay quiet under a sky the color of old iron. Jonas stood near the well with his hands on his hips, listening to the low murmur of voices from the remaining families. They clustered in small groups near the empty trading post, their bundles tied and ready but going nowhere. The north road still held its barricade of wagons and rifles.

Harlan Pricket stepped out from between two buildings. He wore his usual dark coat, but the cloth hung loose on his frame as if he had lost weight overnight. His face looked drawn, the skin tight across the bones. He walked with purpose toward the center of the square, his boots striking the packed dirt with steady rhythm.

"Listen," he called out. His voice was too steady, too clear in the flat air. "I've been under. It's chosen me. I speak for it now."

Several people stopped their packing. They turned toward him, their faces showing a mix of exhaustion and something sharper. Jonas felt his shoulders tighten. He had never heard Pricket speak in that tone before, the words slow and measured like someone reciting from memory.

"The entity does not seek to destroy," Pricket continued. He raised one hand, palm open. "It seeks witnesses. Those who submit will be preserved. Their minds will remain intact within the greater memory. The Hollow-Eyed are not lost. They are elevated."

A woman near the well clutched her child closer. The boy pressed his face against her skirt. Another man, older, with gray in his beard, took a step forward. His eyes held the look of someone who had run out of better options.

"What does it want from us?" the man asked.

Pricket's mouth twitched into a dry shape. "Just you. Your eyes. What you remember. You don't die, not really. You just go into the dirt with the rest of it."

Jonas moved closer. He kept his hands visible and his movements slow. The families watched him approach, some leaning forward to catch his eye while others pulled their shawls tighter and looked down at the dirt. Widow Grier stood near the edge of the group, her shotgun resting across her forearm. Her mouth had thinned to a hard line.

"This is a lie," Jonas said. His voice cut through the quiet. "Whatever is talking through you is not offering mercy. It is collecting."

Pricket turned. His neck moved with a slow, dry click. "Jonas. You're already tasting the red water. Why keep fighting it?"

The words landed like cold stones. Jonas felt them settle in his chest, but he kept his face still. He had felt the water's pull for weeks now. Hearing Pricket name it out loud changed nothing.

Widow Grier stepped forward. She lifted the shotgun and fired once into the air. The blast cracked across the square, sharp and final. Several families flinched. The sound echoed off the shifted buildings and died away into the trees.

"Disperse," she said. Her voice carried the weight of someone who had buried too many already. "Go back to your homes. Lock your doors. Do not listen to this man."

The families hesitated. The older man with the gray beard looked between Pricket and Widow Grier. His hands worked at his sides, fingers opening and closing. Then he turned and walked toward his cabin. Others followed, their bundles dragging in the dirt behind them. The square emptied slowly, the sound of boots on packed earth fading into the wind.

Pricket remained where he stood. He showed no sign that the gunshot had affected him. His eyes stayed fixed on Jonas, the pupils slightly enlarged against the gray light.

"It's already moving," Pricket said, his voice dropping an octave. "It learns. Every time someone looks, it learns. It's almost done."

Jonas studied the man's face. Something about the eyes looked wrong. The usual sharp focus had softened, the irises taking on a milky cast around the edges. The change was subtle, but it held. The same film that covered the Hollow-Eyed had begun to form there.

Sera appeared at his side. She had come from the direction of the creek, her dark hair braided back and her face set in concentration. She approached Pricket without hesitation and stopped an arm's length away. Her eyes moved over his features with clinical attention.

"Look at me," she said.

Pricket turned his head toward her. The movement came in segments, as if each part of his neck had to remember its function. Sera leaned closer. She studied the clouded film across his eyes, the way the pupils did not contract properly in the light.

"The entity has touched him," she said. Her voice stayed low, meant for Jonas alone. "Not fully. Not yet. But it has claimed part of him. He speaks for it now because it uses his mouth."

Pricket's eyelids fluttered, out of sync. "The last one is coming. Someone has to carry the memory. Then the ground just... opens."

Widow Grier kept her distance, the shotgun still ready. She watched Pricket with the same wariness she reserved for wounded animals that might still bite. "How long has this been happening?"

"In the dark," Pricket said. "Under the creek. It saw me. It needs people. It always uses people."

Footsteps approached from the direction of Widow Grier's cabin. Paul Murdock walked with his head down, his hands still stained with creek mud. He carried a folded sheet of paper, the edges creased from being carried too long. He stopped when he saw Pricket, his eyes widening slightly.

"I know him," Paul said. His voice came out hoarse, as if he had not spoken in hours. "From the drawings. The ones that come when the ground shifts."

He unfolded the paper with shaking hands. The drawing showed a man standing in a square much like this one, surrounded by pale figures. The face matched Pricket's features, though the clothing in the sketch looked older, from another time. The eyes in the drawing held the same milky cast that now spread across the real man's gaze.

"He did this before," Paul said, his finger scratching at the paper. "In the old days. He tried to make a deal to save himself. It just took him. Used him to call the others in."

Pricket showed no reaction to the words. He stood with his hands at his sides, the fingers slightly curled. The wind moved through his thinning hair, but he did not blink against the dust it carried.

"The entity remembers its tools," Sera said. She stepped back from Pricket, putting distance between herself and the clouded eyes. "It keeps certain patterns. Certain people who prove useful across cycles. He is one of them."

Jonas felt the weight of that knowledge settle across his shoulders. If Pricket could be claimed so completely, others might follow. The entity was learning to work through human agents rather than relying solely on the Hollow-Eyed. The settlement had become a testing ground for new methods of control.

"What happens when it finishes with him?" Jonas asked.

Sera shook her head. "The vessel breaks. The mind goes first. The body follows. What remains becomes another extension, another set of eyes for the thing below."

Pricket turned toward the tree line. His head moved in that same segmented way, each motion deliberate and slightly delayed. Beyond the edge of the settlement, among the dark trunks, the Hollow-Eyed stood in loose formation. Their pale forms blended with the shadows, their attention fixed on the square.

Eliza Penhaligon stood among them. She wore her dark mourning dress, the hem stained with red water from the creek. Her hands hung at her sides, the stone beads still embedded in her palms. She watched Pricket's transformation without surprise, without concern. Her face held the same detached interest she had carried since her arrival in the valley.

Jonas followed her gaze back to Pricket. The man's posture had changed. He stood straighter now, his shoulders squared as if something else held him upright. The milky film across his eyes had spread further, covering more of the iris.

"You're too late anyway," Pricket said. His tongue looked thick and gray. "It wants the kids first. They don't fight the quiet. They go down easy."

Widow Grier's grip tightened on the shotgun. Her knuckles showed white against the dark wood. "If you touch one of those children, I will put you down myself."

Pricket's mouth stretched again. "You can't kill a tool, Grier. It'll just find another hand."

Paul took a step backward. The drawing trembled in his hands. "I saw this before. In the mine. When the walls came down. There was a man like him. He gathered people. Told them the same things. They followed him into the dark and never came back."

The wind picked up across the square. It carried the metallic scent of the red water, the smell of something old and wrong rising from beneath the soil. Jonas felt the ground shift slightly beneath his boots, a subtle tremor that traveled up through his legs and settled in his chest.

Sera moved closer to Pricket. She studied him with the same careful attention she gave to the ancestral texts. "How much of you remains?" she asked.

Pricket's head lolled to the left. "Just enough to talk. To bring you in. The rest of me is gone."

Jonas felt his hands clench at his sides. The entity was using Pricket as a bridge, a way to reach the remaining settlers through familiar words and faces. The pattern was clear now. Each cycle refined the approach. Each witness added new understanding. The thing below learned from every encounter, adapting its methods with each awakening.

"We need to isolate him," Jonas said. His voice stayed low, meant only for Sera and Widow Grier. "Before he reaches anyone else."

Widow Grier nodded. She kept the shotgun ready, her eyes never leaving Pricket's face. "The old root cellar. It still has a door that locks."

Pricket did not resist when they approached. He stood where he was, his eyes tracking their movement with that same delayed precision. Jonas took one arm. Widow Grier took the other. They walked him toward the edge of the square where the root cellar door sat half-buried in the shifted earth.

The descent took them down narrow steps cut into the ground. The air grew colder with each foot. The walls pressed close on either side, the smell of damp soil and old wood filling the space. At the bottom, a single room opened out, the ceiling low enough that Jonas had to duck his head.

They placed Pricket on a wooden bench against the far wall. He sat without protest, his hands resting on his knees. The milky film across his eyes had reached the edges of the pupils now, leaving only small circles of darkness in the center.

"It'll get another mouth," Pricket whispered from the dark. "There are plenty of us left."

Sera stood near the steps, her hand resting on the rough wall. "Then we deal with each one as it comes."

They left him there. Widow Grier turned the key in the lock above, the metal scraping against stone. The sound carried through the small space, final and heavy. Pricket did not call after them. He sat in the darkness, his clouded eyes fixed on nothing.

Above ground, the square had emptied completely. The families had retreated to their cabins, their doors closed against the wind. Only Eliza remained at the tree line, her dark form visible between the trunks. She watched the root cellar door with the same calm attention she had shown throughout. The Hollow-Eyed stood motionless around her, their pale shapes blending into the shadows.

Jonas felt the weight of the decision settle across his shoulders. Pricket had been the first to be claimed in this cycle. He would not be the last. The entity was learning to use human agents, to speak through familiar faces and trusted voices. The pattern had shifted. The threat had evolved.

Sera stood beside him, her dark eyes fixed on the tree line. "We need to warn the others. Before it finds another vessel."

Widow Grier shouldered her shotgun. Her face had hardened into the expression she wore when facing impossible choices. "The children first. We keep them close. We watch for any sign of change."

Paul remained near the well, the drawing still clutched in his hands. He stared at the paper as if the lines might offer answers. The wind moved through his hair, carrying the scent of red water and damp earth.

Jonas turned toward the remaining cabins. The ground felt uneven beneath his boots, rising in places where it had been flat the day before. He marked each change in his mind, counting the shifts that had occurred since morning. The entity continued its slow work, reshaping the valley one tremor at a time.

They walked together toward the first cabin. The door opened before they reached it. A woman stood in the threshold, her face pale in the gray light. Behind her, two children peered around her skirts, their eyes wide with the same fear that had settled into every face in the settlement.

"What did he mean?" the woman asked. Her voice trembled slightly. "About the children going first?"

Widow Grier stepped forward. She kept her shotgun low, the barrel pointed at the ground. "We don't know. But we won't let it happen."

The woman studied their faces. She looked between Jonas and Sera, searching for something she could trust. Then she nodded and stepped aside, letting them enter the cabin. The children moved back into the shadows, their small hands clutching at their mother's dress.

Inside, the cabin smelled of wood smoke and dried herbs. A single window let in the gray light from outside. Jonas stood near the door, his shoulders nearly brushing the low ceiling. Sera moved to the center of the room, her presence filling the small space without effort.

"We need to gather everyone," Jonas said. "In one place. Where we can watch each other."

The woman nodded. She gathered her children close, one hand resting on each small head. "The meeting hall. It has room for all of us. And only one door."

They moved through the settlement cabin by cabin. Each family listened with the same exhausted attention. Each one agreed to gather in the meeting hall when the sun dropped lower. The fear had become a constant presence, settling into the spaces between words and actions.

By the time they reached the last cabin, the light had begun to fade. The wind carried a colder edge now, the promise of night settling across the valley. Jonas felt the ground shift again beneath his boots, a subtle tremor that traveled up through his legs and settled in his chest like a second heartbeat.

They returned to the square. The meeting hall stood at the far edge, its door open to the wind. Inside, the families had already begun to gather. They sat on the wooden benches, their bundles piled at their feet. The children stayed close to their parents, their eyes tracking every movement.

Widow Grier positioned herself near the door. She held the shotgun across her lap, her finger resting near the trigger guard. Jonas took a place near the center of the room, where he could see every face. Sera stood beside him, her dark eyes moving across the gathered settlers with careful attention.

Paul entered last. He carried his drawing with him, the paper folded and tucked into his shirt. He found a place on the floor near the wall, his knees drawn up to his chest. His hands still showed traces of mud from the creek, the dirt worked deep into the lines of his palms.

The door closed against the wind. The room grew quiet except for the sound of breathing and the occasional whisper of cloth against wood. Outside, the Hollow-Eyed gathered among the trees, their pale forms visible through the gaps in the walls. Eliza stood among them, her dark dress blending with the shadows.

Jonas felt the entity's presence pressing against the edges of his thoughts. It waited just beyond the reach of conscious awareness, patient and hungry. The thing below had learned to use human voices. It had found a way to speak through familiar faces. The cycle had evolved again.

He looked across the room at the gathered families. Their faces showed the same exhaustion that had settled into his own bones. They had survived the sinkholes and the red water. They had endured the Hollow-Eyed and the shifting ground. But this new threat, this use of human agents, required a different kind of vigilance.

Sera touched his arm. Her fingers pressed against the rough fabric of his sleeve. "We watch each other," she said. "We trust no one completely. Including ourselves."

Jonas nodded. The decision had formed between them without need for further words. The entity would continue to adapt. It would find new vessels, new patterns, new ways to reach the remaining witnesses. Their only defense lay in constant attention, in the refusal to let any single voice go unchallenged.

The wind moved against the walls of the meeting hall. It carried the metallic scent of the red water, the smell of something old and wrong rising from beneath the soil. Jonas felt the ground shift again, a subtle tremor that traveled up through the floorboards and settled in his chest.

They sat together in the gathering darkness. The children had fallen silent, their small forms pressed against their parents. The adults watched the door, their eyes tracking every sound from outside. Widow Grier remained near the entrance, the shotgun resting across her lap. Paul sat with his back against the wall, his hands moving through small patterns on the wooden floor.

Jonas felt the weight of the choice settle across his shoulders. Pricket had been claimed. Others might follow. The entity was learning to work through human agents, to speak through familiar faces and trusted voices. The pattern had shifted. The threat had evolved.

They would face it together. They would watch each other. They would refuse to let any single voice go unchallenged. The entity had found a new method. They would find a new defense. The cycle had changed. So would they.

The wind continued to move against the walls. The ground continued its slow work beneath them. The Hollow-Eyed waited among the trees, their pale forms visible through the gaps in the wood. Eliza stood among them, her dark dress blending with the shadows.

Jonas closed his eyes. The entity's presence pressed against his thoughts, patient and hungry. It waited for the next opening, the next vessel, the next witness to claim. He would not be that vessel. He would not be that witness. The choice remained his, for now.

The families settled into uneasy rest. The children slept fitfully, their dreams disturbed by the constant tremor of the ground. The adults kept watch in shifts, their eyes moving between the door and each other's faces. Widow Grier remained near the entrance, the shotgun ready across her lap. Sera sat beside Jonas, her presence a steady weight in the darkness.

They waited for morning. They waited for whatever the entity would send next. The thin place offered a chance. Whether it offered survival remained to be seen. The choice stood before them, as clear as the barricade on the road and the symbols carved into the stone.

The ground shifted once more beneath the meeting hall. A low tremor moved through the floorboards, subtle but unmistakable. Jonas felt it travel up through his boots and settle in his chest like a second heartbeat. The entity continued its work, reshaping the valley one tremor at a time. They had bought time. How they used that time remained to be seen.

CHAPTER EIGHTEEN

The Shared Vision

The four of them sat around Widow Grier's table with the oil lamp burning low between them. The room felt smaller than it should have been, the walls pressing in with each breath they took. Jonas kept his hands flat on the scarred wood. Across from him, Sera stared at the flame without blinking. Paul Murdock sat hunched forward, his shoulders drawn up around his ears. Widow Grier poured water from a tin pitcher into four cups, her movements slow and deliberate.

Paul stared down at his twitching fingers. “It’s coming up. Through the floorboards. Right now.”

Widow Grier set the pitcher down. She did not sit. Instead she stood with one hand resting on the back of her chair, the shotgun leaning against the wall within easy reach. The children had already been moved to the meeting hall with the other families. The house felt empty without their small voices.

Jonas pushed his cup away. The water was too still. "How long?"

Sera didn't look up from the flame. "The graves were warm this morning. The soil is turning."

Paul pressed both palms flat against the wood, trying to stop the vibration. "Like the mine. Just before the timbers cracked."

The lamp flickered. Jonas watched the light shift across their faces. Widow Grier's mouth had set into a hard line. Sera's dark eyes reflected the flame, two small points of gold against the black. Paul looked younger than his years, his face drawn tight with fear he could not hide.

Then the air changed.

It happened between one breath and the next. The room stayed the same. The lamp still burned. But something else pressed against the edges of Jonas's mind, heavy and cold. He tried to stand. His legs would not move. Across the table, Sera's hand froze halfway to her cup. Widow Grier's fingers tightened on the chair back. Paul made a small sound in his throat.

The vision took them all at once.

The valley appeared around them, but it was not the valley they knew. The buildings stood in the same places. The creek ran in its usual path. Yet the faces were different. Men and women moved through the square with the same weariness Jonas had seen in the remaining settlers. Their clothes belonged to another time. Their eyes held the same exhausted fear.

A woman stood near the creek bank. She wore a dark dress and held stone beads in her palms. Her face was not Eliza's, but the eyes were the same. The same flat stare that seemed to make the weeds around her boots wither and turn gray. The same cold patience that slowed the very flow of the creek, turning the water sluggish and heavy. She watched the water turn red beneath the surface and did nothing to stop it.

Another man argued with a small group near the trading post. His coat was older, the cut different, but the desperation in his face matched Harlan Pricket's. He gestured toward the trees. His mouth moved, though no sound reached Jonas. The people around him listened. Some nodded. Others turned away. The man kept speaking. His hands shook. The same ambition twisted his features into something ugly and familiar.

The ground began to pulse.

It started beneath the old graves. Dirt rose and fell in a slow rhythm. Roots shifted under the soil. The tremor traveled outward, reaching the creek, the square, the cabins. People stopped what they were doing. They looked down at their feet. A child near the well began to cry.

Then the entity pushed upward.

It did not break through the surface. It pressed against the minds of every person still standing. Jonas felt it inside his own skull, cold and vast. Memories that were not his own flooded through him. A man falling into a sinkhole. A woman waking with red water on her lips. A boy hearing footsteps beneath his bed. Each image carried the weight of grief, fear, and something older. Something hungry.

The woman with the stone beads smiled. She lifted her hands. The beads caught the light. Around her, the pale figures gathered. Their eyeless faces turned toward the settlement. They waited.

The man near the trading post fell to his knees. His eyes clouded over. He spoke to the people still listening, his voice hollow and flat, promising preservation, promising memory. The listeners didn't move. Their jaws went slack, and their eyes glassy and vacant, reflecting the grey sky like muddy puddles as they drank in his words. Some stepped forward. Others ran. The ground kept breathing.

Jonas tried to pull away. The vision held him. He saw the entity gathering every witness it had touched across the cycles. Their minds became its eyes. Their grief became its strength. The thing below did not need to rise physically. It rose through them.

The vision shattered.

Jonas gasped. Air filled his lungs. The kitchen returned around him, the lamp still burning, the table still solid beneath his hands. Across from him, Sera blinked hard. Widow Grier released her grip on the chair. Paul remained hunched forward, his breathing ragged.

Then Paul screamed.

He clawed at the table with both hands. His fingernails dug into the wood. Splinters broke away. Blood welled from under his nails and spread across the grain. He carved without looking, his eyes unfocused, his mouth open in a sound that did not sound human. Lines appeared beneath his fingers. Shapes. A square. Trees. Pale figures standing in a loose circle. A woman with beads. A man on his knees.

Widow Grier moved first. She grabbed Paul's wrists. "Stop. Paul, stop."

He did not hear her. His hands kept moving. Blood smeared across the table. The carving deepened. Jonas stood and reached across. He caught one of Paul's arms. The younger man's strength surprised him. Paul pulled against the grip, still carving, still bleeding.

Sera came around the table. She took Paul's other arm. Between the three of them they pulled him back. His body went limp. He slumped forward, his forehead resting on the edge of the table. Blood dripped from his fingers onto the floor.

The carving remained. Jonas stared at it. The lines matched what he had seen. The square. The creek. The woman with the beads. The man with the desperate face. The pale figures waiting among the trees. Paul's blood filled the grooves, turning the wood dark.

Widow Grier stepped back, wiping her hands on her apron. The linen stained dark red. “What was that?”

Sera’s fingers hovered over the fresh cuts in the wood. “Before. It’s happened here before.”

Jonas looked at the boy’s bleeding hands. “He saw them first.”

“He can’t block it.” Sera’s shoulder rose and fell. “It’s too loud for him.”

Widow Grier wrung out the wet rag. The water in the basin turned pink. “Like Pricket. Same promises.”

Sera shook her head. “There’s a seam. A weak spot.”

Jonas turned toward her. "How?"

“The graves.” Sera tapped the carved lines. “The ground hasn’t settled there yet. If we get there before the next shift, we can plug it.”

Paul blinked, looking down at his torn nails. “Did I…”

Widow Grier tied a knot in the clean bandage. “Keep still. You were gone.”

Paul stared at the dried blood in the grooves. “The woman. She wanted it. And the man… he thought he could make a deal.”

Jonas rubbed his face. Pricket’s face came to him, pale and desperate. “Eliza.”

"She's waiting for the end of it." Sera tightened the straps on her pack. "She isn't fighting."

The lamp flickered again. Jonas looked toward the window. Outside, the night pressed against the glass. No stars showed through the clouds. The wind had died. The settlement lay silent beyond the walls.

Widow Grier picked up her coat. "Then we go to the graves."

Paul tried to stand, but his knees buckled. Jonas caught him by the elbow. "He's too weak."

"I'm going." Paul's voice was barely a whisper. "If I stay here, the noise gets inside."

Sera gathered her pack from the corner. She checked the contents. The ancestral texts lay wrapped in oilcloth at the bottom. She added a small knife and a length of rope. "We go now. Before the next shift."

Widow Grier retrieved her shotgun. She checked the shells, then slung the weapon over her shoulder. "The children are safe in the meeting hall. I left instructions with the mothers. No one leaves until we return."

Jonas supported Paul toward the door. The younger man leaned against him, his breathing still uneven. The bandages on his hands had already begun to stain. "What happens if we cannot reach the graves in time?"

Sera opened the door. Cold air flowed into the kitchen. "Then the vision becomes truth. The entity claims another cycle. We become part of it."

They stepped outside. The settlement square stretched before them, empty and dark. The cabins stood silent. No lamps burned in the windows. The families waited in the meeting hall, their presence felt rather than seen. Jonas smelled the metallic tang of red water on the wind. It came from the creek, thick and wrong.

Paul stumbled. Jonas tightened his grip. "Stay with me."

"I am." Paul's head lifted. His eyes focused on the path ahead. "The voice is quieter out here. It does not like the open air."

They moved together toward the old graves. The path wound between empty cabins and the remains of the trading post. Jonas kept his eyes on the ground. The soil had shifted in places, small ridges rising where the earth had settled unevenly. He marked each change, counting the tremors that had altered the landscape since morning.

Sera walked ahead. She held the lamp high, its light barely cutting through the dark. Widow Grier followed, the shotgun ready in her hands. Paul stayed close to Jonas, his steps slow but steady.

The graves appeared ahead. Stones leaned at odd angles. Some had fallen completely. The ground between them looked disturbed, as if something had tried to push upward and failed. Jonas felt the air grow colder as they approached.

Sera stopped at the edge of the burial ground. She set the lamp on a flat stone. "This is the thin place. The entity has not reached it yet. We have time."

Widow Grier scanned the dark tree line. “How long?”

“Minutes.” Sera knelt, clearing wet leaves from the flat stone. “Help me clear this.”

Paul slid down against a leaning marker. “It's starting again. It knows.”

Jonas moved to stand beside Sera. He watched her open the pack and remove the wrapped texts. She unfolded the oilcloth carefully. The pages inside looked old, the ink faded but still legible. She turned to a section near the back. Her finger traced the symbols written there.

"Jonas." Sera reached for her knife. "The stone needs to be marked."

Widow Grier did not hesitate. She drew a small knife from her belt. She cut across her palm, a shallow line that welled with dark blood. She pressed her hand to the largest stone. The mark left behind looked small against the gray surface.

Jonas took the knife next. He cut his own palm. The sting felt distant. He pressed his hand beside Widow Grier's mark. The blood mixed, turning the stone darker.

Sera followed. She cut without flinching. Her blood joined theirs on the stone. She turned to Paul. "Your turn."

Paul held out one bandaged hand. Widow Grier unwrapped the cloth. The cuts beneath had not closed. Fresh blood welled from beneath his nails. He pressed his palm to the stone. The mark smeared, but it held.

Sera began to speak. The words came from the text, old and unfamiliar. Jonas did not understand their meaning. He felt their weight. The air around the graves grew still. The wind died completely. The lamp flame stood straight and tall.

Then the ground pulsed.

It came from beneath the creek. A low tremor traveled through the soil. Jonas felt it in his boots. The stones around them shifted slightly. One of the fallen markers rolled a few inches. Paul gasped. His eyes rolled back. He slumped against the stone behind him.

Sera kept speaking. Her voice did not waver. The words filled the space between the graves. Jonas felt something press against his mind again. Not the full vision this time. Just a presence. Cold. Patient. Watching.

The entity offered.

Jonas saw it clearly. If he stopped Sera, if he walked away, the cycle would continue without him. He would be left untouched. The others would be claimed. The settlement would fall. But he would live. The offer came with images. A cabin in the hills. A quiet life. No more red water. No more Hollow-Eyed. No more responsibility.

He pushed the offer away.

The presence withdrew. It left behind a cold anger. The ground pulsed again. Stronger this time. Jonas staggered. Widow Grier caught his arm. Sera finished the last line of the ritual. She closed the text and wrapped it in the oilcloth.

Paul opened his eyes. He looked at the marks on the stone. His breathing steadied. "It tried to stop us. I heard it. It offered me silence. I said no."

Sera stood. She looked toward the creek. The red water gleamed in the darkness. "We have delayed it. Not stopped it. The thin place will hold for a while. Not forever."

Widow Grier pressed a rag to her palm. "How long will this buy us?"

"A few days. Enough to get the children out." Sera stood up, shaking.

Jonas looked at the marks they had left. Four handprints on the stone. Blood drying in the night air. The ritual had worked. He felt the difference in the ground beneath his boots. The pulse had weakened here. The entity had not claimed this place yet.

Paul got his feet under him. "The humming stopped. For now."

They turned back toward the settlement. The path stretched ahead, dark and empty. Jonas walked beside Paul, ready to catch him if he fell. Widow Grier carried the shotgun low. Sera held the lamp, its light casting long shadows across the ground.

The square appeared ahead. The meeting hall stood at the far side, its door closed against the wind. No sound came from inside. The families waited. Jonas wondered how much they had heard. How much they would believe.

Sera stopped at the edge of the square. She looked toward the tree line. The shadows there seemed deeper than before. "We need to tell them what happened. What we saw."

"They won't believe us," Widow Grier said. "But we're moving them anyway."

Jonas nodded. The decision settled between them without further words. They had bought time. How they used it remained to be seen. The entity had shown them the pattern. It had shown them the cost of failure. Now they would carry that knowledge to the others.

The wind picked up again. It carried the scent of red water and damp earth. Jonas smelled pine needles and blood on his own hands. The marks on the stone would fade. The ritual would hold. For now.

They walked toward the meeting hall. The door opened before they reached it. A woman stood in the threshold, her face pale in the lamplight. Behind her, the gathered families watched in silence. The children slept on blankets near the back wall. Their small forms looked fragile in the dim light.

Jonas stepped inside. The warmth of the room pressed against his skin. He smelled wood smoke and dried herbs.

The families waited. Their eyes tracked every movement. He felt the weight of their attention settle across his shoulders.

Sera moved to the center of the room. She set the lamp on a bench. Widow Grier stood near the door, the shotgun resting across her forearm. Paul found a place near the wall. He sat with his bandaged hands in his lap.

Jonas looked at the gathered faces. He saw the same exhaustion he felt in his own bones. They had survived the sinkholes and the red water. They had endured the Hollow-Eyed and the shifting ground. Now they would hear what came next.

He began to speak.

CHAPTER NINETEEN

The Last Witnesses

The old graves sat quiet under a sky the color of wet slate. Jonas stood with his hands loose at his sides and watched the ground between the stones. It did not move the way it had the night before. The marks they left still showed on the largest marker, four handprints dark against the gray. Blood had dried into the rock and left faint lines that the rain had not washed away.

Sera knelt beside the marker with her pack open at her feet. She pulled the oilcloth bundle free and set the ancestral texts on a flat stone. The pages crackled when she turned them. Her fingers moved slow and careful over the faded ink. Jonas could see the tension in her shoulders, the way she held her breath between each turn of the page.

Paul Murdock sat with his back against a leaning headstone a few yards off. His bandaged hands rested in his lap. The white cloth had already picked up dirt and faint smears of old blood. He kept his eyes on the ground in front of him, listening to something none of them could hear. Every few minutes his head tilted like he was trying to catch a distant voice.

Widow Grier had already gone. She left before the first gray light showed in the east, her shotgun slung across her back and her coat buttoned tight against the cold. The remaining families waited in the meeting hall with what little they could carry. She would get them moving before the next shift hit the valley floor. Jonas had watched her go without saying much. There was nothing left to say that had not already been said.

Eliza Penhaligon stood at the far side of the burial ground. She had appeared while they worked, stepping out from between two crooked markers without a sound. Her dark dress hung heavy with dew. The veil covered her face, but Jonas could see the stone beads moving between her fingers. She did not come closer. She watched. The air around her felt thicker somehow, like the cold had gathered there and refused to leave.

Sera looked up from the texts. Her eyes found Eliza and stayed there for a long moment. Then she turned to Jonas.

Sera gestured toward the far markers with her chin. "She knows the pattern. She has seen this before."

Jonas studied the woman at the edge of the graves. The beads clicked once, a small dry sound that carried farther than it should have.

"She waited for the last cycle to end." Jonas spat into the dead grass. "She did not stop it."

"No." Sera closed one of the books and set it aside. "But she knows how the thin places break. She can tell us where the next one will open."

Paul shifted against the headstone, his raw throat making the words sound dry and cracked. "She wants the same thing we want. For now."

"She wants the same thing we want. For now."

Jonas walked over to the boy. Paul's face looked thinner than it had the day before. The skin under his eyes had gone dark, and his hands trembled even when they lay still. Jonas crouched so their faces were level.

"You heard something new?"

Paul nodded once. "It is using Pricket's voice now. The words are the same, but the sound is different. Like the ground is talking through his mouth."

Jonas glanced toward the tree line beyond the graves. The shadows under the pines looked deeper than they had an hour earlier. He could not see movement yet, but the feeling of being watched had grown stronger. The same feeling that had followed him since the vision in Widow Grier's kitchen.

Sera stood and brushed dirt from her knees. She walked to where Eliza waited. The two women faced each other across ten feet of uneven ground. Neither spoke at first. The beads in Eliza's hands kept their slow rhythm.

Sera took a step closer, her hand resting on the hilt of the knife at her belt. "You offered help. Tell us what you know."

Eliza lifted the veil. Her face showed no expression, only the same flat patience Jonas remembered from the vision. The same face that had watched the water turn red without raising a hand to stop it.

Eliza lifted the veil, her gaze flat and unblinking. "The seam near the old graves is the weakest point left. The entity has not pressed through here yet. If you mark the stones again and speak the second binding, the ground will hold for another cycle."

Sera studied her for a long moment.

"And after that?"

"After that the cycle begins again somewhere else. Or it waits. The choice is not mine to make."

Jonas joined them. He kept his distance from Eliza, but close enough to hear every word. The air smelled of wet leaves and the faint metallic tang that always came with the red water.

Jonas stepped between them, his hand instinctively dropping to his pocket. "Pricket is with them now. We saw him at the edge of the trees last night. His eyes were gone. His suit was torn."

Eliza's fingers paused on the beads.

"He made the same choice the last time. He always does. The promise of memory is stronger than the fear of what comes after."

Paul pushed himself to his feet. He swayed once, then steadied. He walked over to the flat stone where Sera had set the texts. His bandaged hands hovered above the open pages without touching them.

Paul traced a cracked line in the stone marker. "The words are different this time. They want more than blood on stone. They want the memory of the place itself."

Sera moved to stand beside him. She traced one of the faded symbols with her fingertip.

"The second binding requires the ground to remember what it was before the entity touched it. We give it that memory back."

Jonas looked at the marks they had left the night before. The handprints had dried to a dark crust. He could still see where each of them had pressed their palms. Four witnesses. Four names the entity already knew.

"How do we do that?" he asked.

Eliza stepped closer. She stopped at the edge of the cleared space around the largest marker. The beads had gone still in her hands.

"You speak the names of those who died here before the first cycle. You speak the names of the land itself. The stones, the roots, the water that ran before the red came. Then you mark the ground with what remains of the old settlement."

Sera opened another book. She turned pages until she found the section she wanted. The ink here was darker, the symbols larger. She read in silence for a moment, then looked up at Jonas.

"We need something from the old buildings. Wood. Iron. Anything that still carries the smell of the people who lived here first."

Jonas nodded. He turned toward the path that led back to the square. The meeting hall stood at the far end, its windows dark. Beyond it, the cabins sat empty. Widow Grier had already moved the last families out. The only things left behind were the tools they could not carry and the memories that clung to every wall.

He walked the short distance to the nearest cabin. The door hung open on leather hinges that had begun to rot. Inside, the single room held a table, two chairs, and a stove that had not been lit in days. A coat still hung on a peg by the door. Jonas took it down. The wool felt stiff under his hands. He searched the shelves until he found a small iron kettle and a length of rope that had been left behind. He gathered what he could carry and walked back to the graves.

Sera had cleared a wider space around the largest marker. She had drawn a circle in the dirt with the tip of her knife. Paul stood at the edge of the circle, his head tilted again, listening. Eliza remained outside the circle, her veil lowered once more.

Jonas set the kettle and the rope beside the marker. He held out the coat.

"This belonged to the man who built the cabin. He left before the sinkholes started."

Sera took the coat. She folded it once and placed it on the flat stone. Then she opened the ancestral text to the page she had marked and began to read. The words came slow, each syllable shaped carefully. Jonas did not understand the language, but he felt the weight of it settle into the air around them.

Paul moved closer to the circle. His bandaged hands shook as he reached for the iron kettle. He set it inside the circle beside the coat. The metal rang once against the stone, a thin sound that seemed to hang longer than it should have.

The ground under their feet gave a single, low tremor. It was not the steady pulse they had felt before. This was different. Sharper. Like something testing the surface from below.

Eliza took one step forward. She stopped at the edge of the circle.

Eliza pointed a pale, bead-wrapped finger at the circle. "The names. Speak them now."

Sera looked at Jonas. He nodded. He had learned the names from the old records Widow Grier kept in the meeting hall. The first families. The ones who had cleared the land and built the first cabins before the creek turned wrong.

He spoke them one at a time. Each name felt heavier than the last. When he finished, the air inside the circle had grown colder. The kettle on the stone had begun to sweat, small beads of moisture forming on the iron even though the morning remained dry.

Paul spoke next. His voice was quiet, almost lost beneath the sound of the wind moving through the pines. He spoke the names of the land itself. The creek before it carried red water. The ridge where the first trees had stood. The soil that had once been black and rich before the entity pressed upward.

The tremor came again. Stronger this time. A crack appeared in the dirt just outside the circle, a thin line that ran toward the nearest headstone and stopped. Red water seeped up from the crack and pooled in the low places. It smelled of metal and old blood.

Sera finished the last line of the text. She closed the book and set it on the stone beside the coat. Then she took her knife and cut across her palm again. Fresh blood welled up. She let it fall onto the iron kettle. The drops hit the metal and hissed, though the kettle had not been heated.

Jonas cut his own palm and added his blood. Paul followed, his bandaged hands clumsy but steady. The three of them stood together inside the circle while the ground beneath them shifted again.

Eliza did not enter the circle. She remained at the edge, her beads moving once more between her fingers. But she spoke the final binding with them, her voice clear and cold.

The words she used were different from the ones in Sera's text, older, rougher. They carried the sound of stone grinding against stone.

The crack in the dirt widened. Red water poured up from the ground in a sudden rush. It reached the edge of the circle and stopped, as if an invisible wall held it back. The water rose in a thin sheet, then fell back into the crack. The smell of it filled the air, thick and wrong.

Paul gasped. His knees buckled. Jonas caught him before he fell. The boy's eyes had rolled back, showing only the whites. His body convulsed once, twice, then went still. Blood seeped through the bandages on his hands and dripped onto the dirt inside the circle.

Jonas lowered him to the ground. Paul's breathing came shallow and fast. His lips moved, but no sound came out. Jonas stayed beside him, one hand on the boy's shoulder, and watched the circle.

The ground gave one final, violent shake. The headstones around them tilted. One of the smaller markers toppled and landed with a dull thud. The red water that had pooled outside the circle sank back into the earth. The crack sealed itself. The smell of metal faded.

Inside the circle, the air grew still. The kettle on the stone had gone cold. The coat lay folded as Sera had left it. The handprints on the largest marker had begun to darken further, the blood sinking into the rock like it belonged there.

Sera stood with her hands at her sides. Her face had gone pale, but her eyes remained steady. She looked at Eliza.

"It held."

Eliza nodded once. She did not step inside the circle. She remained at the edge, the beads still now in her hands.

"The second seal is in place. The thin place will not open for another cycle. Perhaps longer."

Jonas helped Paul sit up. The boy's eyes had returned to normal, though they looked unfocused. He blinked several times and wiped his mouth with the back of one bandaged hand.

Paul touched his temples, his shoulders dropping as the tension left his frame. "The voice stopped. For the first time since the mine. It is quiet."

Jonas looked toward the tree line. The shadows under the pines had not changed. He could not see Pricket or the Hollow-Eyed yet, but he could feel them. The same presence that had pressed against his thoughts the night before. It had not left. It had only stepped back.

Sera gathered the texts and wrapped them in the oilcloth. She placed the bundle in her pack and stood. The circle in the dirt remained, a faint line that would not wash away with the next rain. The kettle and the coat stayed on the stone. The iron had begun to rust at the edges where the blood had touched it.

They walked back toward the square together. Paul leaned on Jonas for support. Eliza followed at a distance, her veil lowered once more. The meeting hall stood empty now. Widow Grier had already led the last families out through the forest toward the main road. The path they had taken showed in the disturbed leaves and the broken branches along the tree line.

Jonas stopped at the edge of the square. He looked back toward the graves. The stones stood in their crooked rows. The largest marker caught the weak morning light. The handprints had almost disappeared into the gray surface.

Sera stood beside him. She did not speak. The wind moved through the empty cabins and carried the smell of damp earth and pine. Somewhere in the distance, a single bird called and then fell silent.

Paul sat on the steps of the meeting hall. He held his bandaged hands in his lap and stared at the ground. His breathing had steadied, but the exhaustion showed in every line of his face. Jonas wondered how much longer the boy could carry the weight the entity had placed on him.

Eliza remained at the far side of the square. She did not approach. She watched the tree line with the same flat patience she had shown at the graves. The beads moved once in her hands, a small sound that carried across the empty space.

Jonas turned away from the graves. The valley stretched out around them, quiet now in a way it had not been for weeks. The ground did not pulse. The red water had receded. The air felt colder, cleaner, though the metallic smell still lingered beneath the scent of pine.

He walked to the well at the center of the square. The bucket hung on its rope, untouched since the last time anyone had drawn water. He lowered it into the darkness and pulled it up again. The water that came up was clear. No red tint showed in the morning light. He poured it out and watched it soak into the dirt.

Sera joined him. She carried her pack over one shoulder. The ancestral texts rested at the bottom, wrapped and waiting for the next time they would be needed.

Sera adjusted her pack, looking down the empty trail. "Widow Grier will reach the road by midday. The children will be safe there."

Jonas nodded. He set the bucket back on the well's edge and wiped his hands on his coat. The blood from the ritual had dried on his palm. He could still feel the sting where the knife had cut.

Paul stood and walked over to them. His steps were slow but steady. He looked at the empty square, the silent cabins, the meeting hall with its door standing open.

Paul stared down at his boots, kicking a loose pebble into the dirt. "They will come back. When the ground starts to move again."

Sera did not answer. She looked toward the tree line where Eliza stood. The woman had not moved. The beads in her hands caught the light and threw small reflections across the dirt.

Jonas studied the valley one last time. The graves sat quiet at the edge of the settlement. The creek ran clear for the moment. The thin place had been sealed. The cost had been paid in blood and memory, but the entity had not claimed this cycle. Not yet.

He turned toward the forest path that Widow Grier had taken. Sera walked beside him. Paul followed a few steps behind. Eliza remained where she was, a dark figure against the gray morning light. The beads clicked once more, then fell silent.

The three of them entered the trees. The path wound between the pines and led toward the main road. The ground beneath their feet felt solid. No tremor rose to meet them. The valley behind them had gone quiet, but Jonas knew the silence would not last. The entity waited. It remembered. And it would come again when the time was right.

They walked until the settlement disappeared behind them. The sound of the creek faded. The smell of red water gave way to pine and damp earth. Jonas kept his eyes on the path ahead. Sera walked in silence beside him. Paul stayed close, his bandaged hands swinging at his sides.

The forest opened onto the main road at midday. Widow Grier stood with the remaining families at the edge of the trees. The children sat on blankets, their faces pale but calm. The mothers gathered what little food they had carried. No one spoke. The only sound came from the wind moving through the branches above them.

Widow Grier turned as they approached. Her face showed the same exhaustion Jonas felt in his own bones. She carried the shotgun low, the barrel pointed at the ground. Her coat was streaked with dirt and leaves from the journey through the forest.

She looked at Jonas, then at Sera, then at Paul. Her eyes asked the question she did not speak aloud.

Jonas nodded once. The second seal held. The thin place near the graves would not open again for another cycle. The valley had been given time. How they used it remained to be seen.

Widow Grier turned back to the families. She spoke in a low voice, giving instructions for the journey ahead. The children stood and gathered their blankets. The mothers shouldered their packs. They moved out onto the main road in a single line, their footsteps quiet against the packed dirt.

Jonas watched them go. Sera stood beside him, her pack still slung over her shoulder. Paul leaned against a tree at the edge of the road, his eyes half-closed. The exhaustion had caught up with him at last.

The road stretched ahead, empty and gray under the midday sky. The settlement lay behind them, silent and waiting. The entity had been delayed. The witnesses had done what they could. The cost remained, but the cycle had been broken for now.

Jonas turned away from the road. He looked back toward the valley one last time. The trees hid the graves and the creek and the empty cabins. The wind moved through the branches and carried the smell of pine and damp earth. Somewhere beneath the surface, the entity waited. It remembered every name they had spoken. It remembered every witness it had touched.

He walked back into the trees. Sera followed. Paul pushed himself away from the tree and joined them. The three of them returned to the settlement square as the afternoon light began to fade. The meeting hall stood empty. The cabins sat silent. The graves at the edge of the trees caught the last of the sun and held it for a moment before the shadows claimed them.

Jonas stopped at the well. He looked down into the darkness. The water at the bottom remained clear. No red tint showed. The second seal had done its work. The thin place had been claimed, but not by the entity. Not yet.

He turned away from the well and walked toward the meeting hall. Sera and Paul followed. The three of them entered the empty building and closed the door against the coming night. The wind moved through the square outside, carrying the smell of pine and damp earth and the faint metallic tang that would never fully leave the valley.

Inside the hall, the lamp burned low. Jonas sat at the table where Paul had carved the vision the night before. The lines remained in the wood, dark with dried blood. He traced one of the shapes with his fingertip and felt the weight of everything they had done and everything they still had to do.

Sera sat across from him. She opened her pack and removed the ancestral texts. She did not open them. She simply set them on the table and rested her hands on the oilcloth wrapping. Paul took a place at the end of the table and laid his bandaged hands on the wood. The three of them sat in silence while the lamp flickered and the night pressed against the windows.

The entity waited beneath the valley. It had been delayed, but it had not been stopped. The witnesses had done what they could. The cost had been paid. The cycle had been broken for now.

Jonas closed his eyes and listened to the quiet. The ground beneath the hall did not pulse. The red water did not rise. The voices that had filled Paul's head had gone silent. The valley held its breath, and the witnesses waited with it.

The night deepened. The lamp burned lower. Outside, the wind moved through the empty square and carried the smell of pine and damp earth. Somewhere in the distance, a single bird called and then fell silent. The settlement waited. The graves waited. The entity waited beneath the surface, patient and hungry and remembering every name it had ever claimed.

Jonas opened his eyes. Sera watched him from across the table. Paul's head rested on his folded arms, his breathing slow and even. The ancestral texts lay between them, wrapped in oilcloth and waiting for the next time they would be needed.

The second seal had held. The thin place near the graves had been claimed. The valley had been given time. How they used it remained to be seen. The witnesses sat together in the quiet hall while the night deepened and the entity waited beneath the earth, patient and hungry and remembering.

CHAPTER TWENTY

The Second Seal

The old graves waited in their crooked rows, and the largest marker still carried the faint outline of four hands pressed into stone. Jonas stood beside it with his coat open to the cold air. The ritual circle remained visible in the dirt, a faint ring that rain had not yet washed clean. Inside that ring lay the iron kettle and the coat left behind by a man who had built one of the first cabins. Both had begun to rust where blood had touched them.

Sera knelt at the edge of the circle. She held one of her ancestral texts open across her knees, though she did not read from it now. Her fingers rested on the page as if the weight of her hands could keep the words from escaping. The second seal had taken hold. The thin place near the graves had gone quiet. Yet something in the stillness felt wrong, as if the ground were holding its breath rather than resting.

Paul Murdock lay on a blanket inside Widow Grier's spare room. His breathing came shallow and quick, and the skin along his jaw had taken on the same pale, stone-like cast that marked the Hollow-Eyed. Jonas had helped carry him there after the ritual ended. The boy's bandaged hands had stopped shaking, but his eyes remained closed, and no amount of calling his name brought any response.

Eliza Penhaligon stood outside the meeting hall with her veil lowered. She had not entered the building since the seal was completed. Her stone beads moved slowly between her fingers, the only motion she allowed herself. The burn on her arm from the invisible force still showed through the dark fabric of her sleeve, yet she had not flinched when the force struck her again. She had simply stepped forward and shielded the markers with her own body until the words were spoken and the ground fell still.

Jonas walked the short distance to the creek bank. The water ran clear now, no red tint showing in the morning light. He crouched and plunged his hand into the flow. The cold bit at his fingers, but the metallic smell that had followed them for weeks was gone. He scoured his palm against his trousers and stood again. The silence pressed against his ears. No pulse rose from the soil. No distant voices called his name from the tree line. The absence of sound felt heavier than the noise had been.

Sera joined him at the water's edge. She carried her pack slung over one shoulder, the oilcloth bundle of texts resting inside. She set the pack down on a flat rock and opened it. Her fingers moved through the contents until she found the small leather pouch that held the ritual markers. She opened the pouch and counted the stones inside, then closed it again without removing any.

Sera looked down at her hands, then back at the water. "The ground fought harder this time. The sinkholes... they opened before we even finished the last line."

Jonas nodded. He had seen the cracks widen around them, had felt the tremor that nearly threw Paul to the ground before the boy collapsed on his own. The resistance had been stronger than during the first seal, as if the entity had learned from what they had done and was already preparing its next move.

They walked together back toward the settlement square. The meeting hall stood empty, its windows dark. Widow Grier had taken the last families out through the forest before dawn, and the path they had followed showed in the disturbed leaves and broken branches along the tree line. Jonas stopped at the well and looked down into the darkness. The water at the bottom remained clear, the same clear water he had drawn earlier. He pulled the bucket up and poured it out onto the dirt. The liquid soaked in without resistance, leaving only a dark patch that would dry before midday.

Eliza remained at the far side of the square. She watched them approach without moving closer. The beads in her hands had stopped their slow rhythm. She lifted her veil slightly, enough for Jonas to see the flat patience in her eyes. The same patience she had shown when she offered her help with the ritual, when she claimed she had delayed the entity's awakening before and could do so again.

Eliza didn't look at them. "It's down. For now." She pulled her shawl tighter over her burned arm. "Unless someone breaks it."

Jonas studied her face. The burn on her arm had not stopped her from stepping into the force again. She had used her own body to shield the ritual markers when the entity struck. The cost of that choice showed in the way she held her arm close to her side, yet she did not ask for help or show any sign of pain.

Sera picked up her pack and walked toward the meeting hall. Jonas followed. They entered the building together and closed the door against the morning chill. The lamp on the table burned low, the same lamp that had burned through the night while they prepared the ritual. Sera set her pack on the floor beside the table and pulled out one of the chairs. She sat and rested her hands on the wood, her fingers tracing the carved lines Paul had left there during his vision.

Jonas remained standing. He walked to the window and looked out toward the tree line. The shadows under the pines had not changed since he last looked. No figures moved among them. No voice called his name from the darkness. Yet the feeling of being watched had not left him. It pressed against the back of his neck, the same sensation that had followed him since the shared vision in Widow Grier's kitchen.

They ate what little food remained in the hall. Sera had brought dried meat and hard biscuits from her pack. They shared the meal in silence, each bite tasting of dust and the faint metallic tang that still lingered in the air. Jonas chewed slowly and watched the window. The light outside had grown brighter, but the shadows under the trees remained deep.

After the meal, Sera opened one of her texts and began to read. The pages crackled as she turned them. Jonas listened to the sound without understanding the words. The language was older than the settlement, older than the families who had first cleared the land. Yet the weight of it settled into the air around them, the same weight he had felt when she read the binding at the graves.

Paul's condition had not improved by midday. Jonas walked back to Widow Grier's spare room and checked on the boy. Paul's breathing remained shallow, and the pale cast to his skin had spread to his throat and the backs of his hands. Jonas touched the boy's forehead. The skin felt cool, almost cold, and the pulse beneath it moved too slowly. Paul did not stir at the touch. His eyes remained closed, and no sound came from his throat.

Jonas returned to the meeting hall. Sera still sat at the table with her text open before her. She looked up when he entered, and her eyes asked the question she did not speak aloud. Jonas shook his head. Paul's condition had not changed. The entity's voice had gone quiet inside the boy's head, but the cost of that silence showed in the stone-like pallor spreading across his skin.

They returned to the ritual site near the old graves. Sera wanted to check the markers, to make certain the seal had taken hold completely. Jonas walked beside her along the path that wound between the empty cabins. The wind moved through the branches above them, carrying the smell of pine and damp earth. No metallic tang followed them now. The red water had receded, and the ground beneath their feet felt solid.

The largest marker still carried the faint outline of four hands. The blood had sunk deeper into the stone, the lines almost invisible against the gray surface. The circle in the dirt remained, a faint ring that would not wash away with the next rain. The iron kettle and the coat lay on the flat stone where they had left them. Rust had begun to spread across the kettle's surface, eating into the metal where blood had touched it.

Sera knelt beside the circle and studied the ground. She ran her fingers along the edge of the ring, feeling for any break in the pattern. Her hand stopped at a point near the largest marker. A small crack had appeared in the dirt, barely visible, a thin line that ran from the circle's edge toward the nearest headstone. Red water seeped up from the crack, a single drop that pooled in the low place and then sank back into the soil.

"The seal is already weakening," Sera said. She stood and brushed dirt from her knees. "The entity has learned from the first binding. It knows how to press against the thin places now."

Jonas looked at the crack. It had not been there when they finished the ritual. The ground had sealed itself, the red water had receded, and the air had grown still. Yet something had changed in the hours since. The entity had found a way through, a small weakness in the pattern they had drawn.

They walked the perimeter of the circle together. Sera checked each marker, each stone they had touched during the binding. The handprints on the largest marker had almost disappeared, the blood sinking deeper into the rock. The smaller markers remained upright, though one had tilted slightly during the final tremor. The crack near the largest marker was the only visible sign of weakness.

Eliza joined them at the ritual site. She had followed them from the square without speaking, her veil lowered and her beads moving slowly between her fingers. She stopped at the edge of the circle and studied the crack in the dirt. Her fingers paused on the beads, and she lifted her veil slightly to see more clearly.

"The entity has learned to use human agents more effectively than in previous cycles," Eliza said. Her voice carried the same flat patience it always did. "Pricket may only be the first of many. The promise of memory draws them in, and the ground takes what remains."

Jonas turned toward the tree line. The shadows under the pines still showed no movement, yet the feeling of being watched had grown stronger. He could sense the presence there, the same presence that had pressed against his thoughts during the vision. Pricket stood among the Hollow-Eyed now, his expensive suit torn and stained, his eyes clouded and his voice joined to theirs in calling Jonas's name. The entity's strategy had shifted. It no longer relied on the Hollow-Eyed alone. It had found a way to use the living as vessels, to infiltrate the settlement from within.

The ground gave a single, low tremor. It was not the steady pulse they had felt before the seal. This was different, sharper, like something testing the surface from below. The crack near the largest marker widened slightly, and another drop of red water seeped up from the soil. The drop pooled and then sank back into the earth, leaving a faint stain on the dirt.

Sera stepped back from the circle. She kept her hand on the hilt of the knife at her belt, her fingers tight around the handle. The tension in her shoulders showed in the way she held herself, ready to move if the ground shifted again. Jonas stood beside her, his own hand resting on the knife he carried. They watched the crack in the dirt, waiting for the next tremor, the next sign that the seal was failing.

The tremor did not come again. The crack remained narrow, the red water did not rise further. The ground fell silent once more, the same heavy silence that had followed the ritual. Jonas felt the familiar sensation of missing time approaching, the same disorientation that had struck him before. The world around him seemed to stretch and then contract, the trees shifting position by inches, the morning sun casting long, sharp shadows that angled back toward the east, its light curdled into a bruised, unnatural purple. He gripped Sera's arm to anchor himself in the present moment, his fingers tight around her wrist.

The sensation passed. The trees remained where they had been, the light steady in the morning sky. Jonas released Sera's arm and stepped back. His breathing came faster than before, and the sweat on his palms felt cold against his skin. Sera watched him without speaking, her eyes steady and her face pale. She had seen the missing time before, had watched him struggle against the entity's pull on his thoughts.

They returned to the settlement square. Eliza followed at a distance, her veil lowered once more. The beads in her hands had resumed their slow rhythm, the sound carrying across the empty space. Jonas walked to the well and looked down into the darkness. The water at the bottom remained clear, no red tint showing in the light that filtered down from above. He pulled the bucket up and poured it out onto the dirt, watching the liquid soak in without resistance.

Widow Grier returned from guiding the evacuation. She walked into the square with her shotgun slung across her back and her coat streaked with dirt and leaves from the journey through the forest. Her face showed the same exhaustion Jonas felt in his own bones. She carried the weight of the families she had led out, the children she had promised to protect, the mothers who had looked to her for strength when the ground began to shift beneath their feet.

She stopped at the well and looked at Jonas. Her eyes asked the question she did not speak aloud. Jonas nodded once. The second seal had held, though the crack near the largest marker showed that the entity's resistance had already begun to test the pattern. Widow Grier's shoulders dropped slightly, the tension leaving her frame for the first time since she had returned.

Widow Grier unslung her shotgun and set it against the well's stone rim. "Some of them turned back. Once the shaking stopped, they just... went back to their cabins. Idiots."

Jonas looked toward the forest path. The disturbed leaves and broken branches showed where the families had gone, where some had turned back and returned to the settlement. The empty cabins waited for them, the meeting hall stood ready to receive those who had chosen to stay. The silence of the valley had drawn them back, the absence of the pulse they had felt for weeks. They did not understand that the silence was not peace. It was the entity gathering its strength, preparing its next move.

Widow Grier walked to the meeting hall and entered. Jonas followed her inside. Sera remained outside for a moment longer, her eyes on the tree line where Eliza stood. Then she turned and joined them in the hall. The lamp on the table had burned lower, the oil nearly gone. Jonas lit a second lamp from the shelf and set it beside the first. The light pushed back the shadows in the corners, though it did not reach the windows where the gray morning pressed against the glass.

They sat together at the table. Widow Grier's hands rested on the wood, her fingers tracing the carved lines Paul had left there. Sera opened one of her texts and placed it between them, the page open to the section describing the second binding. Jonas studied the symbols without understanding them, feeling the weight of the words settle into the air around them.

The cost of the seal had been paid in blood and memory. Paul's condition showed the price the boy had paid, the stone-like pallor spreading across his skin. Eliza's burn showed the price she had paid, the force that had struck her when she shielded the markers. Jonas felt the missing time pressing against his thoughts, the entity's attempt to claim him as it had claimed Pricket. The witnesses had done what they could. The cycle had been broken for now. Yet the entity waited beneath the valley, patient and hungry, remembering every name it had ever claimed.

Jonas stood and walked to the window. He looked out toward the tree line. The shadows under the pines remained deep, and the feeling of being watched had not left him. Pricket stood among the Hollow-Eyed somewhere in that darkness, his voice joined to theirs in calling Jonas's name. The entity's strategy had shifted. It had learned to use human agents, to infiltrate the settlement from within. Pricket was only the first. Others would follow, drawn by the promise of memory, consumed by the ground's hunger.

The ground gave another tremor, barely perceptible, a faint shift that traveled up through the floorboards and into the soles of Jonas's boots. The sensation lasted only a moment, then faded. The lamps on the table flickered but did not go out. The shadows in the corners deepened for a breath, then returned to their previous depth.

Sera closed her text and stood. She walked to the window and stood beside Jonas. Her shoulder brushed against his arm, the contact brief and solid. They watched the tree line together, the shadows that held no movement yet carried the weight of everything that waited beneath the valley. The second seal had taken hold. The thin place near the graves would not open for another cycle. The cost had been paid. The witnesses remained. The entity waited, patient and hungry, remembering every name it had ever claimed.

CHAPTER TWENTY ONE

The Vessel's Price

The settlement square held a thin layer of frost when Jonas stepped out of the meeting hall. His boots left dark prints in the white crust as he crossed to the well. The bucket rope creaked against the pulley wheel, and the sound carried farther than it should have in the empty air. He lowered the bucket, heard it splash once against water that still ran clear, then hauled it up hand over hand. The liquid inside smelled of cold stone and nothing else. He poured it out against the packed dirt where it soaked away without leaving any stain.

Sera came out a moment later with her pack slung across one shoulder. She stopped beside him and looked toward the forest path where Widow Grier had taken the last families at dawn. The broken branches and scuffed leaves still marked their passage, but fresh footprints showed in the frost now. Three sets of tracks led inward from the trees instead of outward.

"Someone came back," Sera said.

Jonas followed the prints with his eyes. They split near the well, one set turning toward the old boarding house, another toward the Penhaligon cabin, the third disappearing behind the meeting hall where the Murdock boy had once kept his tools. He set the empty bucket down and wiped his palms on his coat. The frost had already begun to melt where the water had spilled.

They found the first family at the boarding house. The Connors stood in the doorway with their youngest wrapped in a blanket and their older boy holding a rifle across his chest. Mrs. Connor's face looked drawn, her eyes red from lack of sleep, but she held her chin up when Jonas approached. Mr. Connor kept his hand near the rifle stock without touching it.

"We heard the ground go quiet," Mr. Connor said. "Figured whatever it was had passed."

Sera shifted her pack higher on her shoulder. "The seal bought time. It didn't end anything."

“That man Pricket,” Mrs. Connor said, her voice dropping to a harsh whisper. “He was out there. By the birch stand. He called to us when we went by. Said the worst was done with, if we just stayed in our beds and didn't make a fuss.”

Jonas studied the frost melting along the porch boards. "Pricket isn't Pricket anymore. The ground took him the way it took the others."

Mr. Connor’s jaw worked. “He looked like himself. Mostly. The eyes... they were like river glass. But he knew our names. He called out to the boy. Said the ground doesn't want our blood, just our names. Said we could trade the memories of the bad years for peace.”

The boy with the rifle looked between his parents and Jonas. His knuckles showed white around the stock. Jonas remembered that rifle from the first night the Hollow-Eyed appeared. It had belonged to the oldest Connor son before he walked into the creek and came back without his eyes.

"You can't bargain with it," Jonas said. "It doesn't trade. It collects."

Mrs. Connor pulled the blanket tighter around the child in her arms. "We've got nowhere else to go. The wagons won't take us without payment, and Pricket said payment could be made in other ways now."

Sera stepped forward until she stood level with the porch rail. "The entity chose him because he had something to lose. A position. A name. It needed someone people would listen to when the time came."

Mr. Connor looked past her toward the tree line where the shadows still held their depth. "He said the second seal wouldn't hold. Said the cracks were already showing and that fighting them only made the collection come faster."

Jonas felt the familiar pull behind his thoughts, the same stretching sensation that had come before the missing time. He set his hand against the porch post and felt the grain of the wood under his palm. The sensation faded after a few breaths, but the cold sweat on his neck remained.

"Stay inside after dark," he said. "Keep the lamps lit and don't answer if something calls your name from outside."

They left the Connors at the boarding house door and walked toward the second set of footprints. These led to the small cabin where the Trasks had lived since spring. Smoke rose from the chimney now, thin and gray against the morning sky. Jonas knocked once on the door frame and waited.

Mr. Trask opened the door with a shotgun held low. He recognized them and lowered the barrel, though he didn't invite them inside. His wife stood behind him holding their youngest by the hand. The child's eyes were wide and fixed on something beyond the doorway.

"We saw the others turn back," Mr. Trask said. "Couldn't see the sense in running if the shaking had stopped."

Sera glanced at the child, then back at the man. "The silence means it's gathering strength, not leaving."

Mrs. Trask pulled her daughter closer, her hands shaking against the wool. “Pricket was at the clearing. Last night, late. He didn't sound like he used to. He sounded... like a crowd. He said the thing down there didn't need the dead anymore. Said it has enough of us now to speak through the living.”

Jonas felt the weight of that statement settle in his chest. The entity had taken Pricket deliberately, had shaped him into something that could walk among the living and be heard. The Hollow-Eyed had always been warnings. Now the warnings had learned to speak with familiar tongues.

"Did he say anything else?" Jonas asked.

Mr. Trask checked the shotgun’s breech, his thumb clicking the metal. “Said we only make it hard on ourselves. Said the ground’s going to take what we remember anyway. Fighting just makes the teeth dig deeper.”

The child pulled at her mother's hand until Mrs. Trask lifted her into her arms. The girl's face pressed against her mother's shoulder, and Jonas saw the small pale marks along her jaw where the skin had begun to take on the same cast as Paul's. Not as deep yet, but the pattern was there.

"Keep her inside," Sera said quietly. "Don't let her near the creek."

They found the third family at the meeting hall itself. The Raines had claimed the back room where the extra blankets were stored. Mr. Raine sat on an overturned crate while his wife sorted through the remaining supplies. Their oldest daughter stood at the window watching the square.

"We came back because the ground stopped moving," Mr. Raine said. "Couldn't keep the little ones walking through the dark when everything went quiet."

Jonas looked at the girl by the window. She had wrapped her arms around herself and kept her forehead pressed against the glass. "What did Pricket tell you?"

Mrs. Raine dropped a bundle of wool onto the crate. “He said some of us belong to this place now. That the dirt remembers us from when we first cleared the timber. Running doesn't do anything but tire the horses.”

Sera set her pack down on the nearest bench. "The entity was here before any of us. It doesn't mark people. It consumes them."

“He said if we all stay, it won't take so much from any one of us,” Mr. Raine muttered, looking at his boots. “Like... sharing the weight. A few years of a man's life instead of the whole thing.”

Jonas walked to the window where the girl stood. Outside, the square remained empty except for the frost melting in patches where sunlight reached the ground. He placed his hand on the glass beside hers and felt the cold seep through his palm.

"The missing time will come for you if you stay," he said. "You'll lose hours, then days. Eventually you'll lose yourself."

The girl's forehead smeared the condensation on the pane. "He said the missing hours are just the start. He said it's like sleeping without the dreams. You don't even feel it go."

They left the Raines in the meeting hall and walked back toward Widow Grier's house. The frost had melted completely now, leaving dark patches of earth where the water had soaked in. Jonas kept his hand near his knife hilt, though he didn't draw it. The air carried a faint metallic scent that hadn't been there earlier, the smell of red water rising somewhere beneath the surface.

Widow Grier met them at her door with her shotgun already in hand. She stepped aside to let them enter, then closed the door and dropped the latch into place. The house smelled of wood smoke and the bitter herbs she kept drying by the stove.

"Three families came back," she said. "I saw their tracks when I returned from the evacuation route."

Jonas nodded. "We spoke to them. They won't leave again."

Widow Grier set the shotgun against the wall beside the door. "Idiots. The silence won't last, and when the ground starts moving again, they'll have nowhere to run."

She led them through the main room to the spare bedroom where Paul lay. The boy remained on the narrow bed with a blanket pulled up to his chin. His breathing came shallow and slow, and the pale cast had spread from his jaw down his throat and across the backs of both hands. The skin looked tight, almost translucent, like stone that hadn't fully hardened yet.

Sera knelt beside the bed and placed her palm against Paul's forehead. The skin felt cool under her fingers, and the pulse at his temple moved in an uneven rhythm. She withdrew her hand and stood again.

"The entity's voice has gone quiet inside him," she said. "But the cost shows in his skin."

Widow Grier crossed her arms over her chest. "He woke once while I was gone. Spoke a single sentence about the ground using living people as doors. Then he went under again."

Jonas studied the boy's face. The stone-like quality had reached his eyelids now, turning the skin a shade paler than the rest of his face. Paul's chest rose and fell in the same shallow pattern, but the movement seemed slower than before, as if each breath required more effort than the last.

They returned to the main room. Widow Grier poured water from a pitcher into three cups and set them on the table. The liquid looked clear, but Jonas caught the faint metallic scent again when he lifted his cup. He set it down without drinking.

"The second seal is already weakening," Sera said. "A crack opened near the largest marker. Red water came through."

Widow Grier's mouth tightened. "How long before it fails completely?"

"Days at most. The entity learned from the first binding. It knows how to press against the pattern now."

Jonas walked to the window that faced the square. The meeting hall stood across the open space with its windows dark. The Raines would be inside sorting supplies and trying to convince themselves that Pricket's words meant safety instead of surrender. The Connors and Trasks would be doing the same in their own homes, waiting for a voice they recognized to tell them the danger had passed.

"The entity chose Pricket deliberately," Jonas said. "It needed someone the others would listen to when the time came. Someone with authority left to lose."

Sera joined him at the window. "The Hollow-Eyed were warnings. Now the warnings have learned to speak with living voices. The next vessels will be easier to create because the first one showed them the way."

Widow Grier picked up her shotgun and checked the breech again, though both barrels remained loaded. "If Pricket comes close enough, I'll put both loads in his chest. See if the ground can speak through a body that's been opened up."

They left Widow Grier's house and walked toward the ritual site near the old graves. The path wound between empty cabins where frost still clung to the shaded sides of the roofs. Jonas kept his hand near his knife, and Sera walked with her pack held close against her side. The metallic scent grew stronger as they approached the creek, though the water itself still ran clear when they crossed the narrow bridge.

The largest marker stood in its crooked row with the faint outline of four hands barely visible against the stone. The ritual circle remained in the dirt, a faint ring that the morning light picked out in sharp relief. Sera knelt at the edge and studied the crack that had appeared during the night. It had widened slightly, and another drop of red water had seeped up from the soil to pool in the low place before sinking back down.

She touched the edge of the crack with one finger. The dirt felt warm despite the morning chill, and the metallic scent rose stronger from the small depression where the water had pooled. She wiped her finger on her trousers and stood again.

"The pattern is holding, but barely," she said. "The entity is testing every weak point now."

Jonas walked the perimeter of the circle. The smaller markers remained upright, though one had tilted further during the night. The iron kettle and the coat lay where they had been left, both showing more rust than before. He stopped at the largest marker and placed his palm against the stone. The surface felt cold, but the faint warmth from the crack reached him through the ground beneath his boots.

They returned to the settlement square as the sun climbed higher. The frost had melted completely now, leaving the ground dark and soft underfoot. Jonas stopped at the well and looked down into the darkness. The water at the bottom remained clear, but the metallic scent rose from the opening like breath from a sleeping animal.

Eliza Penhaligon stood at the far side of the square with her veil lowered. She watched them approach without moving closer, her stone beads moving slowly between her fingers. The burn on her arm showed through the dark fabric of her sleeve, the skin beneath still raw from where the invisible force had struck her during the ritual.

“It has a taste for them now,” Eliza said, her fingers clicking the heavy stone beads. “The ones who want to keep things the same. Pricket was easy. He wanted his town back so bad he let the roots in through his ears.”

Jonas studied her face. The flat patience in her eyes had not changed since the ritual, but something new moved behind that patience now. Something that watched them the way the entity watched from beneath the soil.

"You knew this would happen," he said.

Eliza’s mouth showed beneath the black lace, thin and dry. “The cycle doesn't care about our names, Mr. Farlow. It only cares about the weight we leave behind. The question is how much you'll give up to keep your eyes."

Sera shifted her pack higher on her shoulder. "The second seal will hold for now. But the cracks are already showing, and the entity will press against them until they widen."

Eliza let her veil fall back into place. "Then the witnesses must decide how much of themselves they're willing to lose before the ground takes the rest."

They left her standing at the edge of the square and walked toward the tree line. The shadows under the pines remained deep despite the morning light, and the feeling of being watched pressed against Jonas's neck the way it had since the shared vision in Widow Grier's kitchen. He stopped at the place where the forest path began and looked into the darkness between the trunks.

Pricket stood among the Hollow-Eyed figures, his expensive suit torn and stained, his eyes clouded like water that had stood too long. His voice joined theirs in calling Jonas's name, the sound carrying across the empty square with the same patient hunger that had always marked the entity's presence. The figures moved closer to the tree line, their pale forms visible now in the shadows, and Pricket's voice rose above the others.

"Why keep the weight?" Pricket's voice was dry, like dead leaves scraping a cellar floor. It didn't sound like it came from his chest; it came from the trees behind him, from the frost under their boots. "The ground remembers the winter of '52, Jonas. It remembers your mother. It's easier to let it have her."

Jonas felt the missing time approaching again, the same disorientation that had struck him before. The world stretched and contracted, the trees shifting position by inches, the morning light curdled into a bruised purple that angled back toward the east. He reached out and gripped Sera's arm, his fingers tight around her wrist until the sensation passed.

The trees remained where they had been. The light steadied in the morning sky. Jonas released Sera's arm and stepped back, his breathing faster than before, the sweat on his palms cold against his skin. Sera watched him without speaking, her eyes steady and her face pale from what she had seen in his expression.

They turned away from the tree line and walked back toward the meeting hall. The Raines would still be inside sorting supplies and trying to convince themselves that the silence meant safety. The Connors and Trasks would be doing the same in their own homes, waiting for a voice they recognized to tell them the danger had passed. The entity's strategy had shifted. It no longer relied on the Hollow-Eyed alone. It had found a way to use the living as vessels, to infiltrate the settlement from within.

Paul Murdock lay unconscious in Widow Grier's spare room with his skin taking on the same pale, stone-like quality as the Hollow-Eyed. The second seal was already weakening, with small cracks appearing around the markers. The entity had learned to use human agents more effectively than in previous cycles, and Pricket may only be the first of many. Jonas felt the familiar sensation of missing time approaching and gripped Sera's arm to anchor himself in the present moment.

The witnesses had done what they could. The cycle had been broken for now. Yet the entity waited beneath the valley, patient and hungry, remembering every name it had ever claimed. The ground remained still, but the air carried the metallic scent of red water rising beneath the soil, and the silence pressed against their ears like something testing the surface from below.

CHAPTER TWENTY TWO

The Returned

The settlement square held frost in thin patches when Jonas stepped out of Widow Grier's house. His boots left dark marks where the white crust broke under his weight. The bucket at the well creaked against the pulley when he lowered it, and the splash came back quieter than it should have. He hauled the rope hand over hand until the water sat level at the rim, then poured it out against the dirt. The liquid smelled of cold stone and nothing worse. It soaked away without staining the ground darker than it already was.

Sera waited near the porch with her pack resting against one hip. She watched the forest path where Widow Grier had led the last families at dawn. The broken branches still showed the way they had gone, but fresh prints cut across the frost in the opposite direction. Three sets. One turned toward the old boarding house. Another headed for the cabin where the Trasks had settled in the spring. The third set disappeared behind the meeting hall where the Raines had claimed the back room.

"They came back," Sera said.

Jonas set the empty bucket down and wiped his palms on his coat. The frost had begun to thin where the water touched it. He followed the prints with his eyes until they split near the well, then looked toward the boarding house first. The Connors stood in the doorway when he approached. Mrs. Connor held their youngest wrapped in a blanket. Their older boy kept a rifle across his chest with both hands on the stock.

The exhaustion sat in her like gray water in an old well, but her chin stayed up when Jonas stopped at the bottom step. Mr. Connor kept his hand near the rifle without quite touching it. The boy glanced between his parents and the two figures on the path, knuckles pale against the wood.

"We heard the ground go quiet," Mr. Connor said. "Figured the worst had passed."

Sera shifted her pack higher on her shoulder. "The seal bought time. It did not end anything."

Mrs. Connor pulled the blanket tighter around the child. "That man Pricket. He was out by the birch stand last night. Called to us when we went by. Said the worst was done if we stayed in our beds and did not make a fuss."

Jonas studied the frost melting along the porch boards. "Pricket is not Pricket anymore. The ground took him the way it took the others."

Mr. Connor's jaw worked. “He looked like himself. Mostly. The eyes were... like river glass. But he knew our names. Called out to the boy.” He rubbed a hand over his mouth, his fingers trembling slightly. “Said we could trade. The bad years. For peace.”

The rifle stayed where it was. Jonas remembered that same weapon from the first night the Hollow-Eyed appeared. It had belonged to the oldest Connor son before he walked into the creek and came back without his eyes. The boy holding it now looked at the ground instead of meeting anyone's stare.

"You cannot bargain with it," Jonas said. "It does not trade. It collects."

Mrs. Connor's voice dropped. "We have nowhere else to go. The wagons will not take us without payment, and Pricket said payment could be made in other ways now."

Sera stepped forward until she stood level with the porch rail. "The entity chose him because he had something to lose. A position. A name. It needed someone people would listen to when the time came."

Mr. Connor looked past her toward the tree line. "He said the second seal would not hold. Said the cracks were already showing and that fighting them only made the collection come faster."

Jonas felt the familiar pull behind his thoughts, the stretching sensation that always came before missing time. He set his hand against the porch post and felt the grain under his palm. The feeling faded after a few breaths, but the cold sweat on his neck stayed. "Stay inside after dark," he said. "Keep the lamps lit and do not answer if something calls your name from outside."

They left the Connors at the boarding house door and walked toward the second set of footprints. Smoke rose thin and gray from the Trask chimney. Jonas knocked once on the door frame. Mr. Trask opened it with a shotgun held low. He recognized them and lowered the barrel, though he did not invite them inside. His wife stood behind him holding their youngest by the hand. The child's eyes stayed wide and fixed on something beyond the doorway.

"We saw the others turn back," Mr. Trask said. "Could not see the sense in running if the shaking had stopped."

Sera glanced at the child, then back at the man. "The silence means it is gathering strength, not leaving."

Mrs. Trask pulled her daughter closer, her knuckles white against the girl's wool coat. “Pricket was at the clearing last night. He didn't sound right, Jonas. It was like... like a crowd talking all at once. Said the ground doesn't need the dead anymore. Not now.”

Jonas felt the weight of that statement settle in his chest. The entity had taken Pricket deliberately and shaped him into something that could walk among the living and be heard. The Hollow-Eyed had always been warnings. Now the warnings had learned to speak with familiar tongues.

"Did he say anything else?" Jonas asked.

Mr. Trask checked the shotgun's breech, thumb clicking against metal. "Said we only make it hard on ourselves. Said the ground is going to take what we remember anyway. Fighting just makes the teeth dig deeper."

The child pulled at her mother's hand until Mrs. Trask lifted her into her arms. The girl's face pressed against her mother's shoulder. Jonas saw the small pale marks along her jaw where the skin had begun to take on the same cast as Paul's. Not as deep yet, but the pattern was there.

"Keep her inside," Sera said quietly. "Do not let her near the creek."

They found the third family at the meeting hall. The Raines had claimed the back room where the extra blankets were stored. Mr. Raine sat on an overturned crate while his wife sorted through the remaining supplies. Their oldest daughter stood at the window watching the square.

"We came back because the ground stopped moving," Mr. Raine said. "Could not keep the little ones walking through the dark when everything went quiet."

Jonas looked at the girl by the window. She had wrapped her arms around herself and kept her forehead pressed against the glass. "What did Pricket tell you?"

Mrs. Raine dropped a bundle of wool onto the crate. “He said some of us belong to this place now. From when we first cleared the timber. Said running...” She swallowed hard, staring at the dark floorboards. “Running just tires the horses.”

Sera set her pack down on the nearest bench. "The entity was here before any of us. It does not mark people. It consumes them."

“He said if we all stay, it won't take so much,” Mr. Raine muttered. He didn't look up from his boots. “Like sharing the weight. A few years of a man’s life. Not the whole thing.”

Jonas walked to the window where the girl stood. Outside, the square remained empty except for frost melting in patches where sunlight reached the ground. He placed his hand on the glass beside hers and felt the cold seep through his palm. "The missing time will come for you if you stay," he said. "You will lose hours, then days. Eventually you will lose yourself."

The girl’s forehead smeared the condensation on the pane. “He said the missing hours are just the start. Like sleeping. You don't even feel it go.”

They left the Raines in the meeting hall and walked toward Widow Grier's house. The frost had melted completely, leaving dark patches of earth where the water had soaked in. Jonas kept his hand near his knife hilt, though he did not draw it. The air carried a faint metallic scent that had not been there earlier, the smell of red water rising somewhere beneath the surface.

Widow Grier met them at her door with her shotgun already in hand. She stepped aside to let them enter, then closed the door and dropped the latch into place. The house smelled of wood smoke and the bitter herbs she kept drying by the stove.

"Three families came back," she said. "I saw their tracks when I returned from the evacuation route."

Jonas nodded. "We spoke to them. They will not leave again."

Widow Grier set the shotgun against the wall beside the door. "Idiots. The silence will not last, and when the ground starts moving again, they will have nowhere to run."

She led them through the main room to the spare bedroom where Paul lay. The boy remained on the narrow bed with a blanket pulled up to his chin. His breathing came shallow and slow, and the pale cast had spread from his jaw down his throat and across the backs of both hands. The skin looked tight, almost translucent, like stone that had not fully hardened yet.

Sera knelt beside the bed and placed her palm against Paul's forehead. The skin felt cool under her fingers, and the pulse at his temple moved in an uneven rhythm. She withdrew her hand and stood again. "The entity's voice has gone quiet inside him," she said. "But the cost shows in his skin."

Widow Grier crossed her arms over her chest. "He woke once while I was gone. Spoke a single sentence about the ground using living people as doors. Then he went under again."

Jonas studied the boy's face. The stone-like quality had reached his eyelids now, turning the skin a shade paler than the rest of his face. Paul's chest rose and fell in the same shallow pattern, but the movement seemed slower than before, as if each breath required more effort than the last.

They returned to the main room. Widow Grier poured water from a pitcher into three cups and set them on the table. The liquid looked clear, but Jonas caught the faint metallic scent again when he lifted his cup. He set it down without drinking.

"The second seal is already weakening," Sera said. "A crack opened near the largest marker. Red water came through."

Widow Grier's mouth tightened. "How long before it fails completely?"

"Days at most. The entity learned from the first binding. It knows how to press against the pattern now."

Jonas walked to the window that faced the square. The meeting hall stood across the open space with its windows dark. The Raines would be inside sorting supplies and trying to convince themselves that Pricket's words meant safety instead of surrender. The Connors and Trasks would be doing the same in their own homes, waiting for a voice they recognized to tell them the danger had passed.

"The entity chose Pricket deliberately," Jonas said. "It needed someone the others would listen to when the time came. Someone with authority left to lose."

Sera joined him at the window. "The Hollow-Eyed were warnings. Now the warnings have learned to speak with living voices. The next vessels will be easier to create because the first one showed them the way."

Widow Grier picked up her shotgun and checked the breech again, though both barrels remained loaded. "If Pricket comes close enough, I will put both loads in his chest. See if the ground can speak through a body that has been opened up."

They left Widow Grier's house and walked toward the ritual site near the old graves. The path wound between empty cabins where frost still clung to the shaded sides of the roofs. Jonas kept his hand near his knife, and Sera walked with her pack held close against her side. The metallic scent grew stronger as they approached the creek, though the water itself still ran clear when they crossed the narrow bridge.

The largest marker stood in its crooked row with the faint outline of four hands barely visible against the stone. The ritual circle remained in the dirt, a faint ring that the morning light picked out in sharp relief. Sera knelt at the edge and studied the crack that had appeared during the night. It had widened slightly, and another drop of red water had seeped up from the soil to pool in the low place before sinking back down. She touched the edge of the crack with one finger. The dirt felt warm despite the morning chill, and the metallic scent rose stronger from the small depression where the water had pooled. She wiped her finger on her trousers and stood again.

"The pattern is holding, but barely," she said. "The entity is testing every weak point now."

Jonas walked the perimeter of the circle. The smaller markers remained upright, though one had tilted further during the night. The iron kettle and the coat lay where they had been left, both showing more rust than before. He stopped at the largest marker and placed his palm against the stone. The surface felt cold, but the faint warmth from the crack reached him through the ground beneath his boots.

They returned to the settlement square as the sun climbed higher. The frost had melted completely now, leaving the ground dark and soft underfoot. Jonas stopped at the well and looked down into the darkness. The water at the bottom remained clear, but the metallic scent rose from the opening like breath from a sleeping animal.

Eliza Penhaligon stood at the far side of the square with her veil lowered. She watched them approach without moving closer, her stone beads moving slowly between her fingers. The burn on her arm showed through the dark fabric of her sleeve, the skin beneath still raw from where the invisible force had struck her during the ritual.

"It has a taste for them now," Eliza said. The heavy stone beads clicked between her fingers. "The ones who want to keep things the same. Pricket was easy. He wanted his town back. He let the roots in."

Jonas studied her face. The flat patience in her eyes had not changed since the ritual, but something new moved behind that patience now. Something that watched them the way the entity watched from beneath the soil.

"You knew this would happen," he said.

Eliza's mouth showed beneath the black lace, thin and dry. "The cycle doesn't care about our names, Mr. Farlow. It only cares about the weight we leave. How much will you give up to keep your eyes?"

Sera shifted her pack higher on her shoulder. "The second seal will hold for now. But the cracks are already showing, and the entity will press against them until they widen."

Eliza let her veil fall back into place. "Then the witnesses must decide how much of themselves they are willing to lose before the ground takes the rest."

They left her standing at the edge of the square and walked toward the tree line. The shadows under the pines remained deep despite the morning light, and the feeling of being watched pressed against Jonas's neck the way it had since the shared vision in Widow Grier's kitchen. He stopped at the place where the forest path began and looked into the darkness between the trunks.

Pricket stood among the Hollow-Eyed figures, his expensive suit torn and stained, his eyes clouded like water that had stood too long. His voice joined theirs in calling Jonas's name, the sound carrying across the empty square with the same patient hunger that had always marked the entity's presence. The figures moved closer to the tree line, their pale forms visible now in the shadows, and Pricket's voice rose above the others.

"Why keep the weight?" Pricket's voice was dry, like dead leaves scraping a cellar floor. It did not sound like it came from his chest. It came from the trees behind him, from the frost under their boots. "The ground remembers the winter of fifty-two, Jonas. It remembers your mother. It is easier to let it have her."

Jonas felt the missing time approaching again, the same disorientation that had struck him before. The world stretched and contracted, the trees shifting position by inches, the morning light curdled into a bruised purple that angled back toward the east. He reached out and gripped Sera's arm, his fingers tight around her wrist until the sensation passed. The trees remained where they had been. The light steadied in the morning sky. Jonas released Sera's arm and stepped back, his breathing faster than before, the sweat on his palms cold against his skin.

Sera watched him without speaking, her eyes steady and her face pale from what she had seen in his expression. They turned away from the tree line and walked back toward the meeting hall. The Raines would still be inside sorting supplies and trying to convince themselves that the silence meant safety. The Connors and Trasks would be doing the same in their own homes, waiting for a voice they recognized to tell them the danger had passed.

The entity's strategy had shifted. It no longer relied on the Hollow-Eyed alone. It had found a way to use the living as vessels, to infiltrate the settlement from within. Paul Murdock lay unconscious in Widow Grier's spare room with his skin taking on the same pale, stone-like quality as the Hollow-Eyed. The second seal was already weakening, with small cracks appearing around the markers. The entity had learned to use human agents more effectively than in previous cycles, and Pricket may only be the first of many.

Jonas felt the familiar sensation of missing time approaching and gripped Sera's arm to anchor himself in the present moment. The witnesses had done what they could. The cycle had been broken for now. Yet the entity waited beneath the valley, patient and hungry, remembering every name it had ever claimed. The ground remained still, but the air carried the metallic scent of red water rising beneath the soil, and the silence pressed against their ears like something testing the surface from below.

CHAPTER TWENTY THREE

The Memory Collector

Jonas opened his eyes to gray stone and frost. The old graves stretched in uneven rows around him, their markers leaning at odd angles from years of weather and shifting soil. He did not remember leaving his cabin. His boots pressed into the cold ground without any memory of the path that had brought him here, and his coat hung heavy across his shoulders like something borrowed from another man.

The Hollow-Eyed stood in a perfect ring. Their empty sockets locked onto him with the same patient attention they always showed, but this time the circle felt tighter, more deliberate. They had hemmed him in completely, bodies frozen like carved wood, faces angled inward like observational organs pinning a specimen down for examination. The morning air carried no sound except the faint rasp of his own breathing.

Pricket stood at the center of the circle. His expensive suit showed tears along the seams and dark stains across the front that had not come from ordinary dirt. The man who had once controlled the settlement's future now moved with the slow certainty of something else wearing his skin. His clouded eyes fixed on Jonas without blinking.

"It collects," Pricket said, his voice dry as rust, rising from his throat and the soil beneath. "Grief. Fear. Every scrap of it left in the dirt. The stone down there... it keeps it. Like a dog with a bone."

Jonas tried to step backward. His boots would not move. The circle had closed too tightly around him, and the Hollow-Eyed shifted only slightly when he tested their boundary. Their empty faces remained fixed on him with that same unblinking focus.

Pricket stepped closer, his boots sinking into the frost. "Everything you carry. The deaths. The shaking hands before the cold took them. It doesn't wash away. It stays in the cracks. It feeds."

The cold pressed against Jonas's skin through his coat. He could feel the entity's presence in the way the air moved, in the way the ground beneath his boots seemed to hold its breath. His thoughts stretched thin, and for a moment he could not remember why he had come to this place or how long he had been standing among these figures.

Footsteps broke through the quiet. Sera moved between two of the Hollow-Eyed, her pack slung across her shoulder and her face set in the same grim determination she carried whenever the entity showed its hand. She reached Jonas without hesitation, her hand closing around his wrist with enough force to pull him forward. The circle parted just enough to let them through, and she did not release him until they stood several yards beyond the outermost figure.

Sera didn't look back at the ring. She kept her grip tight on his sleeve, dragging him toward the tree line. “Your cabin was empty. I saw the frost broken. You walked straight here.”

Jonas rubbed his wrist where her fingers had gripped him. The skin felt cold, and his pulse beat too fast against his palm. "I do not remember walking."

"The missing time is getting worse."

They moved away from the graves together. The Hollow-Eyed did not pursue them, but their faces remained turned in their direction, empty sockets tracking the retreat with that same patient observation. Pricket stayed at the center of the circle, his voice carrying across the distance without effort.

"The collection continues whether you fight it or not," Pricket called after them. "The ground remembers every name. Every fear. Every moment of surrender. It is patient. It has always been patient."

Jonas did not look back. The path to the settlement square wound through bare trees and frost-stiffened grass. His boots left clear prints in the soft earth, and Sera walked close enough that their shoulders nearly touched. The metallic scent of red water rose from the ground in faint traces, stronger near the low places where the soil had begun to sink.

They found Paul Murdock in Widow Grier's spare room. The young man's condition had changed since the previous day. Pale calcification spread along his forearms in thin, hard patches that caught the morning light like unfinished stone. The same texture had begun to show along the sides of his neck, the skin pulled tight and translucent over the bone beneath. His breathing came shallow and irregular, each breath requiring visible effort.

Widow Grier stood near the doorway with her shotgun resting against the wall. She had not left the house since the returned families had appeared, and her eyes showed the exhaustion of someone who had spent the night watching for movement outside. She nodded once when Jonas and Sera entered, then gestured toward the bed with her chin.

Widow Grier didn't look up from her shotgun. "He was talking to the floorboards around midnight. Then he went stiff. The grey stuff... it's crawling up his arms."

Sera knelt beside the bed and studied the calcification without touching it. The hard patches extended from Paul's wrists nearly to his elbows, and smaller spots had appeared across his collarbone where the blanket had slipped. She pulled the fabric higher to cover the exposed skin and remained kneeling for several long moments.

Sera let go of the blanket. Her fingers were trembling slightly. "It's not just a voice anymore. It's taking him."

Jonas stood at the foot of the bed. Paul's face looked younger in sleep, the lines of exhaustion smoothed away by whatever held him under. The calcification had not yet reached his features, but the skin along his jaw showed the same pale cast that marked the beginning of the change. Jonas had seen this pattern before in the Hollow-Eyed, though never in someone still breathing.

"We can't let Pricket's men see this," Grier said, her thumb tracing the hammer of her gun. "They'll put him in a cellar. Call him a plague."

"They're too scared to listen," Jonas said.

Widow Grier picked up her shotgun and checked the breech without opening it. The weapon had become an extension of her presence in the room, a constant reminder that she would not surrender this space without a fight. "I have already turned two away this morning. They wanted to see the boy. Said Pricket offered payment for information about anyone showing signs of change."

The room held the smell of wood smoke and bitter herbs. Jonas moved to the window and looked out at the empty yard behind the house. The trees stood still, and no figures moved among them, but the feeling of being watched pressed against the glass like breath from something standing just out of sight.

Sera stood, her hand resting on her pack. “It’s moving fast. Whatever happened during his missing hours... it’s hardening. He’s turning to rock, Jonas.”

Paul stirred. His eyelids fluttered without opening, and a low sound escaped his throat that did not sound entirely human. The calcification along his forearms shifted slightly with the movement, the hard surface catching the light in a way that made Jonas's stomach turn. Paul settled again after a few seconds, his breathing returning to the same shallow rhythm.

“We have to stop it,” she whispered. “Before he’s solid.”

Jonas studied the boy's face. The missing time had claimed Paul more thoroughly than anyone else in the settlement, and the cost showed in his skin. The entity had chosen him early, had spoken through him when it still needed a voice that would not be recognized. Now it seemed to be using him for something else, something that required physical presence rather than words.

Jonas stared at the boy's grey wrist. "It's done waiting. It's using the water. The ones who came back. It's pulling them in."

Widow Grier spat out a piece of tobacco. "More came back last night. Walked right past my porch like sheep. No use talking to them. They've got that look in their eyes."

Jonas felt the familiar pressure building behind his thoughts. The missing time approached like a wave, and he gripped the windowsill to steady himself. The sensation lasted only a few seconds before receding, but it left behind the same cold sweat that always followed. He released the wood and wiped his palms on his coat.

"Pricket was there," Jonas said, his hand dropping to his side. "At the graves. He said the stone holds us. Like teeth."

Sera looked back at the boy. "The memory of this place. Every bad year we've had. It stays down there."

"And now it wants the living," Jonas said.

Paul's eyes opened. They focused on nothing at first, staring at the ceiling with the same empty attention the Hollow-Eyed showed. Then his gaze shifted to Jonas, and his mouth moved without sound for several seconds before words emerged.

"It knows you, Jonas," Paul whispered. His teeth clicked together, dry and hollow. "It knows everyone who saw it. It doesn't forget."

The calcification along his forearms seemed to pulse with each word. Jonas watched the hard surface shift, and his hands tightened on the windowsill. Paul continued speaking without appearing to notice the change in his own skin.

"The creek... there's people under it," the boy muttered, his eyes rolling back toward the ceiling. "Older than us. The dirt keeps them. It's getting heavy."

Sera leaned down. "Paul. How does it reach you?"

"The red stuff," he wheezed, his chest straining. "The well water. The people who came back from the woods... they have it in their mouths. They're calling the rest of us."

Paul's breathing grew more labored. The calcification had spread further up his neck during the time he spoke, and the skin along his collarbone showed new hard patches forming beneath the surface. He closed his eyes again, and his body went still except for the shallow rise and fall of his chest.

Widow Grier wiped her brow with her sleeve. "They're not taking him. Not while I've got lead left."

Jonas nodded. The decision had already formed in his mind, though he had not yet put words to it. Paul represented something the entity wanted, and that made him valuable in ways that went beyond his own survival. The calcification spreading through his body was both a warning and a map, showing the path the entity took when it claimed new territory.

"He stays," Jonas said. "We watch him."

Sera watched the yard. "It's not waiting anymore. It's reaching up through the wells. Through anyone who drank."

Jonas moved to stand beside her. The trees beyond the yard remained still, but the metallic scent of red water rose from the ground in stronger traces now. Somewhere beneath their feet, the entity continued its work, pressing against the second seal and testing every weak point it could find.

"Pricket told me to stop fighting," Jonas said. "Said the ground wins anyway."

"You tell him no?"

"For now."

The admission hung between them. Jonas had felt the pull of the missing time more strongly at the graves, and the entity's voice had reached him through Pricket's borrowed tongue. The choice remained, waiting for the moment when his resistance would weaken or his exhaustion would overcome his will to fight.

Grier looked out toward the porch. “Something was scraping the side of the house last night. Heavy steps. Didn't sound like boots. Went down toward the water.”

Jonas studied the yard through the glass. The frost had melted in patches where sunlight reached the ground, leaving dark soil exposed in irregular shapes. The metallic scent grew stronger near those exposed places, as if the red water had found new paths to the surface during the hours of darkness.

“It’s getting stronger,” Sera said. “Every person it takes... it’s like a hand reaching further up.”

Paul stirred again on the bed. His eyes remained closed, but his mouth moved in the same silent pattern as before. The calcification along his forearms had spread further, and new hard patches appeared along his neck with each shallow breath. Jonas watched the change without moving closer, his hands resting on the windowsill with enough pressure to make the wood creak.

“We can’t stop it,” Sera said, her voice dropping. “But we can keep Paul out of the red mud. Keep him dry.”

Grier clicked the safety. “Let them try.”

Jonas released the windowsill and stepped back from the glass. The pressure behind his thoughts had returned, and he recognized the familiar stretching sensation that preceded the missing time. He gripped the edge of the nearest chair and held on until the sensation passed. The room remained steady. The light through the window stayed the same pale gray as before.

"It's in my head, Sera," Jonas said, his voice barely a whisper. "The lost hours. The dreams. It's figuring me out."

Sera didn't look at him. "Then we don't have much time."

They left Widow Grier at the doorway and moved through the main room toward the front of the house. The shotgun remained within reach of her hand, and her eyes tracked every shadow that passed the windows. Jonas opened the door and stepped out into the cold air, Sera following close behind him. The settlement square lay empty in the morning light, and the metallic scent of red water rose from the ground in stronger traces than before.

The path to Jonas's cabin wound through the same bare trees and frost-stiffened grass. His boots left clear prints in the soft earth, and Sera walked with her pack held close against her side. The feeling of being watched pressed against the back of his neck, and he did not need to look to know that the Hollow-Eyed had shifted their attention to follow their retreat.

At the cabin door, Jonas paused. The wood felt cold under his palm, and the metallic scent rose stronger from the ground near the threshold. He pushed the door open and stepped inside, Sera moving past him to set her pack against the wall. The room held the same sparse arrangement as always, the bed unmade and the stove cold, but something had changed in the air between his leaving and his return.

Jonas closed the door and dropped the latch into place. The feeling of being watched remained, pressing against the walls from outside, but the cabin offered the only shelter they had left. He moved to the small table and rested his hands on the scarred surface, his thoughts turning to the graves and the circle of empty faces that had surrounded him there.

"It's not waiting," Jonas said. "It's coming through the wells. It's in the water."

Sera leaned against the glass. "How much do we give up before we run?"

The words hung in the cold air between them. Jonas studied the grain of the table beneath his palms and felt the weight of the choice settling into his chest. The entity had shifted its strategy, and the collection had begun in earnest. The witnesses who remained would face the same decision Pricket had already made, and the cost of resistance would only grow heavier as the cycle continued.

Outside the cabin, the morning light crept across the frost-stiffened grass. The metallic scent of red water rose from the ground in steady traces, and somewhere beneath the settlement the entity continued its patient work, gathering memories the way a predator gathers prey. The Hollow-Eyed waited in their circle among the old graves, and Pricket stood at the center with his clouded eyes fixed on the path that led back to the living. The ground remained still, but the pressure built beneath the surface like water behind a dam, waiting for the moment when the collection would begin again.

CHAPTER TWENTY FOUR

The Child's Warning

The creek bank held a stillness that pressed against the skin like cold hands. Jonas stood where the water met the stones, his boots planted in the soft mud that had replaced the usual gravel. The morning had dragged on since he left the cabin, and now the light sat gray across everything, thin and without warmth. He had come here because the child needed to be buried proper, and the settlement square offered no such mercy. The boy's body lay wrapped in an old blanket, weighted down with river rocks to keep the current from taking it. Sera stood a few paces back, her pack resting against a fallen log, her dark eyes fixed on the water that moved too slowly.

They had carried the child down together in the quiet hours before most people stirred. No one followed them. The returned settlers stayed near the wells, their movements slow and aimless, and Pricket's guards had not ventured this far from the square. Widow Grier remained at her house, shotgun within reach, watching over Paul Murdock as the calcification crept further across his skin. Jonas had promised to return before nightfall, though promises felt thin against the weight of what pressed upward from below.

The metallic scent of the water rose stronger here than anywhere else. It clung to the back of the throat, thick and warm even in the cold air. Jonas crouched near the body and adjusted one of the stones that had shifted during the walk. The blanket had come loose at one corner, exposing a small pale hand. He covered it again without looking too long at the fingers.

Sera moved closer, her boots dragging in the mud. She stared down at the water.

"The ground is too soft."

Jonas didn't look up from the rocks. "It's been giving way all morning."

"Not like this," she said. "It's hollow."

Jonas nodded but did not answer. He had felt it too, the subtle give beneath his feet that spoke of hollow spaces opening in the dark. The child had died three days ago, one of the first to return from the woods with the empty look in his eyes. Now the body rested here because the living had nowhere else to put it. The settlement could not afford another grave that might collapse inward during the night.

They worked in silence for a time, piling more stones around the blanket until the shape beneath looked less like a child and more like a cairn. The water lapped at the edges of their work, red-tinged and sluggish. A dead fish floated past, belly up, its scales dulled to the color of old iron. Jonas watched it drift until the current took it around the bend.

When the cairn stood finished, Sera stepped back and wiped her hands on her trousers. "We should say something," she said. "Even if no one else will hear it."

Jonas remained crouched beside the stones. His knees ached from the damp, and the cold had worked its way into his bones. He thought about the boy's face before the blanket covered it, the way the skin had looked stretched too tight across the cheekbones. The child had been eight, maybe nine. Old enough to know fear when it came for him, young enough that the fear stayed pure and undiluted.

“He shouldn’t have come back.” Jonas stood up, his knees cracking in the quiet. “Whatever took him should’ve kept him.”

Sera watched the muddy water lap against the fresh cairn.

“It wanted him found,” she said. “It wants us looking.”

They turned away from the cairn and started back toward the settlement. The path wound through bare trees and patches of frost that had not yet melted. Jonas kept his pace steady, his eyes on the ground ahead. The metallic scent followed them even as they moved away from the water, rising from the soil in faint traces wherever the earth had begun to sink.

Halfway to Widow Grier's house, Paul Murdock's scream split the morning air.

The sound came from the direction of the settlement, thin and high and wrong. It carried the pitch of a child's voice, though Paul was a grown man. Jonas broke into a run, his boots slapping against the frost-hardened ground. Sera followed close behind, her breath coming hard and fast. They reached the house in time to see Widow Grier standing on the porch, shotgun raised toward the yard as if expecting an attack from the trees themselves.

Inside, Paul lay on the floor of the spare room, his body arched backward in a rigid bow. The calcification along his forearms had spread further overnight, the gray patches now reaching past his elbows and onto his shoulders. His neck showed the same hard texture, and his mouth opened and closed without sound, the words trapped somewhere between his throat and whatever held him. Then the child's voice emerged again, clear and small and terrified.

"The stones remember the names," the voice said through Paul's lips. "Every name that went into the ground. Every fear that soaked into the dirt. It keeps them all. It feeds on them when the cycles turn."

Widow Grier lowered her shotgun but did not set it aside. She stood in the doorway, her face pale beneath the usual scowl, one hand gripping the doorframe so hard her knuckles showed white. Jonas moved past her and knelt beside Paul, careful not to touch the calcified skin. Sera followed, dropping to her knees on the other side of the boy's body.

Paul's eyes remained closed, but his mouth continued to form words that belonged to someone else. "Beneath the valley there are rooms. Caverns carved by water that never sees the light. The walls are lined with the memories of those who died here. They pile up like sediment in a riverbed. Grief. Terror. The slow understanding that no one is coming to help."

The voice paused, and Paul's chest rose and fell in shallow jerks. The calcification along his collarbone pulsed with each breath, the hard surface catching the light from the window in dull flashes. Jonas felt his own stomach turn at the sight, but he forced himself to stay where he was, listening because the warning mattered more than his revulsion.

"It has been growing for generations," the child's voice continued. "Every witness who died added to the weight. Every scream that went unheard. Every moment of surrender when someone realized they were already lost. The entity feeds on these things. It stores them in the stone and draws strength from the accumulation."

Sera leaned closer, her fingers hovering just above Paul's trembling shoulder. Her jaw was set tight.

"Paul. How do we stop it?"

The child's voice came through again, high and dry and flat. "You don't. You delay it."

Paul's fingers twitched against the floorboards.

"The boy's fear was clean," the voice whispered. "No adult lies to dilute the taste. It sinks deep."

Paul's body convulsed once, then went still. The voice faded, leaving only the sound of his labored breathing. Widow Grier stepped fully into the room and set her shotgun against the wall. She moved to the bed and pulled the blanket from it, then draped it over Paul's torso to cover the spreading calcification. Her movements were deliberate, almost gentle, though her jaw remained tight with the effort of holding herself together.

Widow Grier stepped into the room, her boots heavy on the pine. She took up her shotgun and let the barrel rest in the crook of her arm.

"He stays out of the square."

Jonas looked at her. "Pricket's men are looking."

"Let them," Grier said. "They try to quarantine him in one of those cellars, he won't come out."

Jonas stood and moved to the window. Outside, the yard remained empty, but the feeling of pressure beneath the ground had grown stronger. He could sense it even through the soles of his boots, a steady push against the earth that spoke of something building toward release. The child's warning echoed in his mind, the words settling into place alongside everything else they had learned about the entity. It did not simply wait for witnesses to come. It collected them, stored their pain, and used that accumulation to grow stronger with each cycle.

Sera remained kneeling beside Paul. She reached out and brushed a strand of hair from his forehead, careful to avoid the hard patches along his temples. "The entity chose him because children do not know how to lie to themselves," she said. "They do not convince themselves that what they see is not real. Their fear goes straight into the ground."

"And now it's using him to speak," Jonas said. He turned from the window and looked at the boy on the floor. Paul's face had gone slack, the lines of strain smoothed away by whatever held him under. The calcification had not yet reached his features, but Jonas could see the pale cast spreading along his jaw. It would not be long before the change claimed his face as well.

Widow Grier picked up her shotgun again and checked the breech without opening it. The gesture had become a habit, a way of confirming that the weapon remained ready even when there was nothing visible to fight. "I turned away three more this morning. They wanted to see the boy. Said Pricket was offering payment for anyone who could report strange behavior. They're scared enough to sell their neighbors for a few coins."

Jonas nodded. He had expected as much. Pricket's desperation had grown along with the entity's influence, and the man would do whatever it took to maintain the appearance of control. The settlement square had become a place of whispered accusations and guarded doors, the survivors turning inward as the ground itself betrayed them.

They moved Paul back to the bed with careful hands, avoiding the hard patches wherever possible. The blanket slipped during the transfer, and Jonas caught a glimpse of the boy's forearm, the skin now almost entirely gray and smooth as unfinished stone. He pulled the fabric higher to cover the sight, then stepped back as Widow Grier arranged the pillows beneath Paul's head. The boy remained unconscious, his breathing shallow but steady, the child's voice silent for now.

Jonas moved to the doorway and looked out into the main room of the house. The shotgun stayed within reach of Widow Grier's hand, and her eyes tracked every shadow that passed the windows. The house smelled of wood smoke and the bitter herbs she had been burning to keep the metallic scent at bay. It did not work, but the ritual seemed to give her some measure of comfort.

Sera stood by his shoulder, her eyes on the dark hallway. "The caverns. What the boy said about the memories."

Jonas kept his back to her. "Grief."

"Every death," she whispered. "It's like wood for a fire."

"The old foundations under the ridge," Jonas looked at her. "They knew."

"They ran," Sera looked around. "But we have too many people left. Too many witnesses. It's changing how it feeds."

They stood together in the doorway for a moment, the weight of the warning settling between them. Outside, the morning light had begun to shift, the gray giving way to a paler hue that suggested the sun might break through the clouds. It would not last. The entity had claimed the weather along with everything else, turning even the sky into something that felt watched.

Jonas felt the familiar pressure building behind his thoughts. The missing time approached like a wave, and he gripped the doorframe to steady himself. The sensation lasted only a few seconds before receding, but it left behind the same cold sweat that always followed. He released the wood and wiped his palms on his coat.

"It offered me a choice." Jonas didn't look at her. "Down at the graves. It used Pricket's voice."

Sera went still.

"Said I could stop," Jonas muttered. "Said the ground wins anyway."

Sera's hand found the doorframe near his. "Jonas. What did you say?"

"Nothing," he looked forward. "But it's still there."

The ground remained silent beneath their feet, but Jonas could feel the pressure building like water behind a dam. The child's warning had made the entity's strategy clear. It had shifted from passive waiting to active recruitment, using the returned settlers and the contaminated water to pull more witnesses into its collection. Every person who drank from the wells added to the weight. Every fear that soaked into the soil made the entity stronger.

Widow Grier appeared in the doorway behind them, her shotgun resting against her shoulder. "Something moved in the trees an hour ago, not the Hollow-Eyed. Something smaller. It stayed just out of sight, but I could feel it watching."

Jonas nodded. He had felt the same presence on the walk back from the creek. The entity had many eyes now, and not all of them belonged to the figures that stood in silent rings. Some watched from the shadows, some spoke through the water, and some waited in the bodies of those who had been claimed and returned.

They spent the next hour preparing the house for whatever might come. Widow Grier reinforced the shutters on the windows, nailing boards across the glass with steady, practiced movements. Sera checked the supply of water in the barrels, pouring out anything that showed the slightest trace of red. Jonas moved through the rooms, testing the doors and noting which floorboards creaked underfoot. The house had become a fortress of sorts, though they all knew that no walls could keep the entity out if it truly wanted to enter.

Paul remained unconscious on the bed, his breathing steady but shallow. The calcification had spread to his shoulders during the time they worked, the hard patches now visible above the collar of his shirt. Jonas watched the change with a growing sense of dread. The boy's time was running short, and the child's voice had made it clear that the entity would not release him easily.

As the afternoon light began to fade, a knock sounded at the front door. Widow Grier moved to answer it, shotgun in hand, while Jonas and Sera stood ready in the main room. The knock came again, three short raps that echoed through the house like warnings. Widow Grier opened the door a crack, then wider when she recognized the figure on the porch.

Eliza Penhaligon stood in the doorway, her dark mourning dress brushing the floorboards, her veil lifted just enough to reveal the sharp line of her nose. Her hands moved constantly, fingers working the string of stone beads that hung around her neck. She did not step inside, but her eyes took in the scene with a detached, academic interest that made Jonas's skin crawl.

"I heard the child," She didn't look at Widow Grier's gun. "The warning carries. Some of us have been waiting."

Widow Grier raised the muzzle an inch. "Get off my porch."

Eliza's thin lips twitched. "You're fighting the tide, Martha. It's already coming in."

Jonas pushed past Grier. "What do you want, Eliza?"

"The same thing Pricket wanted," Eliza reached out, her fingers brushing the wooden doorframe. "To stop struggling. Give it your memories, Jonas. Or let it take them when you break."

The words hung in the air between them, heavy with the weight of implication. Jonas felt the pressure behind his thoughts intensify, the missing time pressing closer than before. The entity's presence filled the room, though no physical form appeared. It spoke through Eliza's borrowed tongue, the same way it had spoken through Pricket at the graves.

Sera stepped up beside him, her shoulder solid against his. "We're not giving it anything."

Eliza looked at her, then back to Jonas. "You don't have enough time left to choose."

She turned and walked away from the house, her dark dress trailing across the frost-stiffened grass. The door closed behind her, and Widow Grier slid the bolt into place with a sharp click. The house fell silent except for the sound of Paul's shallow breathing from the spare room.

Jonas moved to the window and looked out at the yard. The trees stood still, but the metallic scent of red water rose from the ground in stronger traces than before. Somewhere beneath their feet, the entity continued its work, pressing against the second seal and testing every weak point it could find. The child's warning had made the stakes clear. The entity was no longer content to wait. It had begun active recruitment, and every witness who remained would face the same choice Pricket had already made.

The ground remained silent, but Jonas could feel the pressure building beneath his boots like water behind a dam. The entity's strategy had shifted from passive waiting to active recruitment through the returned settlers and the contaminated water. The collection continued whether they fought it or not, and the cost of resistance would only grow heavier as the cycle continued.

Widow Grier set her shotgun against the wall and moved to the stove, stirring the pot of bitter herbs that had been simmering since morning. The smell filled the house, sharp and acrid, but it could not mask the metallic scent that rose from the floorboards themselves. Jonas remained at the window, his hands resting on the sill, his thoughts turning to the caverns beneath the valley and the memories that accumulated like sediment in those lightless rooms.

Sera joined him at the glass, her reflection faint in the fading light. "We cannot let Pricket's men take Paul. The calcification is spreading too fast. If they imprison him, he will be lost to us entirely."

“He stays and we watch him.”

"And when the choice comes for you?" Her voice stayed low, but the question carried the weight of everything they had avoided saying until now.

Jonas did not answer immediately. He studied the yard through the glass, the frost melting in patches where the weak sunlight reached the ground. The metallic scent grew stronger near those exposed places, as if the red water had found new paths to the surface during the hours of darkness. The entity's presence pressed against his thoughts, offering the same choice it had offered Pricket. The ground wins anyway. The collection continues. The stone holds every name, every fear, every moment of surrender.

Jonas watched a patch of gray mud swallow a dry leaf. “Not today.”

The afternoon light faded into evening, and the house settled into a tense quiet. Widow Grier kept her shotgun close, her eyes never straying far from the windows. Sera sat beside Paul's bed, monitoring the spread of the calcification with a grim determination that spoke of her own fears. Jonas moved through the rooms, checking the doors and testing the floorboards, his thoughts turning again and again to the child's warning and the caverns that waited beneath the valley.

The ground remained silent, but the pressure built steadily beneath their feet. The entity had shifted its approach, and the collection had begun in earnest. The witnesses who remained would face the same decision Pricket had already made, and the cost of resistance would only grow heavier as the cycle continued. Outside the house, the evening light crept across the frost-stiffened grass. The metallic scent of red water rose from the ground in steady traces, and somewhere beneath the settlement the entity continued its patient work, gathering memories the way a predator gathers prey. The Hollow-Eyed waited in their circle among the old graves, and Pricket stood at the center with his clouded eyes fixed on the path that led back to the living. The ground remained still, but the pressure built beneath the surface like water behind a dam, waiting for the moment when the collection would begin again.

CHAPTER TWENTY FIVE

The Fractured Seal

The old graves sat half-hidden beneath a blanket of dead leaves and frost that refused to melt. Jonas moved through them with care, his boots finding the few patches of solid ground between the sunken markers. Sera walked a few steps behind, her breath visible in the cold air that hung over the burial plot like smoke from a dying fire. They had come to check the second seal before the light failed completely, though neither of them said the words out loud. The first seal had already failed, and the child's voice through Paul had made clear that the entity no longer waited for an invitation.

The stakes they had driven into the thin place two days earlier lay scattered across the clearing. Some had snapped near the base. Others had been pulled free and thrown into the surrounding brush as if the ground itself had rejected them. Jonas knelt beside one of the broken pieces and ran his fingers along the splintered end. The wood felt warm despite the chill in the air, and a faint red film clung to the surface like rust that had formed too quickly.

Sera stood near the center of the clearing and studied the soil. Cracks had opened in a rough circle where the markers once stood, and red water seeped from the fissures in slow, steady trickles. The liquid carried the same metallic odor that had begun to rise from every low place in the valley. It pooled in the depressions and ran in thin streams toward the creek, staining the dead grass as it moved.

Jonas picked up another stake and turned it over in his hands. The point had been driven deep once, deep enough that the ground should have held it through any ordinary frost. Now the wood lay on its side, the carved symbols along its length cracked and filled with the same red seepage that came from the soil. He set the stake down and wiped his palm on his coat.

Jonas spat onto the damp dirt. "They didn't pull 'em."

Sera didn't look up from the split wood. "Pushed."

The ground beneath the clearing felt different underfoot, less solid than it should have been. Jonas shifted his weight, his knees automatically bending as his boots slid a fraction of an inch into the spongy, yielding earth. He threw his arms out slightly to catch his balance, his fingers clawing at the empty, cold air. The soil didn't just sink; it drifted sideways, a slow, sickening slide that made his stomach drop. He took a hasty step back onto a patch of frozen weeds and watched the nearest crack widen another fraction.

Footsteps approached through the trees on the north side of the clearing. Jonas turned toward the sound and saw Paul Murdock moving between the trunks, his gait uneven and his arms held stiff at his sides. The young man's face had gone pale, and the gray patches along his jaw had spread upward to touch the corners of his mouth. He stopped at the edge of the clearing and looked at the ruined stakes without surprise.

"It told me you would be here," Paul said. His voice carried a strange resonance, as if more than one person spoke through the same set of lungs. "It wanted me to watch."

Jonas took a slow step forward, keeping his hands down. "Paul. Go back to the house."

Paul's mouth twitched into a shape that wasn't a smile. "Not back. Down."

Sera watched his hands. "Paul. Look at me."

Paul's eyes focused on the red water seeping from the cracks. "The collection is almost complete. Every name, every fear, every moment of surrender. It holds them all now. The next time the ground opens, it won't close again."

The words came out in the same child's voice that had spoken through him earlier, though the pitch had deepened slightly. Paul swayed where he stood, and his hands twitched at his sides as if something tugged at the fingers from beneath the skin. Jonas watched the gray patches on the young man's forearms pulse in time with the slow seep of water from the ground.

"How long?" Jonas asked. His voice was flat, dry.

"Until the permanent awakening?" Paul tilted his head, listening to something the others could not hear. "Three nights. Maybe four. The memories have reached the threshold. After that, the entity will not return to dormancy. It will stay awake and keep gathering."

Sera stepped closer, her boots crunching on the frost. "Did it do this before? In the old records?"

"No." The single word carried a weight that seemed to settle over the clearing like additional frost. "Previous attempts always stopped short. The witnesses fled or died before the collection finished. This time the settlement stayed. The witnesses remained. The accumulation is complete."

Jonas studied the ruined markers and the red water that continued to rise. The thin place had ruptured completely, and the entity's influence now leaked into the air itself. He could taste the metallic bite on his tongue, and the pressure behind his thoughts had grown stronger since they entered the clearing. Missing time waited at the edges of his awareness, ready to claim another stretch of minutes or hours.

Paul took another step forward, his boots leaving faint impressions in the soft soil. "It knows your names now. All of you. The entity remembers every witness who has ever stood in this place. It adds new names with each cycle, and it never forgets."

"What's it want?" Sera asked.

"The same thing it has always wanted. More memories. More fear. More surrender." Paul's voice shifted again, taking on a deeper timbre that Jonas recognized from the graves. "The ground learns from every failed seal. Every attempt to contain it teaches it something new. This time it will not be forced back."

The words hung in the cold air between them. Jonas felt the truth of them like a cold weight dropping into his stomach, a sudden tightening in his chest that made his next breath rattle. The entity had watched every ritual, every desperate attempt to close the thin places, and it had adapted. The stakes in the ground meant nothing to something that existed beneath the stones themselves.

A branch cracked in the woods to the south. Widow Grier emerged from the trees, her shotgun resting in the crook of her arm and her face set in the familiar scowl that meant bad news had arrived. She moved with the careful steps of someone who had learned to watch the ground at all times, and her eyes went first to the ruined markers before settling on Paul.

"Pricket's men have started taking people," she said without preamble. "Anyone who tries to leave gets stopped at the trailheads. They claim the infection spreads through the red water, and they say leaving spreads it further."

Jonas didn't look up from the frost. "How many?"

"Six that I know of. Three families tried to pack up this morning and head east. The guards met them at the old logging road and brought them back to the square." Widow Grier shifted the shotgun to her other arm. "They put them in the root cellars under the old storehouse. Said it was for everyone's protection."

Sera stared down the dark trail. "Under the storehouse?"

"From becoming like the returned ones, according to Pricket." Widow Grier's voice carried a bitter edge. "He says the entity's influence travels through contact. Anyone who leaves carries it with them. Anyone who stays can be watched and contained."

Paul swayed again, and his mouth opened as if another voice wanted to speak. Jonas moved closer and caught the young man's arm before he could fall. The calcified skin felt cold and hard beneath the coat sleeve, and Paul flinched at the touch before steadying himself.

"The collection doesn't need the witnesses to stay in one place," Paul said. His own voice had returned for a moment, thin and frightened. "It only needs them to remain alive and afraid. Pricket is helping without realizing it. The fear in those cellars feeds the entity just as much as the red water does."

Widow Grier studied the young man with a mixture of concern and suspicion. "How much longer before that stuff covers his whole body?"

"Not long," Sera said. "The spread has accelerated since the child's voice came through him. Whatever the entity is doing, it's using Paul as a conduit now."

Jonas released Paul's arm and stepped back. The pressure behind his thoughts had begun to build again, the familiar warning that missing time approached. He gripped the broken stake in his hand and focused on the solid weight of the wood, the rough texture of the splinters against his palm. The sensation helped anchor him for a few more moments.

"The other spots," Jonas started rubbing his temple. "We have to go down there."

Sera shook her head. "The second seal was the strongest of the three. If it failed this quickly, the first and third will not last the night."

Widow Grier moved closer to the cracks in the soil and studied the red water that continued to seep upward. "What happens when all three open?"

"The entity gains direct access to the surface memories," Sera said. "Every person who has ever died in this valley becomes part of its collection. Every fear that soaked into the ground becomes fuel. The awakening becomes permanent."

Paul's eyes had gone distant again, focused on something beyond the clearing. "The stones remember. They always remember. The entity only needs to wait for enough witnesses to accumulate in one place. The settlement provided that accumulation. The cycle will not end this time."

Jonas dropped the broken stake and wiped his hands on his coat. The red film left a faint stain on the leather, and the metallic scent clung to his fingers even after he rubbed them clean. He looked at the ruined markers and the water that flowed from the ground like blood from a wound that would not close.

"We try anyway. Buy some time."

Sera studied the clearing for a long moment before speaking. "My people's knowledge was meant to contain the thin places, not destroy what lies beneath them. We have always known the entity could not be killed. Only held back. I thought that would be enough."

The admission came quietly, without the certainty she usually carried. Jonas turned to look at her and saw the exhaustion in her face, the weight of generations of watchers who had delayed the same awakening only to watch it begin again. She met his eyes briefly before looking back at the red water.

"We buy a few hours," Jonas said.

Sera stared at her muddy boots. "And then?"

Widow Grier shifted her shotgun and scanned the tree line. "Then we fight with whatever we have left. Pricket's guards won't be the only ones with weapons. Some of us still remember how to use them."

Paul's body convulsed suddenly, and the child's voice returned through his mouth. "The entity learns from every attempt. Every seal teaches it where the weaknesses lie. This time it will not be contained by wood and carved symbols. This time it will rise and remain risen."

The words ended with a wet cough that brought flecks of gray stone to Paul's lips. He wiped his mouth with the back of his hand and stared at the small particles that clung to his skin. The calcification had reached his face now, spreading from his jaw toward his temples in slow, visible patches.

Jonas moved to support him as the young man's knees buckled. They lowered Paul to the ground together, careful to avoid the hard patches along his arms and shoulders. Sera knelt beside them and checked the pulse at Paul's throat, her fingers light against the skin that had not yet turned to stone.

"We need to get him back to Widow Grier's house," Jonas glared. "The spread is moving faster now."

"The entity's voice is stronger here," as Sera looked over. "The thin place amplifies it. Every moment he spends in this clearing gives the collection more access to his mind."

Widow Grier slung her shotgun over her shoulder and moved to help lift Paul. The four of them worked together to get him upright, supporting his weight between them as they began the slow walk back through the trees. The red water continued to seep from the ground behind them, marking their passage with thin trails that led toward the creek.

The settlement square came into view as they cleared the last stand of trees. Smoke rose from the chimneys of the remaining occupied buildings, and the sound of voices carried from the direction of the storehouse. Pricket's guards stood at the main trailhead, their rifles visible even from a distance, and the root cellars beneath the old storehouse had been reinforced with new boards across the doors.

Jonas felt the pressure behind his thoughts intensify as they approached the square. The missing time pressed closer, and he focused on the solid weight of Paul's arm across his shoulders, the steady rhythm of their footsteps on the frozen ground. The sensation passed after a few seconds, but it left behind the familiar cold sweat and the knowledge that the entity continued to learn him from the inside.

They reached Widow Grier's house as the light began to fade. The old woman unlocked the door and held it open while Jonas and Sera carried Paul inside. They settled him on the bed in the spare room, and Widow Grier covered him with the blanket she had used earlier. The calcification had spread further during the walk, and the gray patches now covered most of his neck and the lower half of his face.

Sera remained by the bed and watched the young man's shallow breathing. "The entity's memory collection has reached its limit. Paul was the final witness it needed. Once the calcification claims him completely, the awakening will begin."

Jonas stood at the window and looked out at the yard. The frost had begun to melt in patches where the weak sunlight reached the ground, and the metallic scent of red water rose from those exposed places. The entity's presence filled the room, though no physical form appeared. It waited beneath the floorboards, patient and hungry, gathering every moment of fear that had accumulated in the valley since the first witness died.

"The third site," Jonas said. "We go there now. Before Pricket shuts the east trail."

Widow Grier checked the shotgun and set it within reach of the bed. "Some of them won't leave. They've lived here too long. The valley is all they know."

"Then we give them a choice," Sera said. "Stay and become part of the collection, or run and carry the knowledge to other places. Either way, the entity will continue. But the witnesses who flee may delay the next awakening somewhere else."

Paul's eyes opened, and the child's voice spoke one final time through his lips. "The ground remembers every name. Every fear. Every surrender. It will not forget you when the stones open."

The voice faded, and Paul's breathing grew shallower. The calcification had reached his eyes now, turning the whites to the same gray stone that covered his arms and legs. Jonas watched the change with a growing sense of finality. The entity had claimed another witness, and the collection continued whether they fought it or not.

The ground beneath the house remained silent, but Jonas could feel the pressure building like water behind a dam. The entity's strategy had shifted from passive waiting to active recruitment, and the witnesses who remained would face the same decision Pricket had already made. The cost of resistance would only grow heavier as the cycle continued, and the ground would remember every name that had ever been spoken in this place.

Jonas turned from the window and looked at the others. Sera stood beside the bed, her face set in the grim determination that had carried her through every previous awakening. Widow Grier checked the shotgun again, her movements steady despite the exhaustion that showed in the lines around her eyes. Paul lay motionless beneath the blanket, his breathing barely visible now, the child's voice silent at last.

"Get the lanterns," Jonas shouted. "We're running out of dirt."

The others nodded without speaking. Outside, the light faded completely, and the metallic scent of red water rose from the ground in stronger traces than before. The entity continued its patient work beneath the settlement, gathering memories the way a predator gathers prey, and the ground remained still while the pressure built steadily beneath their feet.

CHAPTER TWENTY SIX

The Final Gathering

The Hollow-Eyed stood just beyond the last line of houses, their pale forms crowded shoulder to shoulder in the failing light. Their numbers had grown since the last time Jonas had seen them. Dozens now. Each one once a person with a name and a place in the settlement, now reduced to gray stone and empty sockets. They faced the square without moving, their silent presence more threatening than any shout or weapon.

Jonas kept his distance, his boots planted on the packed dirt between two empty cabins. From this spot he could see the entire line of them, their motionless shapes stretching from the creek side all the way to the northern pasture. Some still wore scraps of clothing. Others had shed everything, their stone skin showing the same pale, featureless surface. The sight turned his stomach, but he forced himself to look. Running would do nothing now. They had already come as far as they could without crossing into the square itself.

Pricket stood among them. The settlement's leader had moved out of the storehouse hours ago, and now he waited with the rest of the returned. His expensive suit hung loose on his frame, the fabric stained with the same red film that coated every low place in the valley. His face had begun to change. Gray patches spread along his jaw and up toward his temples, though his eyes still held their old, desperate focus. When he spoke, his voice carried across the open ground without effort.

"Jonas." The voice was thin, but it carried across the dirt. "Come out here."

Jonas stayed where he was. He had no intention of walking into the open, not while the Hollow-Eyed watched from every direction. Pricket's voice carried again, louder this time.

"I know you're there. The entity knows your name. It has known your name since the first time you stood on this ground. Surrender now, and the settlement stays whole. The children live. The work continues. Fight, and everything burns with the rest of us."

Widow Grier answered from the center of the square. She had gathered the remaining settlers into a loose ring around the well and the storehouse steps. Most carried rifles or shotguns, though everyone understood the weapons would do little against stone that did not bleed. Widow Grier held her own scattergun across her chest, her face set in the same grim scowl she had worn since the first deaths.

"You sold us out," she called back. "You sold every name in this place for the chance to keep your ledger clean. We won't join you."

Pricket's mouth twitched, the skin around his jaw tight and gray. "It's not about the money, Grier. It never was. There's... there's a quiet here. No more of the noise. No more of the pain. It's the only way the valley stays."

Jonas moved along the cabin wall until he could see Sera. She stood near the old smokehouse, her attention fixed on the line of Hollow-Eyed. When she caught his eye she gave a small nod toward the creek path. He understood. She had kept one location secret even from him, a final thin place where the boundary between surface and depth had worn so thin that the entity's voice came through without any vessel. They needed to reach it before the light failed completely.

Paul Murdock sat on the storehouse steps, his back against the wall. The calcification had claimed most of his arms and legs now. His skin had taken on the same gray tone as the Hollow-Eyed, and his breathing had slowed to match the slow rhythm that came from beneath the soil. Every few minutes his chest rose and fell in time with the distant pulse, as if the ground itself controlled his lungs. Widow Grier had tried to move him inside earlier, but he refused. He said the open air helped him hear the warnings before they became too loud to understand.

Sera slipped away from the smokehouse and circled toward the creek path. Jonas followed at a distance, keeping the buildings between himself and the watching figures. The settlers in the square stayed quiet, their eyes moving between the Hollow-Eyed and the two people leaving their defensive line. No one called out. They had learned that noise only drew attention.

The path to the creek followed the same route Jonas had walked a hundred times before. Now the ground felt different under his boots. The soil gave slightly with each step, as if something moved just beneath the surface. Small stones rolled away from his heels without reason. The metallic smell grew stronger as they neared the water, and the dead grass along the bank had taken on a reddish cast that had nothing to do with sunset.

Sera stopped at a place where the creek curved sharply around a stand of dead willows. The thin place here had never been marked with stakes. She had kept it hidden even from the other watchers, a place so compromised that any ritual would only draw more attention to it. Now she knelt beside a patch of bare earth and brushed away the loose dirt with her hands. A narrow crack appeared, no wider than a finger, running from the water's edge toward the trees. Red liquid seeped from it in slow beads that caught the last light like blood.

Sera didn't look up. "This is the last one." She wiped a streak of red mud onto her skirt. "The others are already gone. This one's holding. Barely."

Jonas crouched beside her. The crack felt warm when he placed his palm near it. The heat came from below, not from the air. He could hear something moving under the soil, a slow, wet sound like water finding new channels through stone.

"How long?" Jonas asked.

"Hours. Maybe less. The entity has gathered enough now. It does not need to wait."

They stayed quiet for a moment, listening to the creek. The water moved slower than it should have, the surface thick with the same red film that coated everything else. A dead fish floated past, its belly up and its eyes missing. Sera watched it drift until it caught on a root and stopped.

"The entity speaks through the air here," she said. "Not through Paul or anyone else. Just the space between the ground and the sky. If you listen, you can hear what it remembers."

Jonas leaned closer to the crack. At first he heard only the creek and the wind in the dead branches. Then another sound rose beneath those noises, a voice that seemed to come from everywhere and nowhere at once. It spoke his name. Not the way Pricket had spoken it, as a threat or a summons. This voice spoke it the way someone speaks a word they have carried for years, turning it over and over until every edge wears smooth.

"Jonas Farlow. You walked these ridges before the settlement came. You buried your traps in the same soil that holds us now. You ran from your father's voice, but the voice found you anyway. The ground keeps what it is given."

The words settled into his chest like cold water. He had never told anyone the full story of why he had come west. His father's obsession with the breathing earth had been a heavy, private shame, a physical weight he had tried to leave behind in the old states. Now the entity repeated the story back to him as if it had been present for every argument, every slammed door, every night his father had spent listening to the floorboards.

"You fear you are already inside me," the voice continued. "You are not wrong. The missing hours. The moments that slip between one breath and the next. Those are mine now. I learn you the way I learned every witness who came before. Soon you will not need to wonder what you were doing while the time was gone. You will be with me, and the wondering will end."

Sera placed her hand on his shoulder. The touch pulled him back from the voice, though the words continued in the air around them. She did not ask what he had heard. She had heard versions of it herself, in other places, through other thin spots that had failed over the years.

"It does that," Sera said, her hand dropping from his shoulder. "It gives you the choice. Or it just takes."

Jonas stood and stepped back from the crack. His legs felt unsteady, as if the ground had shifted beneath him while he listened. He wiped his hands on his coat, though nothing visible clung to them. The voice faded when he moved away, but he could still feel its presence pressing against his thoughts, patient and certain.

Footsteps approached from the direction of the square. Widow Grier appeared between the trees, supporting Paul with one arm while she carried her shotgun in the other. Paul's legs dragged with each step, the calcified skin too stiff to bend properly. His breathing had grown shallow, and gray stone now covered the lower half of his face. Only his eyes remained clear, wide and frightened and still his own.

"He wouldn't stay behind," Widow Grier said. "Said the voice was stronger near the water. Said he needed to be here when it spoke again."

They lowered Paul to the ground near the crack. He sat with his back against a dead willow, his arms resting on his knees. The stone had spread to his chest now, and each breath came with visible effort. Still, he managed to speak.

"It wants..." Paul choked, a small puff of gray dust escaping his lips. "It wants you to hear."

The air around the crack changed. The voice returned, but this time it spoke through Paul as well as through the space itself. The two sounds overlapped, one coming from below and one from the young man's mouth.

"Every witness becomes part of the memory. Every fear. Every moment of surrender. The collection is complete. The next opening will not close. The settlement will become part of the whole. Those who join now will keep their names. Those who resist will be taken without choice."

Paul's body convulsed. More stone dust fell from his lips. Widow Grier steadied him with a hand on his shoulder, her face set against the sight of what the entity had done to him.

"The choice is the same one it gave Pricket," the voice continued. "Surrender brings peace. Resistance brings consumption. There is no middle ground. The ground does not bargain."

Jonas felt the pressure against his thoughts grow stronger. The missing time hovered at the edges of his awareness, ready to claim another stretch of minutes. He focused on the solid weight of the shotgun in Widow Grier's hands, the sound of the creek moving past them, the cold air against his face. The sensations helped hold him in place for a few more moments.

"It is already inside you," the voice said. "The premonitions. The moments when you knew what would happen before it occurred. Those are my memories of you, placed ahead of time. Soon there will be no difference between what you remember and what I remember. You will be whole again."

Sera moved closer to the crack. She had remained quiet while the entity spoke, her face set in the same calm expression she wore when facing any truth she could not change. Now she spoke directly to the voice.

"My people delayed you before. We can delay you again."

"Your people delayed nothing. They only taught me where the weaknesses lay. Each ritual showed me how to pull harder the next time. Each witness added to the collection. The delay is over. The awakening is permanent."

Paul's eyes rolled back. His body went rigid against the willow trunk, and a fresh wave of stone dust spilled from his mouth. Widow Grier pulled him away from the crack, her arms straining under his weight. The calcification had reached his throat now, and his breathing came in short, desperate gasps.

Jonas stepped forward. The voice pressed harder against his thoughts, offering the same promise it had made to Pricket. No more loneliness. No more missing time. No more wondering what the entity would take next. All he had to do was stop fighting. All he had to do was let the ground claim what it already held.

He reached into his coat and pulled out the last stake. Sera had carved it the night before, the symbols running along its length in the old language of her people. The wood felt heavy in his hand, though it was no different from the others they had used. He moved to the edge of the crack and drove the point into the soil with both hands. The ground resisted at first, then gave way with a wet, tearing sound. The stake sank to half its length before stopping.

The voice rose in volume. It filled the air around them, no longer speaking through Paul or the crack alone. It came from the trees, from the water, from the soil beneath their feet. The words overlapped until they became a single, continuous sound that pressed against Jonas's chest like a physical weight.

"You cannot seal what has already opened. You cannot contain what has already learned your names. The collection is complete. The witnesses remain. The ground remembers every moment you have ever spent here. It will not forget when the stones open."

The ground convulsed beneath Jonas's boots. The crack widened, red water spilling out in a sudden flood that soaked his legs and ran toward the creek. The stake tilted but did not pull free. He drove it deeper with his heel, forcing the point past the resistance until only the carved top remained visible. The symbols glowed faintly in the dying light, though he could not tell if the glow came from the wood or from something beneath it.

Sera knelt beside the widening crack and placed both hands on the soil. Her lips moved in the old words, though Jonas could not hear them over the voice that filled the air. Widow Grier pulled Paul farther back, shielding his body with her own as the ground shifted and rolled. The young man's breathing had nearly stopped, his chest barely rising now, the stone covering everything except his eyes.

The voice reached a peak, then faded. The air cleared. The pressure against Jonas's thoughts lifted, leaving behind the familiar cold sweat and the knowledge that the entity had taken another piece of him. The ground stopped moving. The crack remained open, but the red water slowed to a trickle. The voice did not return.

Jonas stood over the stake, his breath coming hard. His hands shook from the effort of driving it in, and his legs felt unsteady beneath him. He wiped his palms on his coat and looked at the others. Sera remained kneeling, her hands still pressed to the soil. Widow Grier held Paul upright, her face set in the same grim determination she had shown since the beginning. Paul's eyes stayed open, though his breathing had become so shallow that Jonas could barely see it.

The Hollow-Eyed had not moved closer. They remained at the edge of the settlement, their silent shapes watching the four people by the creek. Pricket stood among them, his gray face turned toward the water. He did not call out again. Whatever the entity had offered him, he had already accepted it. The rest of them would have to make their own choice.

Jonas stepped back from the crack. The stake held for now. The ground had stopped pulsing beneath his boots. The voice had gone quiet. He knew the silence would not last. The entity had gathered enough witnesses to make the next awakening permanent, and the collection continued whether they fought it or not. Every moment they remained in the valley added to what the ground remembered. Every fear they carried became fuel for what waited beneath the stone.

Sera stood and brushed the dirt from her hands. She looked at Jonas without speaking, her face showing the same exhaustion he felt. They had bought a few more hours, maybe a night. The thin place would not hold forever. When it opened again, the entity would rise and remain risen. The choice Pricket had made would be offered to everyone who stayed.

Widow Grier adjusted her grip on Paul. The young man's head had fallen forward, his breathing barely visible now. She looked toward the settlement square, where the remaining settlers waited behind their useless weapons. The Hollow-Eyed watched from the tree line, their numbers too great to count in the failing light. The choice would have to be made soon. Surrender or resistance. Peace or consumption. The ground did not bargain, and it never forgot.

Jonas turned away from the creek. The others followed. Behind them, the stake stood in the widening crack, the carved symbols catching the last of the light. The red water continued its slow seep toward the main channel. The entity waited beneath the soil, patient and hungry, gathering every moment that passed in the valley above. The witnesses remained. The collection continued. The awakening drew closer with each breath they took, and the ground remembered every name that had ever been spoken in this place.

CHAPTER TWENTY SEVEN

The Witness's Choice

The final thin place lay where the creek turned hard against the roots of three dead willows. Jonas stood over the narrow crack with the last stake in his hands, the carved symbols still damp from the red water that had seeped up moments before. The stake had gone in deep, but he could feel the ground shifting beneath it already, testing the wood like something alive feeling for a weak spot.

Sera stayed close, her hands still marked with the same red mud that coated the bank. She had spoken the old words once more after the stake went in, though both of them knew the ritual was running out of strength. The air around the crack felt heavier now, and the slow breathing sound from below had not stopped even after the voice went quiet.

Jonas wiped his palms on his coat. The wood under his fingers still held the warmth from where it had pressed against the soil. He looked at the crack again, watching the way the red liquid gathered at the edges and then slid away toward the main channel. The stake held. For now.

"It said my name like it had carried it a long time," he said. The words came out quieter than he meant them to.

Sera nodded once. She did not ask what else the voice had told him. She had heard enough versions of the same offer over the years to know the shape of it without asking for details.

They heard Widow Grier before they saw her. Her boots crushed the dead grass along the path, and her shotgun barrel caught the last of the light as she moved between the trees. Paul Murdock walked beside her, though his legs barely bent and his breathing came in short pulls that matched the slow rhythm under the ground. Widow Grier kept one arm around his waist, steadying him when the stone in his limbs made him stumble.

"He wouldn't stay at the square," she said when they reached the willows. "Said the voice was pulling harder near the water. Said you needed to hear what it had left to say."

They lowered Paul to the ground near the crack. He sat with his back against one of the dead trunks, his arms resting stiff on his knees. The gray stone had reached his throat now, and every breath pushed small clouds of dust from between his lips. His eyes stayed clear though, still his own even while the rest of him turned to something else.

The air around the crack shifted again. The voice returned, speaking through the space itself and through Paul's mouth at the same time. The two sounds layered over each other until Jonas could not tell which came from below and which came from the young man sitting against the tree.

"Every witness becomes part of the memory," the voice said. "Every fear. Every moment of surrender. The collection is complete. The next opening will not close. The settlement will become part of the whole. Those who join now will keep their names. Those who resist will be taken without choice."

Paul's body jerked once. More stone dust spilled from his mouth and settled on the front of his shirt. Widow Grier kept a hand on his shoulder, her face set hard against what she was seeing.

"The choice is the same one it gave Pricket," the voice continued. "Surrender brings peace. Resistance brings consumption. There is no middle ground. The ground does not bargain."

Jonas felt the pressure against his thoughts grow stronger. The missing time waited at the edges of his awareness, ready to take another stretch of minutes if he let his guard slip. He focused on the weight of the shotgun in Widow Grier's hands, the sound of the creek moving past, the cold air on his face. The sensations helped hold him in place for a few more moments.

"It is already inside you," the voice said. "The premonitions. The moments when you knew what would happen before it occurred. Those are my memories of you, placed ahead of time. Soon there will be no difference between what you remember and what I remember. You will be whole again."

Sera moved closer to the crack. She had stayed quiet while the entity spoke, her face set in the same calm expression she wore when facing any truth she could not change. Now she spoke directly to the voice.

"My people delayed you before," she said. "We can delay you again."

"Your people delayed nothing," the voice answered. "They only taught me where the weaknesses lay. Each ritual showed me how to pull harder the next time. Each witness added to the collection. The delay is over. The awakening is permanent."

Paul's eyes rolled back. His body went rigid against the willow trunk, and a fresh wave of stone dust spilled from his mouth. Widow Grier pulled him away from the crack, her arms straining under his weight. The calcification had reached his throat now, and his breathing came in short, desperate gasps.

Jonas stepped forward. The voice pressed harder against his thoughts, offering the same promise it had made to Pricket. No more loneliness. No more missing time. No more wondering what the entity would take next. All he had to do was stop fighting. All he had to do was let the ground claim what it already held.

He reached into his coat and pulled out the last stake. Sera had carved it the night before, the symbols running along its length in the old language of her people. The wood felt heavy in his hand, though it was no different from the others they had used. He moved to the edge of the crack and drove the point into the soil with both hands.

The ground resisted at first, then gave way with a wet, tearing sound. The stake sank to half its length before stopping. The voice rose in volume. It filled the air around them, no longer speaking through Paul or the crack alone. It came from the trees, from the water, from the soil beneath their feet. The words overlapped until they became a single, continuous sound that pressed against Jonas's chest like a physical weight.

"You cannot seal what has already opened," the voice said. "You cannot contain what has already learned your names. The collection is complete. The witnesses remain. The ground remembers every moment you have ever spent here. It will not forget when the stones open."

The ground convulsed beneath Jonas's boots. The crack widened, red water spilling out in a sudden flood that soaked his legs and ran toward the creek. The stake tilted but did not pull free. He drove it deeper with his heel, forcing the point past the resistance until only the carved top remained visible. The symbols glowed faintly in the dying light, though he could not tell if the glow came from the wood or from something beneath it.

Sera knelt beside the widening crack and placed both hands on the soil. Her lips moved in the old words, though Jonas could not hear them over the voice that filled the air. Widow Grier pulled Paul farther back, shielding his body with her own as the ground shifted and rolled. The young man's breathing had nearly stopped, his chest barely rising now, the stone covering everything except his eyes.

The voice reached a peak, then faded. The air cleared. The pressure against Jonas's thoughts lifted, leaving behind the familiar cold sweat and the knowledge that the entity had taken another piece of him. The ground stopped moving. The crack remained open, but the red water slowed to a trickle. The voice did not return.

Jonas stood over the stake, his breath coming hard. His hands shook from the effort of driving it in, and his legs felt unsteady beneath him. He wiped his palms on his coat and looked at the others. Sera remained kneeling, her hands still pressed to the soil. Widow Grier held Paul upright, her face set in the same grim determination she had shown since the beginning. Paul's eyes stayed open, though his breathing had become so shallow that Jonas could barely see it.

The Hollow-Eyed had not moved closer. They remained at the edge of the settlement, their silent shapes watching the four people by the creek. Pricket stood among them, his gray face turned toward the water. He did not call out again. Whatever the entity had offered him, he had already accepted it. The rest of them would have to make their own choice.

Jonas stepped back from the crack. The stake held for now. The ground had stopped pulsing beneath his boots. The voice had gone quiet. He knew the silence would not last. The entity had gathered enough witnesses to make the next awakening permanent, and the collection continued whether they fought it or not. Every moment they remained in the valley added to what the ground remembered. Every fear they carried became fuel for what waited beneath the stone.

Sera stood and brushed the dirt from her hands. She looked at Jonas without speaking, her face showing the same exhaustion he felt. They had bought a few more hours, maybe a night. The thin place would not hold forever. When it opened again, the entity would rise and remain risen. The choice Pricket had made would be offered to everyone who stayed.

Widow Grier adjusted her grip on Paul. The young man's head had fallen forward, his breathing barely visible now. She looked toward the settlement square, where the remaining settlers waited behind their useless weapons. The Hollow-Eyed watched from the tree line, their numbers too great to count in the failing light. The choice would have to be made soon. Surrender or resistance. Peace or consumption. The ground did not bargain, and it never forgot.

Jonas turned away from the creek. The others followed. Behind them, the stake stood in the widening crack, the carved symbols catching the last of the light. The red water continued its slow seep toward the main channel. The entity waited beneath the soil, patient and hungry, gathering every moment that passed in the valley above. The witnesses remained. The collection continued. The awakening drew closer with each breath they took, and the ground remembered every name that had ever been spoken in this place.

They moved back along the path toward the square. The buildings stood quiet, their windows dark. No one called out when they appeared between the cabins. The remaining settlers had learned to keep their voices low, to move carefully, to watch the ground for any sign that it was about to shift again. Widow Grier led Paul to the storehouse steps and settled him there, propping his back against the wall so he could breathe easier. His eyes stayed open, but the stone had covered his mouth now, and every breath came with visible effort.

Jonas walked to the well and checked the bucket. The rope felt rough under his fingers, the wood of the crank worn smooth from years of use. The water below had gone silent, but he could still smell the metallic tang that had replaced the usual clean scent of the valley. He pulled the bucket up anyway, checking the level before letting it drop back down. The sound of it hitting the surface echoed once and then faded.

Sera stood near the smokehouse, her attention fixed on the line of Hollow-Eyed that waited beyond the last houses. She had not spoken since they left the creek. Jonas could see the exhaustion in the way she held her shoulders, the way her hands stayed still at her sides instead of moving constantly as they usually did. Her ancestral knowledge had run out at the final thin place, and the admission had cost her something she could not name.

"It knew things about my father," Jonas muttered, staring down at his boots. "Things I never told anyone."

Sera didn't look at him. "It learns from what we carry. What we try to bury."

"Same offer it gave Pricket." Jonas rubbed the back of his neck, his knuckles raw. "No more missing time. No more waiting for the next piece of me to go."

Sera finally turned her head. "But you didn't take it."

"I drove the stake."

She stared at him, her dark eyes hollowed out by the shadows of the smokehouse. "That was the choice. The voice only asks once. After that..." She let the sentence trail off into the dark.

Widow Grier approached from the storehouse, her shotgun still in her hands. She had checked the weapon three times since they returned, checking the shells and the hammer and the trigger mechanism as if the familiar motions could keep the fear at bay. Her face showed the same grim set it had worn since the first deaths, but Jonas could see the weariness underneath it now, the way her eyes moved constantly between the watching figures and the people she was trying to protect.

"Paul's worse," Widow Grier said, her voice tight. "The stone's in his chest. He can't talk, but he keeps pointing toward the creek."

Jonas looked toward the storehouse steps. Paul sat with his head tilted back against the wall, his eyes open and fixed on the sky. The calcification had claimed everything below his throat, and his chest rose and fell in the same slow rhythm that came from beneath the soil. Every few minutes his body twitched as if something inside him was trying to break free.

"The entity spoke through him at the creek," Jonas said. "It used his voice along with its own. Maybe it's still using him now."

Widow Grier shook her head. "He's fighting it. I can see it in his eyes. He's still in there, still trying to help even while the stone takes everything else."

The ground trembled once beneath their feet. Not the steady pulse they had grown used to, but a single sharp movement that made the buildings creak and the water in the well slosh against its walls. Several of the remaining settlers cried out, their voices thin in the quiet air. Widow Grier moved toward them without hesitation, her shotgun held ready though everyone knew the weapon would do nothing against what waited beyond the houses.

Jonas stayed by the well. The tremor had passed, but he could feel the ground settling beneath him, adjusting to whatever change had just occurred below. The red water had begun to seep up between the boards of the well cover, small beads that caught the light and then disappeared into the wood.

Sera moved to stand beside him. She placed one hand on the well's rim, her fingers tracing the worn grain of the wood. "The entity heard your refusal," she said. "It will come for you now. For all of us who stood at the thin place and chose resistance."

"We knew that."

Sera watched the well cover. "Knowing isn't facing it."

Jonas nodded. He had known the cost when he took the stake from his coat. He had known the entity would not accept the refusal without consequence. The missing time had already claimed pieces of him, and the premonitions had shown him moments that had not yet arrived. The voice had promised peace, but he had seen what that peace looked like in Pricket's gray face and empty eyes.

The Hollow-Eyed remained where they stood, their pale forms motionless against the failing light. Pricket had not moved either, his gray face still turned toward the water where the stake now held the final thin place. Jonas wondered what the entity had shown him in exchange for his surrender, what memories it had offered to replace the ones he had lost when he chose to join the collection.

Paul made a sound from the storehouse steps. It was not a word, just a low breath that carried the same rhythm as the ground beneath them. Widow Grier moved to his side, checking his pulse and the stone that covered his chest. She looked up at Jonas and Sera, her face tight with the knowledge that they were running out of time.

"He can't hold much longer," she said. "The stone's in his throat now. If it reaches his lungs..."

She did not finish the thought. They all knew what would happen if the calcification reached Paul's lungs. They had seen it happen to others, had watched as breathing became impossible and the body turned to stone while the eyes remained open and aware.

Jonas walked to the storehouse steps and crouched in front of Paul. The young man's eyes tracked him, still clear despite the stone that covered everything else. Jonas could see the fear there, but he could also see something else, a kind of desperate urgency that had nothing to do with his own survival.

"What are you trying to tell us?" Jonas asked.

Paul's eyes moved toward the creek path. His hand twitched once, the stone fingers scraping against the wood of the steps. He could not speak, but the message was clear enough. The entity was still active at the thin place. The stake had bought them time, but not enough.

"We need to move him inside," Widow Grier said. "Get him away from the square where the Hollow-Eyed can see him. Maybe the distance will slow whatever's happening to him."

Jonas nodded. He and Widow Grier lifted Paul between them, careful not to jar the stone that had become his body. The weight was different now, heavier than it should have been, as if the calcification had added density along with the gray surface. They carried him into the storehouse and settled him on a blanket near the back wall, where the shadows were deeper and the sound of the ground breathing was less noticeable.

Sera remained in the square, watching the line of Hollow-Eyed as the light continued to fail. Jonas joined her after they had settled Paul, his boots crunching on the packed dirt. The air had grown colder as the sun dropped below the ridge, and the metallic smell of the red water seemed stronger in the gathering dark.

"The entity will not wait long," Sera said. "It has what it needs now. The witnesses. The collection. The thin places are all that stand between us and what waits below."

"And we sealed the last one."

"We delayed it. Nothing more."

Jonas looked at the line of figures standing beyond the houses. Pricket had moved closer to the others, his gray form blending with the rest until Jonas could not tell him apart from the Hollow-Eyed he had once led. The settlement's leader was gone now, replaced by something that wore his shape but held none of his old ambitions or fears.

The ground trembled again, stronger this time. The buildings creaked and shifted, and several of the remaining settlers cried out as the well bucket swung on its rope. Widow Grier appeared in the storehouse doorway, her shotgun ready, her face set against whatever was coming next.

Jonas felt the pressure against his thoughts return. The missing time pressed at the edges of his awareness, waiting for him to slip, waiting for the moment when his refusal would cost him more than he had already given. He focused on the solid weight of the well beneath his hands, the sound of Sera's breathing beside him, the cold air against his face. The sensations helped hold him in place for a few more moments, but he could feel the entity's patience wearing at his defenses.

"It knows we're exhausted," he said. "It knows we've used everything we had at the thin place."

Sera nodded. "That is when it strikes. When the witnesses are worn down and isolated. When hope has been worn away to nothing."

The ground pulsed once more beneath their boots, stronger than before. The stake at the creek would hold for a while longer, but Jonas could feel the entity's attention turning toward the square now, toward the people who had gathered there to make their final stand. The choice Pricket had made would be offered to everyone who remained, and the entity would not wait much longer to make that offer.

Widow Grier moved to stand with them, her shotgun held across her chest. Her face showed the same grim determination she had carried since the beginning, but Jonas could see the exhaustion underneath it now, the way her shoulders had begun to sag under the weight of protecting people who could not be protected from what waited below.

"The children are in the storehouse," she said. "The ones who haven't been taken yet. I've got them barricaded in the back room with what food we could gather. If the Hollow-Eyed come for the square, at least they'll have to go through me first."

Jonas nodded. He had no words to offer that would change what was coming. The entity had gathered its witnesses, had learned their names and their fears, and now it waited for the moment when resistance would cost more than surrender. The ground remembered everything, and it would not forget the names that had been spoken in this place.

The air around them grew heavier. The metallic smell of the red water filled Jonas's lungs with each breath, and the sound of the ground breathing seemed louder now, closer to the surface. The Hollow-Eyed had not moved, but Jonas could feel their attention shifting, their empty sockets turning toward the square as the entity prepared to make its final offer.

Sera placed her hand on his arm. The touch was light, but it carried the weight of everything they had faced together since the first deaths at the creek. Her ancestral knowledge had run out at the thin place, and the admission had left her with nothing but the same choice that faced everyone else who remained in the valley.

"It'll come for you first," she said. "You broke the cycle at the creek. It won't let that stand."

"I know."

"And you'll do it again?"

Jonas looked at her, at the exhaustion lining her face. The ritual words were gone, leaving only the quiet weight between them.

"As long as I have hands to hold the wood."

The ground pulsed once more beneath their boots, stronger than before. The buildings creaked and the well bucket swung on its rope, and the remaining settlers cried out as the tremor passed through the square. Widow Grier raised her shotgun, though they all knew the weapon would do nothing against what waited beyond the houses.

Jonas felt the pressure against his thoughts grow stronger. The missing time hovered at the edges of his awareness, ready to claim another stretch of minutes if he let his guard slip. He focused on the solid weight of the well beneath his hands, the sound of Sera's breathing beside him, the cold air against his face. The sensations helped hold him in place for a few more moments, but he could feel the entity's patience wearing at his defenses.

The choice would have to be made soon. Surrender or resistance. Peace or consumption. The ground did not bargain, and it never forgot the names of those who stood against it. Jonas stood with the others in the square, the last witnesses to the entity's gathering, and waited for the moment when the voice would return to offer its final terms.

CHAPTER TWENTY EIGHT

The Last Stand

The settlement square had gone quiet in a way that made every small sound carry. Jonas stepped between the last of the cabins with Sera beside him, and the silence pressed against his ears like something physical. Widow Grier's barricade of barrels and rope still stood in front of the storehouse, but two of the barrels had already tipped over. The Hollow-Eyed moved between the houses without hurry, their pale shapes sliding across the packed dirt as if the ground itself guided their steps.

Widow Grier stood near the well with her shotgun raised, her body angled to cover the storehouse door where the children waited inside. She fired once as a figure reached the first overturned barrel. The shell tore through the Hollow-Eyed without resistance. The shape kept moving, untouched, its empty face turned toward the sound of the blast. Widow Grier lowered the weapon and pulled another shell from her pocket with steady hands.

Widow Grier didn't look back at them. She spat into the dirt, her thumb tracing the cold metal of the breach lever.

"Nothing," she muttered. "Right through the damn thing."

Jonas watched the figures advance. The Hollow-Eyed had reached the square in numbers he had not seen before. They moved together, each step matched to the slow rhythm that rose from the soil. One of them stepped through the smokehouse wall as if the boards held no more substance than fog. Another passed beneath the well rope without disturbing it. Their coordination felt wrong, as though one mind directed all of them at once.

Sera stood close to Jonas, her hands empty at her sides. She had no more carved stakes left. The last one rested at the creek, holding the final thin place closed for now. She watched the approaching figures without expression, her dark eyes following the way they circled the remaining settlers.

Paul Murdock sat on the storehouse steps where they had left him. The stone had reached his throat, and his head rested at an angle against the wooden post. His eyes stayed open. They tracked the Hollow-Eyed as they drew closer, and his chest rose and fell in small movements that matched the pulse beneath the ground. Widow Grier had tried to move him inside earlier, but the weight of the stone made it impossible to carry him far.

One of the Hollow-Eyed reached Paul first. The figure stopped three steps away and tilted its head as though listening. Paul's body jerked once. His mouth opened, and stone dust spilled out across his shirt. A low sound came from his throat, not a word, just the same rhythm that rose from the soil. His eyes rolled back until only the whites showed, and his hands clenched against the steps.

The stone spread faster after that. It moved up his throat in a visible wave, covering his jaw and then his cheeks. Paul's breathing stopped. His eyes remained clear for another moment, staring past the Hollow-Eyed toward the creek path. Then the gray surface claimed them too. His body settled against the post, rigid and complete, another vessel added to the collection.

Widow Grier made a sound low in her throat. She stepped forward, then stopped. There was nothing left to protect. Paul had become part of what they fought, his face blank now, his body joined to the others that waited in the square.

Harlan Pricket stood at the center of the open space between the buildings. The gray had reached his eyes as well, but his mouth still moved. His voice carried across the square without effort, the words forming in the air as though the entity spoke through him directly.

"There's no sense in it," Pricket said. His voice was too thin, too flat, like grease spread over dry wood. "Just... let go. It's easier if you don't fight it. We're keeping the names. Most of them."

Jonas felt the pressure against his thoughts grow heavier. The missing time waited at the edges of his awareness, ready to claim another stretch of minutes if he let his guard slip. He focused on the weight of the well rope in his hands, the cold air on his face, the sound of Widow Grier reloading her shotgun even though the shells did no good. The sensations helped hold him in place.

Sera moved closer to him. Her hand found his arm, and her fingers pressed against the buckskin sleeve. She did not speak. There was nothing left to say that had not already been said at the creek. The entity had gathered its witnesses, had learned their names and their fears, and now it waited for the moment when resistance would cost more than surrender.

The ground pulsed beneath their feet. The movement came stronger than before, a single deep shift that made the well bucket swing on its rope and the storehouse walls creak. Several of the remaining settlers cried out. One woman dropped to her knees near the smokehouse, her hands pressed to the dirt as though she could feel the breathing through her palms. The Hollow-Eyed continued their slow advance, unaffected by the tremor.

Jonas realized the entity had been waiting for exactly this. The witnesses stood exhausted and isolated. Their hope had worn down to nothing through days of watching the land change and the water turn red. The thin places had been sealed one by one, but each seal had shown the entity where the weaknesses lay. The collection was complete. The next opening would not close.

Pricket's voice rose again. "The ground does not bargain. It remembers every moment spent here. Every fear. Every surrender. Those who accept now will keep something of themselves. Those who wait will lose even that."

Widow Grier raised her shotgun once more. She aimed at the nearest Hollow-Eyed and pulled the trigger. The blast echoed across the square. The figure kept moving, the shell passing through its chest without leaving a mark. Widow Grier lowered the weapon and stared at the advancing shapes with the same grim determination she had carried since the first deaths.

"They're not stopping," she said again. Her voice stayed steady. "Nothing stops them now."

Jonas watched Paul's stone body among the others. The young man's face had gone blank, his eyes empty sockets now. Another vessel added to the collection. The entity had used him at the creek, speaking through his mouth while he still fought to stay himself. Now the stone claimed everything. Jonas wondered what Paul had tried to tell them in those final moments before the calcification reached his throat.

Sera's grip on his arm tightened. She leaned closer, her voice low enough that only he could hear.

"It's done," Sera said. Her fingers dug hard into his sleeve. "The seals. We shut the doors, Jonas. We shut them all in."

Jonas nodded. He had known the cost when he drove the final stake into the soil at the creek. The entity would not accept refusal without consequence. The missing time had already taken pieces of him, and the premonitions had shown him moments that had not yet arrived. The voice had promised peace, but he had seen what that peace looked like in Pricket's gray face.

The ground pulsed again, stronger this time. The buildings shifted on their foundations, and dust fell from the storehouse roof. The well bucket swung hard enough to strike the wooden frame. Widow Grier stumbled but kept her footing. She moved toward the storehouse door, her shotgun held ready, her body positioned between the Hollow-Eyed and the children inside.

Pricket took a step forward. His gray form moved with the same unnatural coordination as the others. The voice that came from his mouth grew louder, filling the square.

"Come on," Pricket rasped. A trickle of gray fluid ran from the corner of his left eye, but he didn't wipe it away. "It's already here. Just... come on."

Jonas felt the pressure against his thoughts grow stronger. The missing time pressed at the edges of his awareness, waiting for him to slip, waiting for the moment when his refusal would cost him more than he had already given. He focused on the solid weight of the well beneath his hands, the sound of Sera's breathing beside him, the cold air against his face. The sensations helped hold him in place for a few more moments.

Sera released his arm. She turned to face him fully, her dark eyes meeting his with the same calm expression she had worn when facing any truth she could not change. Her hand stayed near his sleeve, close but not touching now.

"There's one more thing," Sera said. She stared at his jaw, refusing to look him in the eye. "One card left. But it's bad, Jonas."

Jonas waited. The ground pulsed beneath them again, and the Hollow-Eyed drew closer to the well. Widow Grier fired her shotgun once more, the blast useless against the advancing shapes. The children inside the storehouse had gone quiet, their voices silenced by the fear that filled the square.

"It wants a name," Sera whispered. She looked toward the dark water. "A big one. Someone to hold the weight of it while the rest of us... while we finish the stakes. But you don't come back from that. Not you. Not any of it."

Jonas looked at the line of Hollow-Eyed that surrounded the square. Pricket stood among them, his gray face turned toward the well. The remaining settlers had gathered near the storehouse, their bodies pressed together as though closeness could protect them from what came next. Widow Grier stood with her shotgun lowered now, her face set against the truth that no weapon would help them.

"The entity has been waiting for this moment," Sera said. "When the witnesses are exhausted. When hope has been worn down to nothing. When resistance costs more than surrender. It learns from what we carry. What we try to bury. It knows we have nothing left to fight with."

Jonas felt the pressure against his thoughts grow heavier. The missing time waited at the edges of his awareness, ready to claim another stretch of minutes if he let his guard slip. He focused on the weight of the well rope in his hands, the cold air on his face, the sound of Widow Grier's breathing across the square. The sensations helped hold him in place.

Jonas spat a bit of grit from his teeth. "Get the stakes ready."

Sera nodded once. She did not argue. She had known the cost when she spoke the words. Her ancestral knowledge had run out at the final thin place, and the admission had left her with nothing but the same choice that faced everyone else who remained in the valley.

Widow Grier heard the exchange. She turned from the storehouse door, her shotgun held across her chest. Her face showed the same grim determination she had carried since the beginning, but Jonas could see the weariness underneath it now. She moved toward them with heavy steps.

"Like hell," Grier snapped, her boots grinding into the gravel. "You've already got half your head full of water, Jonas. We aren't doing this."

Jonas didn't look at her. "Look around, Grier. You got a better idea? Because they're almost at the porch."

Widow Grier's hands tightened on the shotgun. She looked at the Hollow-Eyed that surrounded them, at Pricket's gray form standing at the center of the square, at Paul's stone body among the others. Her face set harder against what she saw.

"We go together," Grier said, raising the stock back to her shoulder. "We don't leave people behind in the dark."

"It doesn't work that way," Sera said. Her voice cracked, then went cold again. "It needs one. If we all go, it just takes us all at once."

The ground pulsed again. The movement came stronger than before, a deep shift that made the well bucket swing hard enough to strike the wooden frame twice. Dust fell from the storehouse roof in a steady stream. One of the remaining settlers cried out as the ground shifted beneath their feet.

Jonas felt the pressure against his thoughts grow stronger. The missing time pressed at the edges of his awareness, waiting for him to slip. He focused on the solid weight of the well beneath his hands, the sound of Sera's breathing beside him, the cold air against his face. The sensations helped hold him in place for a few more moments.

"I will go to the thin place," he said. "The entity will follow. While it focuses on me, the others can complete the ritual. The settlement may survive. The children may have a chance."

Widow Grier stared at him. Her face showed the same grim set it had worn since the first deaths, but Jonas could see the conflict underneath it now. She had sworn to protect the settlement's children, and now the only path forward required one of their own to sacrifice everything.

"The children are in the storehouse," she said. "The ones who haven't been taken yet. If the Hollow-Eyed come for the square, at least they'll have to go through me first."

Jonas nodded. He had no words to offer that would change what was coming. The entity had gathered its witnesses, had learned their names and their fears, and now it waited for the moment when resistance would cost more than surrender. The ground remembered everything, and it would not forget the names that had been spoken in this place.

Sera placed her hand on his arm again. The touch was light, but it carried the weight of everything they had faced together since the first deaths at the creek. Her ancestral knowledge had run out at the thin place, and the admission had left her with nothing but the same choice that faced everyone else who remained in the valley.

"It's going to hurt," she said.

"Yeah," Jonas frowned.

"You sure?"

Jonas looked at her, at the exhaustion lining her face. The ritual words were gone, leaving only the quiet weight between them.

"As long as I have hands to hold the wood."

The ground pulsed once more beneath their boots, stronger than before. The buildings creaked and the well bucket swung on its rope, and the remaining settlers cried out as the tremor passed through the square. Widow Grier raised her shotgun, though they all knew the weapon would do nothing against what waited beyond the houses.

Jonas turned toward the creek path. The Hollow-Eyed watched him move, their empty faces turning to follow his steps. Pricket's gray form stood among them, his voice still carrying across the square with the entity's words. The pressure against Jonas's thoughts grew stronger with each step he took. The missing time waited at the edges of his awareness, ready to claim another stretch of minutes if he let his guard slip.

Sera began the final ritual behind him. Her voice rose in the old language of her people, the words carrying across the square as the ground pulsed beneath their feet. Widow Grier stood with her shotgun held ready, her body positioned between the Hollow-Eyed and the storehouse door. The children inside had gone quiet, their voices silenced by the fear that filled the square.

Jonas walked toward the creek path alone. The Hollow-Eyed followed him like witnesses to their own resurrection, their pale forms moving with the same unnatural coordination. The ground pulsed beneath his boots with each step, stronger than before, as the entity prepared to fully emerge through the collected memories of everyone it had ever touched.

The entity had been waiting for this moment. The witnesses stood exhausted and isolated. Their hope had worn down to nothing. The thin places had been sealed one by one, but each seal had shown the entity where the weaknesses lay. The collection was complete. The next opening would not close.

Jonas reached the edge of the square and stepped onto the path that led to the creek. The Hollow-Eyed followed. Pricket's voice faded behind him as the distance grew. The ground pulsed once more beneath his boots, and the missing time pressed harder against his thoughts. He focused on the solid weight of the ground beneath his feet, the cold air against his face, the sound of Sera's voice carrying the final ritual across the square.

The entity prepared to emerge. The witnesses remained. The collection continued. The awakening drew closer with each breath they took, and the ground remembered every name that had ever been spoken in this place.

Jonas walked toward the thin place with the Hollow-Eyed following behind him. The ground pulsed with increasing violence, and the missing time waited at the edges of his awareness. He had refused the entity's offer at the creek. Now the entity would come for him, and the final ritual would either seal the awakening permanently or fail completely.

The settlement square fell behind him. The remaining settlers gathered near the storehouse, their bodies pressed together as though closeness could protect them from what came next. Widow Grier stood with her shotgun held ready. Sera's voice rose in the old language, the words carrying across the square as the ground pulsed beneath their feet.

Jonas reached the creek path. The red water had begun to seep up between the stones, small beads that caught the last of the light and then disappeared into the soil. The stake stood in the widening crack, the carved symbols catching the failing light. The Hollow-Eyed followed him like witnesses to their own resurrection, their pale forms moving with the same unnatural coordination.

The entity had been waiting for this moment. The witnesses stood exhausted and isolated. Their hope had worn down to nothing. The thin places had been sealed one by one, but each seal had shown the entity where the weaknesses lay. The collection was complete. The next opening would not close.

Jonas stepped onto the creek bank. The ground pulsed beneath his boots, stronger than before, as the entity prepared to fully emerge through the collected memories of everyone it had ever touched. The Hollow-Eyed gathered around him, their empty faces turned toward the thin place where the stake held the final barrier closed.

The choice Pricket had made would be offered to everyone who remained. The entity would not wait much longer to make that offer. The ground remembered every name that had been spoken in this place, and it would not forget the witnesses who had stood against it.

Jonas stood at the edge of the thin place with the Hollow-Eyed surrounding him. The ground pulsed with increasing violence, and the missing time pressed harder against his thoughts. Sera's voice carried the final ritual across the square, and Widow Grier stood with her shotgun held ready. The entity prepared to emerge, and the witnesses remained to face what came next.

CHAPTER TWENTY NINE

The Memory's Price

Jonas stood at the thin place and felt the stake beneath his boot shift slightly in the loosened soil. The carved symbols along its length caught what little daylight remained, but the wood itself had begun to darken where the red water touched it. He could hear Sera's voice carrying from the square behind him, the old language rising and falling in rhythms that belonged to another time. Each word she spoke seemed to press against the air itself, pushing something back that wanted to come forward.

The Hollow-Eyed had gathered in a loose circle around the creek bank. Their pale forms stood without movement, empty faces turned toward the water that seeped between the stones. Some of them still wore the clothes they had died in. Others had lost even that, their bodies reduced to smooth gray surfaces that caught the light like wet stone. Jonas recognized a few faces among them. A woman who had worked the storehouse. A man who had helped raise the first cabin walls. Their names sat somewhere in his memory, but he could not pull them forward now. The entity had taken those details along with everything else.

Sera's voice grew louder. She had moved closer to the well, her hands raised as she continued the ritual. The remaining settlers pressed against the storehouse door, their bodies packed together as though physical closeness could offer protection. Widow Grier stood apart from them, her shotgun held across her chest, her face set in the same grim line she had worn since the first deaths. She watched Jonas with an expression that mixed anger and resignation.

Widow Grier didn't lower the barrel. "Jonas. Get back from the edge."

Jonas did not turn around. He kept his attention on the thin place, on the way the ground seemed to rise and fall in small movements that matched the rhythm beneath his feet. The entity's presence pressed against his thoughts, a weight that grew heavier with each passing moment. He could feel it testing the boundaries of what he would allow, pushing at the edges of his awareness to see where the resistance might break.

Sera didn't look up from the dirt. "He has to. If we don't pin it to one mind, it takes the whole valley. It takes everyone."

Grier spat, her boots grinding into the damp gravel. "I'm not watching another boy go into the dark alone."

"It's not a choice, Grier," Sera muttered, her fingers tracing the dark wood of the stake. "It already knows our names. It's just waiting for the one who'll carry them."

Jonas felt the pressure against his mind increase. The missing time waited there, ready to claim another stretch of minutes if he let his focus slip. He could feel the entity's voice gathering behind his thoughts, the words forming in a language that was not his own. The sensation reminded him of standing too close to a fire, the heat pressing against his skin even when he could not see the flames.

"Jonas." Sera's voice was barely a whisper over the rushing water. "Stop fighting it. Let it in."

He understood what she was asking. The final option required him to become the vessel, to let the entity's collected memories pour into his mind while Sera completed the sealing. The process would consume his identity, replacing it with something older and hungrier. But it would also give them the window they needed. The entity would focus on its new vessel, leaving the remaining thin places vulnerable for the few minutes required to close them permanently.

Jonas looked at the stake driven into the soil. The carved symbols had begun to glow with a faint light, the wood itself seeming to warm beneath his boot. He could feel the entity's presence growing stronger, the ground pulsing with increasing violence as it prepared to claim its witness. The Hollow-Eyed watched him with their empty faces, their bodies swaying slightly in time with the rhythm that rose from the soil.

Jonas stared into the red pool. "Just finish it, Sera. Do the stakes."

Grier's hands trembled against the stock of her gun. "You're already half stone, Jonas. Look at your hands."

"That's the point," Jonas answered. He kept his gaze on the thin place, on the red water that seeped up between the stones. "It needs someone willing to carry the weight. Someone who knows what they're giving up."

Sera nodded once. She turned back toward the square, her hands raised as she resumed the ritual. The words flowed from her in the old language, each syllable carrying the weight of generations who had faced this same choice. Widow Grier remained where she stood, her shotgun held ready, her body positioned between the Hollow-Eyed and the storehouse door where the children waited.

The pressure against Jonas's thoughts grew stronger. He could feel the entity's voice pushing forward, the words forming in the space behind his eyes. The sensation was not painful, not exactly, but it carried a weight that made breathing difficult. He focused on the solid ground beneath his boots, on the cold air against his face, on the sound of Sera's voice carrying across the distance.

Then the entity's presence poured into him.

It came all at once, a flood of memories that were not his own. Jonas saw the valley as it had been centuries before, the land empty of settlement, the trees standing in patterns that followed the thin places like markers. He saw the first people who had come here, their faces weathered by travel, their eyes bright with the hope of new ground. He saw them build their cabins and dig their wells, unaware of what waited beneath the soil.

The memories shifted. He saw the first awakening, the ground opening to swallow an entire family. Their bodies had turned to stone before they reached the surface, their faces frozen in expressions of confusion rather than fear. The entity had taken them slowly, learning their names and their fears, storing each detail in the collection that grew beneath the valley.

Jonas felt his own memories being pushed aside. The entity's voice spoke through him now, the words forming in his mouth without his consent. "The valley is a single living memory. It has waited for the right witness. Someone who carries enough weight to hold what comes next."

The ground convulsed beneath his boots. The thin place widened, the crack spreading outward in jagged lines that reached toward the creek. Red water surged up from the soil, soaking through the leather of his boots and staining the buckskin dark. Jonas felt the entity's presence expanding within him, its collected memories pressing against the boundaries of what his mind could hold.

Sera's voice rose in response. She had moved closer to the well, her hands still raised as she continued the ritual. The words came faster now, each syllable building on the last. Widow Grier stood guard near the storehouse, her shotgun aimed at the Hollow-Eyed that had begun to move toward the thin place. The remaining settlers pressed against the door, their voices rising in fear as the ground shook beneath them.

Jonas felt his identity beginning to slip. The entity's memories crowded against his own, replacing the years he had spent in the valley with older images that belonged to people long dead. He saw faces he had never known, heard voices that spoke in languages he could not understand. The sensation was like drowning, his thoughts pulled under by a current too strong to fight.

Then Paul Murdock's stone body stepped forward from the circle of Hollow-Eyed. The young man's face remained blank, his empty sockets turned toward Jonas. The entity's voice spoke through Paul as well, the words overlapping with those that came from Jonas's mouth. "Another vessel added to the collection. The witnesses gather. The awakening draws closer."

Jonas tried to speak, tried to push back against the entity's presence, but his mouth formed words that were not his own. "The ground remembers every name. Every fear. Every surrender. Those who accept now will keep something of themselves. Those who wait will lose even that."

Widow Grier fired her shotgun. The blast echoed across the square, the shell passing through Paul's stone form without leaving a mark. She reloaded with steady hands, her face set against the truth that no weapon would help them now. The children inside the storehouse had gone quiet, their voices silenced by the fear that filled the air.

Sera completed the first part of the ritual. She lowered her hands and moved toward the creek path, her dark eyes fixed on Jonas. "It's working," she said. Her voice carried the exhaustion of someone who had seen too many cycles repeat themselves. "The entity is focusing on you. The thin places are vulnerable now."

Jonas felt the missing time claim another stretch of minutes. When his awareness returned, he stood closer to the thin place, his boots soaked through with red water. The entity's voice continued to speak through him, the words describing the valley as a single living memory that had waited for the right witness to accumulate. He could feel his identity being consumed piece by piece, replaced by something older and hungrier.

"Jonas," Sera called out. She had reached the creek bank, her hands raised as she prepared the final sealing. "Hold on a little longer. We need more time. The entity has to commit fully before the seal can hold."

He tried to answer, tried to tell her that he could feel himself slipping away, but the entity's voice spoke instead.

"The collection grows. The witnesses join. The awakening comes through the one who carries the weight."

Widow Grier moved toward the thin place as well. She had left her shotgun behind, her hands empty as she approached Jonas. "You don't have to carry this alone," she said. Her voice carried the same grim determination she had shown since the first deaths. "We can share the burden. We can find another way."

"There is no other way," Sera answered. She moved between Widow Grier and Jonas, her body positioned to block any attempt to interfere. "The entity needs a primary witness. If we all try to share it, the seal fails. Everyone dies."

Jonas felt the entity's presence expand within him. The collected memories pressed against his thoughts, each one carrying the weight of a life that had been taken. He saw the valley as it had been before the settlement, the land empty and waiting. He saw the first thin place open, the ground swallowing those who had come to claim it. He saw the cycles repeat themselves, each awakening claiming more witnesses, each sealing buying only a few more years of peace.

The entity's voice spoke through him again. "The valley is not a place. It is a memory. A single living memory that has waited for the right witness to hold what comes next. The collection is complete. The awakening draws closer with each breath."

Sera began the final sealing. Her voice rose in the old language, the words carrying across the creek bank as the ground convulsed beneath them. Widow Grier stood nearby, her hands clenched at her sides, her face set against the truth that she could do nothing to stop what came next. The Hollow-Eyed watched with their empty faces, their bodies swaying in time with the rhythm that rose from the soil.

Jonas felt his mind filling with foreign memories. The entity's voice described the valley as a single living memory, a collection of every witness it had ever touched. He saw the faces of those who had come before, their eyes empty, their bodies turned to stone. He saw the thin places opening and closing, each cycle buying time while the entity grew stronger beneath the soil.

The ground pulsed with increasing violence. The thin place widened further, the crack spreading outward in jagged lines that reached toward the creek. Red water surged up from the soil, soaking through the leather of his boots and staining the buckskin dark. Jonas felt the entity's presence growing stronger within him, its collected memories pressing against the boundaries of what his mind could hold.

"It's almost done," Sera said. Her voice carried the exhaustion of someone who had watched too many cycles repeat themselves. "The seal is taking hold. The entity is committed to the vessel. We have the time we need."

Jonas tried to speak, tried to tell her that he could feel himself disappearing, but the entity's voice spoke instead. "The collection grows. The witnesses join. The awakening comes through the one who carries the weight. The valley is a single living memory that has waited for the right witness to accumulate."

Widow Grier stepped forward. She moved past Sera, her body positioned between Jonas and the thin place. "You don't have to do this," she said. Her voice carried the same grim determination she had shown since the first deaths. "We can find another way. We always find another way."

"There is no other way," Sera answered. She placed her hand on Widow Grier's arm, her grip firm. "The entity needs a primary witness. Jonas accepted that role. The seal depends on it."

Jonas felt the missing time claim another stretch of minutes. When his awareness returned, he stood at the very edge of the thin place, his boots soaked through with red water. The entity's voice continued to speak through him, the words describing the valley as a single living memory that had waited for the right witness. He could feel his identity being consumed piece by piece, replaced by something older and hungrier.

The Hollow-Eyed had begun to move. Their pale forms stepped closer to the thin place, their empty faces turned toward Jonas. Paul Murdock's stone body stood among them, his empty sockets fixed on the vessel that had taken his place. The entity's voice spoke through Paul as well, the words overlapping with those that came from Jonas's mouth.

"The collection is complete," the entity's voice said. "The witnesses gather. The awakening comes through the one who carries the weight. The valley is a single living memory that has waited for the right witness to accumulate."

Sera completed the final sealing. Her voice rose in the old language, the words carrying across the creek bank as the ground convulsed beneath them. Widow Grier stood nearby, her hands clenched at her sides, her face set against the truth that she could do nothing to stop what came next. The Hollow-Eyed watched with their empty faces, their bodies swaying in time with the rhythm that rose from the soil.

Jonas felt the entity's presence begin to withdraw. The collected memories pulled back from his thoughts, leaving behind a hollow space that his own identity could not fill. He could feel the seal taking hold, the thin place closing around the entity's presence. The process was not gentle. It tore through his mind like a blade, cutting away the foreign memories and leaving only fragments of what he had been.

The ground convulsed one final time. The thin place closed with a sound like stone breaking, the crack sealing over as the entity's presence withdrew. Jonas felt the missing time release its grip, his awareness returning in pieces that did not quite fit together. He stood at the creek bank, his boots soaked through with red water, his mind empty of the entity's voice.

Sera lowered her hands. She moved toward Jonas, her dark eyes searching his face for signs of what remained. "It's done," she said. Her voice carried the exhaustion of someone who had watched too many cycles repeat themselves. "The entity is sealed. The thin place is closed."

Jonas tried to speak, tried to tell her that he could still feel the entity's presence at the edges of his awareness, but his mouth formed words that were not his own. "The collection grows. The witnesses join. The awakening comes through the one who carries the weight."

Widow Grier stepped forward. She moved past Sera, her body positioned between Jonas and the thin place. "That's not Jonas talking," she said. Her voice carried the same grim determination she had shown since the first deaths. "The seal didn't hold. The entity is still in there."

Sera shook her head. She placed her hand on Widow Grier's arm, her grip firm. "The seal held. What you're hearing is the echo. The entity's voice will fade. Jonas will come back to himself."

Jonas felt the entity's presence continue to withdraw. The collected memories pulled back from his thoughts, leaving behind a hollow space that his own identity could not fill. He could feel the seal taking hold, the thin place closed around the entity's presence. The process was not gentle. It tore through his mind like a blade, cutting away the foreign memories and leaving only fragments of what he had been.

The Hollow-Eyed had begun to collapse. Their pale forms fell to the ground, their bodies turning to dust as the connection to the collective consciousness was severed. Paul Murdock's stone body remained standing for a moment longer, his empty sockets turned toward Jonas. Then the stone cracked and crumbled, the dust scattering across the creek bank in the wind that rose from the thin place.

Pricket's body turned to stone completely. His expensive suit crumbled to dust around the calcified remains, the gray surface spreading across his face and hands. The entity's voice faded from his mouth, leaving only the sound of the wind and the red water that seeped between the stones.

Jonas felt his own body beginning to change. The stone spread across his skin in small patches, the gray surface claiming his fingers first, then his hands. He could feel the entity's presence withdrawing, the collected memories pulling back from his thoughts. The process was not gentle. It tore through his mind like a blade, cutting away the foreign memories and leaving only fragments of what he had been.

Sera moved closer to him. She placed her hand on his arm, her grip firm. "The seal is holding," she said. Her voice carried the exhaustion of someone who had watched too many cycles repeat themselves. "The entity is sealed. The thin place is closed. The valley is safe for now."

Jonas tried to speak, tried to tell her that he could still feel the entity's presence at the edges of his awareness, but his mouth formed words that were not his own. "The collection grows. The witnesses join. The awakening comes through the one who carries the weight."

Widow Grier stepped forward. She moved past Sera, her body positioned between Jonas and the thin place. "That's not Jonas talking," she said. Her voice carried the same grim determination she had shown since the first deaths. "The seal didn't hold. The entity is still in there."

Sera shook her head. She placed her hand on Widow Grier's arm, her grip firm. "The seal held. What you're hearing is the echo. The entity's voice will fade. Jonas will come back to himself."

Jonas felt the stone continue to spread across his skin. The gray surface claimed his forearms now, the weight of it pulling at his shoulders. He could feel the entity's presence withdrawing, the collected memories pulling back from his thoughts. The process was not gentle. It tore through his mind like a blade, cutting away the foreign memories and leaving only fragments of what he had been.

The ground beneath the creek pulsed once beneath his boots. The sensation was like a heartbeat, a single deep shift that made the red water surge up from the soil. Then the pulsing stopped. The ground grew still, the thin place sealed, the entity's presence withdrawn from the valley.

Jonas felt the stone stop spreading. The gray surface remained on his hands and forearms, but it did not claim more of him. He could feel the entity's voice fading from his mind, leaving behind only his own memories and the terrible knowledge of what he had become. The seal had held. The entity was contained. The valley was safe for now.

Sera stood beside him, her hand still on his arm. Widow Grier remained nearby, her face set against the truth that the seal had come at a cost none of them could have predicted. The remaining settlers had begun to flee into the forest, their voices rising in fear as they ran from the thin place that had claimed so much.

Jonas looked at his hands, at the gray surface that covered his fingers. The stone felt cold against his skin, a weight that would never leave him. He could feel the entity's presence at the edges of his awareness, a shadow that would always be there. The seal had held. The entity was contained. But Jonas knew the silence was temporary. The valley would never be the same.

The surviving witnesses fled into an uncertain future, leaving Jonas and Sera to face whatever came next. The ground remained still. For now.

CHAPTER THIRTY

The Heartbeat Stops

The final thin place lay before Jonas like an open wound in the earth. Red water still seeped between the stones, but the pulsing had changed. It no longer matched the rhythm of his heart. It had grown slower, heavier, like something drawing one last breath before it slept again.

Sera stood at the creek bank with her hands raised. The old words left her mouth in steady rhythm. Each syllable settled into the ground like a nail driven through wood. The remaining settlers huddled near the storehouse door. Their faces showed the exhaustion of people who had watched too many die and still could not bring themselves to look away.

Widow Grier kept her position between the Hollow-Eyed and the children. Her shotgun rested across her chest, though she knew the weapon would do nothing against what came next. She had accepted that truth somewhere between the first deaths and this final moment.

Jonas took one step closer to the thin place. The stake beneath his boot had darkened where the red water touched it. The carved symbols along its length caught what light remained and held it. He could feel the entity's attention narrowing on him. The pressure against his thoughts grew sharper, more focused, as if the thing below had recognized the vessel it had been waiting for.

"Jonas." Widow Grier's knuckles were white on the stock of her shotgun. "Get back from it."

"Don't touch him," Sera said. She didn't look back, her voice tight and strained. "If anyone interferes now, we all go down with it."

Jonas understood what she meant. The final option required him to accept the entity's presence fully. Not as something he could fight or contain. As something that would move through him, use him as the passage it had sought since the first thin place opened. The process would consume what he had been. It would leave something else behind. But it would also give them the time they needed to close the remaining thin places before the entity could claim more witnesses.

He looked down at his hands. The stone had already begun to claim his fingers. Small gray patches spread across the skin like frost that would never melt. The cold weight pulled at his shoulders. He could feel the entity's memories pressing against his own, each one carrying the weight of a life taken and stored beneath the valley.

"Jonas." Sera's breath hitched. "Let it go. Don't fight."

He closed his eyes. The entity's presence surged forward like water through a broken dam. Memories flooded his mind that did not belong to him. He saw the valley before any settlement existed. The trees stood in patterns that marked the thin places like boundary stones. He saw the first people arrive with their wagons and their hope. He saw them dig their wells and raise their cabins, unaware of what waited beneath the soil.

The memories shifted. He saw the first awakening. The ground opened beneath a family of five. Their bodies turned to stone before they reached the surface. Their faces froze in expressions of confusion rather than fear. The entity had taken them slowly, learning their names and their fears, adding each detail to the collection that grew beneath the valley.

Jonas felt his own memories being pushed aside. The entity's voice formed in his mouth without his consent. The words came out in a voice that was his and not his. "The valley is a single living memory. It has waited for the right witness. Someone who carries enough weight to hold what comes next."

The ground convulsed beneath his boots. The thin place widened. The crack spread outward in jagged lines that reached toward the creek. Red water surged up from the soil and soaked through the leather of his boots. The stone on his hands spread to his wrists. The gray surface claimed more of him with each breath.

Widow Grier took a step forward, her boots sinking into the wet mud. "We can't just let him take the whole weight of it."

"We have to," Sera spat, her shoulders shaking. "Get back, Grier. Just... get back."

Jonas felt the missing time claim another stretch of minutes. When his awareness returned, he stood at the very edge of the thin place. The red water had risen to his ankles. The entity's voice continued to speak through him, describing the valley as a single living memory that had waited for the right witness to accumulate. He could feel his identity being consumed piece by piece, replaced by something older and hungrier.

The Hollow-Eyed had gathered in a loose circle around the creek bank. Their pale forms stood without movement. Empty faces turned toward the water that seeped between the stones. Some of them still wore the clothes they had died in. Others had lost even that, their bodies reduced to smooth gray surfaces that caught the light like wet stone.

Jonas recognized a few faces among them. A woman who had worked the storehouse. A man who had helped raise the first cabin walls. Their names sat somewhere in his memory, but he could not pull them forward now. The entity had taken those details along with everything else.

Paul Murdock's stone body stood among the Hollow-Eyed. The young man's face remained blank. His empty sockets turned toward Jonas. The entity's voice spoke through Paul as well. The words overlapped with those that came from Jonas's mouth. "Another vessel added to the collection. The witnesses gather. The awakening draws closer."

Widow Grier fired her shotgun. The blast echoed across the square. The shell passed through Paul's stone form without leaving a mark. She reloaded with steady hands. Her face set against the truth that no weapon would help them now. The children inside the storehouse had gone quiet. Their voices silenced by the fear that filled the air.

Sera completed the first part of the ritual. She lowered her hands and moved toward the creek path. Her dark eyes fixed on Jonas. "It's working," she said. Her voice carried the exhaustion of someone who had seen too many cycles repeat themselves. "The entity is focusing on you. The thin places are vulnerable now."

Jonas tried to answer. He tried to tell her that he could feel himself slipping away. The entity's voice spoke instead. "The collection grows. The witnesses join. The awakening comes through the one who carries the weight."

The ground convulsed again. The thin place widened further. The crack spread outward in jagged lines that reached toward the creek. Red water surged up from the soil. It soaked through the leather of his boots and stained the buckskin dark. Jonas felt the entity's presence expanding within him. Its collected memories pressed against the boundaries of what his mind could hold.

Pricket emerged from the shadows near the storehouse. His expensive suit hung on his gaunt frame like clothes on a scarecrow. His thinning sandy hair had gone white at the temples. His nervous twitch had become a constant flutter in his left eyelid. He moved toward Jonas with the desperate purpose of a man who had lost everything and still could not accept it.

"You're ruining it," Pricket choked out, his fingers twitching wildly. "We had a deal. The town... we can still save the leases."

Jonas looked down at him. The gray stone had reached his elbows now. "There's nothing left, Harlan."

Pricket grabbed him by the shirt. "I built this! Everything here is mine!"

Sera didn't look up from the dirt. "Let go of him, Harlan. It's over."

Pricket lunged forward. He grabbed Jonas by the arm. His fingers dug into the stone that covered Jonas's skin. "You don't get to decide for all of us. You don't get to take everything I've built."

The stone spread from Jonas's arm to Pricket's hand. It moved like frost across water. Pricket screamed as the gray surface claimed his fingers. He tried to pull away. The stone held him. It spread up his arm and across his chest. His expensive suit crumbled to dust around the calcified remains. The gray surface covered his face last. His eyes turned milky and blank. His body stood frozen in the moment of his final desperate grasp.

Widow Grier watched without moving. Her face showed no surprise. She had seen too many die to be shocked by one more. She kept her position between the Hollow-Eyed and the storehouse door. The remaining settlers pressed against the wood. Their voices rose in fear as the ground shook beneath them.

Jonas felt the entity's presence grow stronger within him. The collected memories pressed against his thoughts. Each one carried the weight of a life that had been taken. He saw the valley as it had been before the settlement. The land empty and waiting. He saw the first thin place open. The ground swallowing those who had come to claim it. He saw the cycles repeat themselves. Each awakening claiming more witnesses. Each sealing buying only a few more years of peace.

The entity's voice spoke through him again. "The valley is not a place. It is a memory. A single living memory that has waited for the right witness to hold what comes next. The collection is complete. The awakening draws closer with each breath."

Sera began the final sealing. Her voice rose in the old language. The words carried across the creek bank as the ground convulsed beneath them. Widow Grier stood nearby. Her hands clenched at her sides. Her face set against the truth that she could do nothing to stop what came next.

The Hollow-Eyed began to collapse. Their pale forms fell to the ground. Their bodies turned to dust as the connection to the collective consciousness was severed. Paul Murdock's stone body remained standing for a moment longer. His empty sockets turned toward Jonas. Then the stone cracked and crumbled. The dust scattered across the creek bank in the wind that rose from the thin place.

Jonas felt his own body changing. The stone spread across his skin in small patches. The gray surface claimed his fingers first. Then his hands. He could feel the entity's presence withdrawing. The collected memories pulled back from his thoughts. The process was not gentle. It tore through his mind like a blade. It cut away the foreign memories and left only fragments of what he had been.

The entity's voice faded from his mouth. The words stopped coming. The pressure against his thoughts eased. He could feel the seal taking hold. The thin place closing around the entity's presence. The process was not gentle. It tore through his mind like a blade. It cut away the foreign memories and left only fragments of what he had been.

Sera lowered her hands. She moved toward Jonas. Her dark eyes searched his face for signs of what remained. "It's done," she said. Her voice carried the exhaustion of someone who had watched too many cycles repeat themselves. "The entity is sealed. The thin place is closed."

Jonas tried to speak. He tried to tell her that he could still feel the entity's presence at the edges of his awareness. His mouth formed words that were not his own. "The collection grows. The witnesses join. The awakening comes through the one who carries the weight."

Widow Grier stepped forward. She moved past Sera. Her body positioned between Jonas and the thin place. "That's not Jonas talking," she said. Her voice carried the same grim determination she had shown since the first deaths. "The seal didn't hold. The entity is still in there."

Sera shook her head. She placed her hand on Widow Grier's arm. Her grip firm. "The seal held. What you're hearing is the echo. The entity's voice will fade. Jonas will come back to himself."

Jonas felt the stone continue to spread across his skin. The gray surface claimed his forearms now. The weight of it pulled at his shoulders. He could feel the entity's presence withdrawing. The collected memories pulled back from his thoughts. The process was not gentle. It tore through his mind like a blade. It cut away the foreign memories and left only fragments of what he had been.

The ground beneath the creek pulsed once beneath his boots. The sensation was like a heartbeat. A single deep shift that made the red water surge up from the soil. Then the pulsing stopped. The ground grew still. The thin place sealed. The entity's presence withdrawn from the valley.

Jonas felt the stone stop spreading. The gray surface remained on his hands and forearms. It did not claim more of him. He could feel the entity's voice fading from his mind. It left behind only his own memories and the terrible knowledge of what he had become.

The remaining settlers had begun to flee into the forest. Their voices rose in fear as they ran from the thin place that had claimed so much. Widow Grier stood guard as they passed. Her empty hands at her sides. Her face set against the truth that the seal had come at a cost none of them could have predicted.

Jonas looked at his hands. The gray surface covered his fingers. The stone felt cold against his skin. A weight that would never leave him. He could feel the entity's presence at the edges of his awareness. A shadow that would always be there.

The seal had held. The entity was contained. But Jonas knew the silence was temporary. The valley would never be the same. The surviving witnesses fled into an uncertain future. Leaving Jonas and Sera to face whatever came next. The ground remained still. For now.

Sera stood beside him. Her hand still on his arm. Widow Grier remained nearby. Her face set against the truth that the seal had come at a cost none of them could have predicted. The children inside the storehouse had begun to emerge. Their small faces pale with fear. They pressed against Widow Grier's legs. Seeking comfort in the only certainty they had left.

Jonas felt his eyes beginning to change. The milky film spread across his vision like frost across glass. The world grew dimmer. The colors faded. He could feel the entity's presence withdrawing completely. The collected memories pulled back from his thoughts. The process was not gentle. It tore through his mind like a blade. It cut away the foreign memories and left only fragments of what he had been.

"Your eyes," Sera said. Her voice carried a note of grief she could not hide. "They're changing."

Jonas nodded. He could not see her clearly anymore. The milky film covered his vision completely. He could feel the stone on his hands and forearms. The cold weight of it. The knowledge that it would never leave him. He could feel the entity's voice fading from his mind. Leaving behind only his own memories and the terrible knowledge of what he had become.

"The seal held," Sera said. She placed her hand on his arm. Her grip firm. "The entity is sealed. The thin place is closed. The valley is safe for now."

Jonas tried to speak. He tried to tell her that he could still feel the entity's presence at the edges of his awareness. His mouth formed words that were not his own. "The collection grows. The witnesses join. The awakening comes through the one who carries the weight."

Widow Grier stepped forward. She moved past Sera. Her body positioned between Jonas and the thin place. "That's not Jonas talking," she said. Her voice carried the same grim determination she had shown since the first deaths. "The seal didn't hold. The entity is still in there."

Sera shook her head. She placed her hand on Widow Grier's arm. Her grip firm. "The seal held. What you're hearing is the echo. The entity's voice will fade. Jonas will come back to himself."

Jonas felt the stone stop spreading. The gray surface remained on his hands and forearms. It did not claim more of him. He could feel the entity's voice fading from his mind. Leaving behind only his own memories and the terrible knowledge of what he had become.

The ground beneath the creek pulsed once beneath his boots. The sensation was like a heartbeat. A single deep shift that made the red water surge up from the soil. Then the pulsing stopped. The ground grew still. The thin place sealed. The entity's presence withdrawn from the valley.

Jonas felt the missing time release its grip. His awareness returned in pieces that did not quite fit together. He stood at the creek bank. His boots soaked through with red water. His mind empty of the entity's voice. The stone on his hands and forearms remained. The cold weight of it. The knowledge that it would never leave him.

Sera stood beside him. Her hand still on his arm. Widow Grier remained nearby. Her face set against the truth that the seal had come at a cost none of them could have predicted. The remaining settlers had fled into the forest. Their voices fading as they ran from the thin place that had claimed so much.

Jonas looked at his hands. The gray surface covered his fingers. The stone felt cold against his skin. A weight that would never leave him. He could feel the entity's presence at the edges of his awareness. A shadow that would always be there. The seal had held. The entity was contained. But Jonas knew the silence was temporary. The valley would never be the same. The surviving witnesses fled into an uncertain future. Leaving Jonas and Sera to face whatever came next. The ground remained still. For now.

ACKNOWLEDGMENTS

Stories like this are never written alone.

Thank you to every reader who stepped into Blackwater Valley and stayed long enough to hear the river moving beneath the ground.

To the readers who embraced the slow dread, the silence, the grief, and the things lurking just beyond the trees—thank you for giving this series a place to breathe.

To the horror readers who still love atmospheric terror, practical characters, and stories willing to take their time building fear instead of rushing toward noise—this book was written for you.

And finally:

Thank you for returning to the valley.

The Hollow-Eyed were waiting.

About the Author

P. Hartwell is an author of mystery and romantic suspense, with a signature blend of atmospheric tension, emotional depth, and a whisper of the uncanny. Drawn to the places where history falters and secrets endure, he crafts stories that linger in the charged space between beauty and terror, love and fear, truth and illusion.

Raised along the windswept shores of Lake Erie and shaped by global travels, ancestral lore, and a reverence for forgotten histories, Hartwell brings a cinematic sense of place to his work. His novels unfold in immersive, shadow-laden landscapes where grief stirs beneath the surface, the past refuses to stay buried, and every silence speaks volumes.

With a keen eye for psychological nuance and elemental unease, Hartwell invites readers into worlds rich with tension, secrets, and haunting echoes—where every clue carries weight, and nothing stays hidden for long.

also by P. Hartwell

Cailleach's Embrace

The Last Inhale

The Sacred Island

Beneath West Seneca

Time in Kilkenny

Brotherhood in Grease and Dust

The Hollow Axle

The Guardian's Hunger

The Darkness We Fell Into

THE HOLLOW-EYED SERIES

When the Hollow-Eyed Come

When the Earth Starts to Wake

Where the Hollow Ones Gather (Coming Soon)

CONTINUE THE SERIES

The valley remembers.
And something beneath the earth is still waking.
Book Three of The Hollow-Eyed Series is coming soon.

AUTHOR'S NOTE

The Hollow-Eyed Series began with a simple fear:

What if the earth remembered everything buried beneath it?

I wanted this story to feel grounded and human—less about heroes fighting monsters and more about exhausted people trying to survive something ancient, patient, and impossible to fully understand.

When the Earth Starts to Wake expands the darkness beneath Blackwater Valley and reveals that the Hollow-Eyed were never the true horror.

Only the warning.

Thank you for returning to the valley.

And thank you for listening closely enough to hear the river.

— P. Hartwell

TEASER FOR BOOK THREE

The first screams came from beneath the snow.

Not above it.

Jonas stopped halfway across the frozen path and listened.

The sound came again.

Muted.

Deep.

Like someone buried under twenty feet of earth was trying to claw their way upward.

Widow Grier slowly raised the lantern.

The ground ahead of them shifted.

Snow slid sideways across the surface.

Then a hand pushed through.

Gray.

Stone-covered.

Still moving.

Sera's voice came low beside him.

"Don't let it touch you."

The fingers kept crawling upward through the frozen dirt.

And somewhere below the valley—far beneath the roots, beneath the caverns, beneath the black water itself—something enormous opened its eyes.

THE HOLLOW-EYED SERIES CONTINUES

www.ingramcontent.com/pod-product-compliance
Lightning Source LLC
LaVergne TN
LVHW041108080826
845145LV00007B/1736

* 9 7 8 1 9 6 9 9 2 9 2 5 0 *